What Mommy Said

BOOKS BY H. PAUL JEFFERS

MYSTERIES

What Mommy Said
Reader's Guide to Murder
A Grand Night for Murder
Adventure of the Stalwart Companions
Rubout at the Onyx
Murder Most Irregular
Murder on Mike
The Ragdoll Murder
Secret Orders

CRIME HISTORY

Gentleman Gerald: America's First Public Enemy No. 1
Bloody Business: the Story of Scotland Yard
Who Killed Precious?

BIOGRAPHY

Colonel Roosevelt: Theodore Roosevelt Goes to War
Commissioner Roosevelt: Theodore Roosevelt
and the New York City Police

What Mommy Said

A NOVEL BY

H. Paul Jeffers

ST. MARTIN'S PRESS ⚏ NEW YORK

Library of Congress Cataloging-in-Publication Data

Jeffers, H. Paul (Harry Paul)
      What mommy said : an Arlene Flynn mystery / H. Paul Jeffers.
        p.   cm.
      ISBN 0-312-15687-1
      I. Title.
    PS3560.E36W43   1997
    813' .54—dc21   97-8808
                                                                CIP

First Edition: November 1997

10 9 8 7 6 5 4 3 2 1

for Al Leibholz,
lord of the lobby.

Prologue

The Other Side

SEBASTIAN STUCK HIS head into his father's den. "Dad, the guys are swimmin' in the lake. Can I go?"

Without looking up from his computer screen to the blond boy in blue trunks with yellow stripes, James Duncan took a sip of tepid decaffeinated instant coffee and said, "Only if your sister goes with you. That way, I'll be sure you won't be diving off the—"

"Yeah, I know. Diving only off of *this* side of Horseman's Head!" Sebastian said impatiently, braced for the familiar horror stories of boys like him who had drowned diving from the far side of the rock—one just last summer.

Resembling a grinning face of a Halloween pumpkin, the large outcropping of black-and-orange stone in Ichabod Crane Lake had been named after the mysterious night rider in Washington Irving's "The Legend of Sleepy Hollow." It marked a precipitous drop of the lake bed on its far side to a depth of sixteen feet. Were terror tales told by parents to be believed, seven boys had gone off the other side in the past twenty years and drowned, each pulled down by a ferocious undertow. Called "the Place of Dangerous Waters" by the local tribe of Iroquois, the lake had been renamed, according to the local lore, because, while on a hike there, Washington Irving had seen the grin in the shore-facing front of the rock and then observed a tall, ungainly fisherman—inspiration for the hapless object of terrifying pursuits by a horseman with a jack-o-lantern for a head.

The truth was, "the Place of Dangerous Waters" had been renamed in 1895 by an entrepreneur who brought the tranquil site in the far

1

northeast corner of Stone County to create a woodland retreat for rich New Yorkers downriver. They had flocked to the lake and may or may not have known that Irving's story had unfolded beyond the Hudson River, many miles to the east. By the Roaring Twenties, the quiet resort had changed ownership several times and its seasonal inhabitants were Jewish. Half a century later, the land had been subdivided and the hotel along with its rustic rows of white cabins and a main lodge with an enormous dining room were gone, replaced by vacation homes and residences of a generation of parents, like James and Jenny Duncan, whose kids were more likely to be diverted by a video game than a tormenting headless cavalier.

At age nine, Sebastian had already learned to entertain himself with the computer in his bedroom in the spacious house his parents had built on a low bluff overlooking the lake. Sebastian's worried mother had done her best to supervise the hours he spent with restless blue eyes studying the electronic creatures animated by the boy's agile hand; a day did not go by without her looking into his room and upbraiding him about it. But when Jennifer Hollander Duncan passed away from an overdose of a powerful sedative two months after her headstrong son turned eight, Sebastian quickly discerned his father had a satisfyingly liberal approach to parenting. In summertime, liberties included afternoons of swimming off Horseman's Head Rock in the lake, with no stricter supervision than his twelve-year-old-sister, Jessica, who exhibited far less interest in her brother than in the good-looking fourteen-year-old son of their widowed father's housekeeper. Because the management of his wife's estate required a great deal of time, James Duncan went into the city twice a week and traveled frequently. This left the care of Sebastian and Jessica to jolly, chubby Cornelia Stewart, whose only child, Richard, was among the half a dozen boys swimming in the lake and waiting for Sebastian.

With a dash to the end of a dock where his father moored a small, trim speedboat, he cannonballed into the ice blue water, leaving Jessica to catch up, then surfaced in an explosion of white foam and stroked strongly toward his friends as they swam around or sunned themselves on Horseman's Head Rock.

Presently, the "betchas" started.

Rick Stewart bellowed to fifteen-year-old Harry Smith, "I'll betcha I can beatcha to Sebastian's dock and back."

Randy Fulmer, twelve, said to his twin brother, "Betcha I do a swan dive better'n you."

"Who's judging?" demanded Sonny, the older by two minutes.

Randy's eyes shifted. "Sebastian."

"Oh no," Sebastian replied with a definitive shake of his damp yellow head. "No way I'm gonna be judge. Anyway, you both stink at swan divin'."

"And you're just great, I suppose," Sonny sneered.

Sebastian puffed his chest. "I'm a better swimmer than you anytime."

"Zat so?"

"Hands down."

"Not in the high dive off the other side of the rock."

Sebastian's eyes sought out Jessica and found her absorbed in Rick Stewart. Satisfied, he surveyed the drop. "I dove off here lots of times."

Sonny grunted a laugh. "Bull! You never high-dived off the other side in your life."

"I have, too," Sebastian said, squaring slim shoulders.

Sonny's jaw jutted daringly. "Oh yeah? When?"

"Once," Sebastian answered softly, still gazing down at the water far down the cliff. "When nobody was around."

Sonny grinned. "Liar!"

"I'm not lyin'," Sebastian muttered, lifting his eyes from the water toward a skimming motorboat in the near distance.

"Okay. Prove it," retorted Sonny, striding to the lip of the precipice. "Betcha you ain't got the guts to dive off this side. Know why? Because your old man would kick your butt if he found out you did."

Sebastian eased closer to the edge, eyes toward the swirl of water lapping the foot of the rock. "How would he find out?"

"Her," Sonny said, jerking his head in Jessica's direction.

"Hey, Jessica," shouted Randy Fulmer, "if Sebastian dove 'off the other side, you'd tell on him, right?"

Irritated at being disturbed in her conversation with Rick, she snapped, "If my stupid brother wants to go and kill himself, let him."

Nudging a pebble with a toe, Sebastian sent it down the side and watched the splash. Looking up, he asked, "How far is it?"

Sonny gazed down. "About twenty-five feet."

"The water's about twelve deep," said his brother.

"So how about it, Sebastian?" Sonny goaded. "Are you goin' in from this side, or what? And I don't mean jumpin' off. I mean a *real* dive. I mean like those guys you see on TV from somewhere down in Mexico."

"Acapulco," Sebastian muttered, remembering seeing the men on television.

"They go off a steeper cliff than this," Sonny said. "And they do it headfirst."

Sebastian pictured them, sleek-limbed and with arched backs, the sun glinting on their skin as they pierced the roiling sea with its surging and battering white foam. But here, the lapping water of Ichabod Crane Lake, in the shade of Horseman's Head Rock, looked more purple than blue as he shifted his weight to his toes at the edge of the rock.

"Dare ya," whispered Sonny through a tight smile.

Sebastian raised his arms stiffly in arcs from his sides in imitation of the graceful poses of the Mexican divers.

"Don't do it, Sebastian," gasped Sonny's twin.

But he pleaded too late, for in that moment, Sebastian was gone, a blur of yellow hair, and a flash of sun-kissed flesh, and blue trunks with yellow side stripes, arms held out like wings in headlong plummet to the purple deep, then swinging forward in the shape of an arrow.

A moment later, he felt startled that diving into mere water could be so hard and hurt so much. But the surprise lasted only a moment, overwhelmed by a sensation of movement as he appeared to have no trouble breathing. Though it was water and not air that filled his lungs, he realized he was not sinking in the cold lake, but rising through it, buoyed toward the sun shimmering through the surface without having to swim.

Seen from above, he popped from the deep into the air while the Fulmer twins and the other boys atop the orange-and-black rock ran around or jumped up and down, waving their arms and screaming down at the slack figure bobbing on the calm surface like a doll made of cork. With a smug look, Jessica seemed pleased to have been proven right. Next, he observed that the motorboat that had been skimming across the lake had turned in the direction of the rock.

Presently, with mounting excitement as to what might happen next, he observed with a detached curiosity as the skipper of the little boat fished him from the water. Wheeled inland, the craft kicked up a rooster tail of water in a mad dash toward the dock and a little knot of agitated, waiting people. Hovering over them, so close he could have touched them if he wanted to, he saw his frantic father and a screaming Cornelia Stewart.

"The paramedics are on the way," James Duncan exclaimed as the boy was lifted from the boat to the dock.

The man from the motorboat bent over the boy, alternately pounding a fist on his chest and breathing into his mouth until he found himself rudely shoved aside by a threesome of purposeful and energetic young men in white uniforms with a pair of what seemed to be table-tennis paddles.

Enthralled by the fascinating tableau a few feet beneath him, and eager to observe the fruits of all the efforts regarding the familiar-looking and motionless young boy, he became aware that the distance between himself and the others had widened. He was being coaxed upward and realized that if he gave into the feeling, he would discover something far more wonderful than what was going on below. Surrendering himself to the inexplicable but pleasant urging, he sped upward without looking back and saw before him what appeared to be a long, dark tunnel with a brilliant light at its beckoning terminus.

Rushing toward it, he saw through the light the vague figure of a very beautiful woman.

As he approached her, she spoke. "Hello, Sebastian."

"Is that you, Mommy?"

"We have only a moment before you must go back," she said.

"I don't want to go back, Mommy. I want to stay with you."

"You can't stay. You don't belong. They will have you back with them in a moment. Listen to me, Sebastian. Tell them that I did not want to go. Tell them I didn't take my life. Tell them it was not an accident. Tell them it was murder."

"Mommy, Mommy, Mommy. Let me stay with you."

"You must go now, Sebastian. They're calling you."

He felt excruciating pain burning in his chest.

Gasping, he cried, "I don't want to go, Mommy!"

"Tell Granny Elizabeth what I said, Sebastian. Tell her that I was murdered. Granny will know what to do."

With narrowing eyes, Sebastian sobbed, "Mommy, there's an awful pain in my chest."

"I know, dearest. But the hurting will stop."

"Mommy, I'm falling!"

"It's all right. You're going back."

"No! Please."

"Just breathe in, darling Sebastian. Just open your eyes and you'll be back on the other side again."

Part One

Sorrow for the Dead

"The sorrow for the dead is the only sorrow from which we refuse to be divorced."

—Washington Irving, *Rural Funerals*

A Mass for the Dead

T HE SADNESS OF death gives way to the bright promise of immortality."

Still, after all the years since the authorization by the Vatican for the replacement of Latin as the language of the Mass in the United States, Arlene Flynn did not feel comfortable hearing English spoken from the altar.

"Lord, for your faithful people, life is changed, not ended."

The celebrant was also unfamiliar to her. In her judgment much too young and good-looking to be a priest, Father Robert Brennan had come straight from St. Joseph's Seminary upstate to the old red-brick pile that was Sacred Heart, keystone of the Roman Catholic Church in Stone County. Tall and slender, with lush brown hair, he bore a remarkable resemblance to the actor who had portrayed Superman in several movies. He had arrived the week after Easter, the last time she had been to Mass.

Had her sweet neighbor, Mrs. Alice Carew, not passed away, Christmas Eve Mass would have been the initial opportunity for Father Brennan to place the Communion wafer on Arlene Flynn's tongue, Rome's permission for communicants to take the Host into their own hands being an innovation toward modernization of the Church that went, in her view, too far.

"When the body of our earthly dwelling lies in death, we gain an everlasting dwelling place in heaven."

As the Mass for the Dead continued, her thoughts drifted from the white-draped casket of her neighbor to the graveyard behind the church, the final resting place of her parents. Before entering the church, she had spent several moments with Michael and Margaret Flynn, for whom all of the choir of angels, of which this handsome young priest was now speaking, had proclaimed their glory in the lovely and mysterious chanted cadences of the religion of the old catechism of strict nuns, patient brothers of a teaching order, and aged priests who saw to the schooling of Mike and Maggie's girl and her brother, Timothy.

The young priest declared, "The Mass is ended. Go in peace."

As the congregation replied, "Thanks be to God," she said the same.

"Go in peace to love," the priest intoned, making a cross in the air with his hand, "and serve the Lord."

Standing, she watched tearfully as Alice's coffin and the slowly moving pairs of the old woman's few survivors moved up the long aisle toward the front door and out to a waiting hearse. It and three black limousines would convey her and her meager mourners to burial far away in a cemetery in Brooklyn. There she would lie next to her cherished husband, whom she had introduced to Arlene Flynn through old photographs shown while remembering the old days over coffee and a wonderful crumb cake.

Among the last out of the church, she found herself shaking hands with the priest and startled by his greeting.

"A very good morning to you, Miss Flynn. But, alas, it is a melancholy one."

"Yes, it is," she said with a puzzled look.

He smiled. "You're wondering how I recognized you." The smile stretched into a grin. "Obviously, it was not from seeing you at Mass on Sundays."

Blushing, she felt as chastened as if a nun had rapped her knuckles with a ruler.

"There's no mystery," he said, beaming. "Alice spoke of you often and fondly when I called on her during her illness. She showed me a photo of herself and you taken at an amusement park."

"Alice loved Ferris wheels."

"She talked a great deal about you. She was very proud to call you her friend. I've also seen your picture in the *Stone County Clarion*. Apparently, there's not been a crime in Stone County that Arlene Flynn,

10

special investigator for District Attorney Aaron Benson, has not had a major role in solving."

"Some of my best friends are reporters. They function in the mistaken belief that if they say nice things about me, I'll help them get their speeding tickets fixed."

"Will you be going to Brooklyn for the interment?"

"I'd like to. But I do have to get back to work."

"Oh yes," he said solemnly, "I read that you're in charge of investigating the murder of that poor woman up at the lake on Sunday. I'll pray for your speedy success in finding the killer."

"Thanks. I'll need all the help I can get."

"When will I see you at Mass again? I hope I won't have to wait till Christmas."

"You *have* spent time talking to Alice!"

"She told me I could count on two things at Christmas Eve Mass— a gift of one of her crumb cakes and Arlene Flynn trying not to be noticed in the very last row. With her passing, I shan't have the former. I'll pray that God will see to the latter."

She watched as a gleaming wooden coffin went in the hearse.

"If Alice were here," she said sadly, "she'd call that a big waste of money, just to stick her in the ground."

"Obviously you don't agree. I know who paid for it."

As the door of the hearse closed, she sighed. "I'm going to miss that feisty old girl."

"You'll see each other again," he said. "You believe, as I do, that death is merely a transition. If not, you wouldn't have taken time away from your case to come here this morning."

2

⁘

Dumb Death Speaks

A LTHOUGH THE MODEST split-level ranch-style house she had
left a couple of hours ago had been painstakingly furnished, perhaps overly, she entered it with a gnawing feeling of emptiness that
grew as she ascended to her bedroom to change from an old black dress
and black shoes bought expressly for the funeral into more sensible
clothes for the office. The sensation was not unfamiliar. She could
count on it overtaking her whenever she returned from Mass. But it
also manifested itself when she investigated a murder, which was, she
had discovered, as solitary an undertaking as confronting one's short-
comings before God. No matter how many people might be around
her at the scene of a homicide, she felt as alone as she did in church.
Each occasion required examination of one's soul.

On the bed, awaiting her return from saying good-bye to her friend
Alice, lay the sensible clothing she had long ago learned to wear to
work: tan slacks, a loose white short-sleeved blouse, a sport jacket with
large pockets, and a pair of low-heeled shoes that would not kill her
feet if she had to walk a great distance and that she would not mind
ruining if she had to trudge in a muddy field in order to have a look
at a spot picked by a killer with a body to dump, as one had sometime
the past weekend.

The woman had been discovered by a pair of weekend hikers from
the city on Sunday afternoon at almost exactly the hour at which Father Brennan had been administering the last rites to Alice Carew.

Slipping out of the funeral dress, she reflected on the coincidence of the priest rushing to Alice's bedside to dispel all the fears of the moment of death, ministering soothing ointments and the comforting promises of resurrection in Christ, while the other young man had found in the second frail old woman a need to inflict the terrors of dying by strangulation with the woman's knotted stockings.

All the evidence glimpsed by her practiced eyes at the site where the body had been dumped had pointed to the killer having been a youthful male, as murderers usually proved to be. In the sorry history of the world, homicide had been an overwhelmingly male endeavor. At what moment in the life of a boy, she wondered as she put on the blouse, could he step across the line to become a murderer? Why not go into the priesthood, as Father Brennan had? Why become a killer and not a doctor? Why not a scientist, a teacher, or any other pursuit that enhanced life and respected it? Why not a cop?

The shoes she had set out had been worn on Sunday. Four days later, they were dried and stiff, but brushed to the highest shine possible after hours slipping and sliding in the muck and mire of the northeastern shore of Crane Lake. As usual, she had not been at the crime scene long when her boss arrived.

As ever, District Attorney Aaron Benson had appeared out of place, crisply dressed in a gray suit and with his hair combed as neatly as that of an altar boy. In ten years of working for him, he seemed not to have aged a day, whereas she was constantly discovering alarming new strands of gray infringing on reddish hair her high school annual had described twenty years earlier as the crowning glory for the girl listed in the book as most likely to become a movie star in roles for which Maureen O'Hara had grown too mature. That she had chosen to attend John Jay College of Criminal Justice in New York City to become a cop had been the talk of her first class reunion. By the tenth-year reunion, she had earned the gold shield of detective third grade of the New York Police Department. At the twentieth, no one had needed to be told she had become District Attorney Aaron Benson's chief investigator. She had tracked down and helped him convict several murderers.

Sunday night, he had asked, "What have we got?"

They had a great deal. The strangled woman had been for a time in a room that had dark blue carpeting. Fibers adhering to her nude body were evident even without a microscope. The body had been driven to the edge of the lake in a car that left the unmistakable imprint of balding tires.

"The killer is a local," she said. "He'd have to be to know this godforsaken spot."

A general psychological criminal profile based on studies by the FBI suggested he would be in his twenties or thirties and in good physical shape. Intelligence probably rated above average. One did not kill and get away with it undiscovered without some smarts. Somewhere along the line, he had probably formed a love-hate feeling for women, which more than likely found its root in fear of them, especially of older women, perhaps imbued in him by his mother or a mother surrogate. Whoever was his father would not have been around much to make a difference. The killer would probably be found to be living alone, this deduction drawn from the unlikelihood of a murder being committed in a home into which a companion might suddenly appear. His abode probably would be in an area in which chances were minimal that he might be observed by a passerby or neighbors whose prying eyes might watch him and ponder what bulky thing he was putting in his car on a Sabbath morning, and why. His job would prove to be a menial one, providing nothing extra in the way of pay to put fresh tires on his car, if he worked at all. "No friends," she continued. "Likely to have had a brush or two, or more, with authority, going back to school days. I wouldn't be surprised to turn up an arrest record in police computer files."

She felt certain he had known the woman he killed.

"Unfortunately, the victim has yet to be identified," she had told the DA. "Once I do that, I'll know the man who did this, and you'll chalk up another murder conviction."

So far, routine procedures to name the dead woman, including fingerprint check, had been fruitless. A story in the *Clarion* on the discovery of the body had produced nothing in the way of a lead. Nor had her partner garnered a clue.

"It's as if this little old lady never existed," Detective Peter Sloan had reported the previous afternoon. Slouching into her office, his face had been as earnest and worried as a hound's, but unlined. "Nobody has filed a missing person's report. There's been no notice at the post office of anyone's mail backed up."

14

"Which tells us she was either a widow," Flynn replied, "or was what my mother used to call—"

"An old maid?"

"A 'spinster lady,' actually. That means she probably lived alone and kept to herself, which is what women like her usually do. As to the mail, what would she get? Utility bills arrive the first of the month. Two weeks ago. A Social Security check comes on the third, if she got one. State welfare assistance? Maybe she wasn't even eligible. If she owned her home, she wouldn't get it, or food stamps. Her children, if there are any, may live elsewhere and would have no way of knowing anything was amiss."

"My mom lives upstate," Sloan said, settling hs lanky frame on the corner of her desk. "I call her every couple of days."

"Not all sons are as good as you, Sloan. But we could hear from a family member any minute. It's only three days since the body was found."

"That's right," the detective said sourly. "And that brings us to the first tenet in the catechism of the Arlene Flynn Church of Homicide Investigation. I remember the day you instructed me in it. I was so fresh out of college that the ink on my degree in criminalistics was still damp. My first day in this job two and a half years ago, you said to me, 'If you haven't solved a murder in three days, Sloan, odds are you never will.' "

Her smile formed crinkles at the corners of her eyes. "Has it been only two and a half years? Then you're long overdue for lesson two of the catechism: 'Forget the first lesson.' "

Sloan barked a laugh.

Smiling, she asked, "Has our beloved friend and brother in right-eousness, the good Dr. Plodder, sent over his autopsy report on the victim?"

Sloan grunted. "Are you kidding? It's only been three days. But so what? We know how she died. The bastard choked her with her own stockings."

"You never know what tales a corpse might tell you," she said. "I've got something to do first thing in the morning. When that's done, I'll pay a visit to Zeligman's charnel house and see if I can goose the report from the lovable old fart."

As promised, having changed from the black dress worn to Alice

Carew's funeral, she arrived at the basement mortuary of Stone County Medical Center, where Dr. Zeligman practiced the catechism of his religion. On the left as she faced his desk was a quote from the poet e.e. cummings:

> Dumb death
> we all inherit.

The other quote was an inscription she had seen often on the wall of the medical examiner's office in New York City:

> This is the place where death delights to help the living.

Jowlish, gray-haired, rumpled, red-eyed, and the picture of the meaning of *avuncular,* Dr. Theodore Zeligman clutched a mug of coffee as if he were a priest handling a chalice of wine that he was about to transubstantiate miraculously into the Blood of Christ. He peered owlishly over the tops of half-moon spectacles.

"I know why you're here," he grumbled. "You've come about the woman up at the lake. Cause of death: strangled from behind with a pair of nylon stockings. She struggled, reaching back and scratching her killer. There are skin scrapings under her nails. No sexual assault. Age: seventyish. She had cancer and about six months to live. If she had initiated a treatment program a year ago, she could have been in remission. She probably lost fifty pounds in that time. Have you identified her yet?"

"Not a clue. I was hoping you might help on that score."

The coroner removed his glasses, tilted back in a squeaky swivel chair, and folded surprisingly delicate hands across his ample belly. "I can't give you a name. But somebody upstairs in hospital records should be able to."

Flynn jerked with surprise. "Really?"

Zeligman pinched the bridge of his bulbous nose where the glasses had left marks. "The X rays show the woman had had a hip replacement. Judging by the scar tissue and other indicia that I won't bore you with, I'd say the surgery was three, maybe four years ago."

"How do you know it was performed here?"

"I don't know. But the type of pin is what they use here. Assuming she was a local resident, she probably had the operation here. Records will tell if I'm right. All the files have been computerized, so it shouldn't take you long to find her name."

Fifteen minutes later, twelve of them spent waiting for someone to run the computer, she had all there was to know about the victim—except who had killed her.

"Her name is Matilda Allen," she declared triumphantly to Peter Sloan after fifteen more minutes. "Address: Five thirteen Traitor's Lair Road. She wasn't a spinster lady, but a widow. There's no next of kin listed in her hospital records. And get this, Peter Sloan! Matilda had no medical insurance and paid for her very expensive hip replacement surgery with a personal check drawn on an account with the Stone County National Bank. Now, given that fact, plus the absence of sexual molestation and that address in the very, very upscale Traitor's Lair neck of our woods, I'd say that the late Matilda Allen had been a lady of means. And where there is money, there is . . ."

Sloan rubbed his hands gleefully. *"Motive."*

"You head up to Traitor's Lair," she said, striding from the office. "I'll relate the happy news of this breakthrough to the boss."

3

The Woman in Blue

L IKE A CROWN, the splendid granite-pillared and domed Stone County Courthouse rested on the crest of a grassy knoll in the center of the city of Newtown and had been designed to express the solidity of American democratic government. The first three floors provided spacious wood-paneled court chambers flooded with sunlight streaming through towering arched windows or from huge elegant crystal chandeliers symbolizing the majestic purpose of illuminating truth and providing fairness and equal justice under God and law for all. On the fourth and fifth stories were found the marriage license bureau, tax collector, records of birth and death, and all other agencies empowered by the county government to oversee the general welfare.

Beneath the gold-leafed dome and a steeply slanting copper roof that eight decades had weathered to green, the uppermost floor's office of the district attorney had been structured into a maze of narrow and meandering corridors and oddly shaped spaces whose only saving grace was their windows, which afforded grand vistas of the city in every direction and the distant Hudson River. The largest of these was a three-room corner suite that had furnished refreshing cross ventilation in the era before air conditioning. Prior to the advent of Aaron Benson, the largest of the offices had been occupied by sixteen men, each of whom in his entire term of service had not prosecuted as many murderers as Aaron Benson had sent to prison in his first three years. Except for meetings requiring confidentiality, his practice, when ensconced behind an antique table that served as a desk in the scrupulously kept office, was to leave the door open.

Hesitating in the doorway, Flynn found the man she called "the boss" coatless and with white shirtsleeves rolled up to elbows that were propped on the arms of a high-back maroon leather chair. Immaculately manicured fingers interlaced into a steeple under the sharp point of his chin. Intent eyes peered across the desk to a silver-haired matronly woman in a royal blue dress who seemed to be in the process of being swallowed by one of a pair of enormous brown leather armchairs.

Benson's eyes shifted from the woman to the doorway. "Ah, Arlene," he exclaimed. "Good. I was just going to call you in. I want you to meet a dear friend, Mrs. Elizabeth Hollander."

As the woman turned slightly, Flynn thought she looked like an errant bluebird who had found a perch on the huge chair.

"It's Miss Flynn, isn't it?" Hollander said in a fittingly chirpy voice. "I've seen you frequently on the television news programs and your picture in the newspapers."

Flynn stepped into the office. "It is a face that's hard to forget, Mrs. Hollander."

The woman accepted the self-effacing humor with a slight smile and turned again to Benson.

"Sit, Arlene. Sit," he urged, waving her into the second chair. "I want your thoughts about an extraordinary experience Elizabeth has just been telling me about, involving her young grandson, Sebastian. Would you mind starting over, Elizabeth?"

"I only hope Miss Flynn won't think I've lost my senses," she said with a sidelong glance.

"Of course I won't," Flynn said, gently touching the woman's cool wrist.

"I assure you I would not be here, Miss Flynn," she said, "were it not for the fact that this matter concerns my grandson and my conviction that he could not possibly have made up the story he has steadfastly related in all the details each time I have asked him to repeat it. Now, it is true that Sebastian has been gifted with intelligence and has an insatiable curiosity, but why should a boy of nine invent such a story? And even if he had made it up, how could he have remained so consistent in all the particulars? I grant that he may have heard about or read of near-death experiences, but why on earth would he pretend to have gone through one and then add something that bears no resemblance to any of these events reported by others? Have you ever heard of anyone who had a near-death experience coming back to say that they'd been told about a loved one being murdered? What you hear from these people is of a long, dark tunnel and a bright light at the end and meeting a deceased loved one. In some cases, they say they were welcomed by Christ. But Sebastian insists he came into the light and met his mother—my daughter—and that Jenny told him she hadn't died from a mistaken overdose of pills last year. That she'd not taken her life. That she had been murdered. I ask you, Miss Flynn, as I asked Aaron before you came in, can you believe a nine-year-old could and would concoct such a fantastic story?"

"Mrs. Hollander, to answer you, I'll need more information."

"Ask anything you wish."

"The obvious first question has to be this: Did your daughter say who murdered her?"

Hollander shook her head slowly. "She told Sebastian only that she had been."

"You said the cause of death was attributed to an overdose of some kind?"

"That's correct."

"What were the circumstances?"

"It was last summer, almost exactly a year ago. To celebrate the consummation of a very important business project she had been working on for months, Jenny invited a number of her associates up from the city to spend a weekend at her house on Crane Lake. On Saturday night, after a day of swimming and boating and a lovely cookout on the deck of the house overlooking the lake at sunset, she complained of one of her migraines coming on. She took one of her pills and soon after excused herself to go to bed early. When her husband, James, went to bed a couple of hours later, he found her sound asleep. But when he attempted waking her in the morning, he discovered she was dead. A blood test during the autopsy showed the presence of a massive dose of the powerful sedative that had been prescribed by the family physician, Dr. Granick."

"For what purpose?"

"For headaches. Jenny had a history of migraines that came on when she was under a great deal of stress. She had been taking the medicine for a year and fully understood she was to take no more than one tablet a day. That evening, she appeared to have taken all of them."

"How many?"

"Dr. Granick had recently prescribed a bottle of six. James said there had been five in the bottle on Saturday. When he found it in the kitchen on Sunday morning, it was empty."

"Excuse me. I want to be clear. Jenny was found dead in bed, but the empty pill bottle was found in the kitchen?"

"Whenever Jenny took a pill of any kind, even an aspirin, she insisted on doing so the way she had always seen her father take medicine—with a cup of coffee. It was a habit I'd never been able to get her to break. She had to have her coffee—the strongest possible. Cup after cup, the way some people chain-smoke. There was always a pot steaming on the stove. That night, she had been drinking it iced. I tried to get her to appreciate that it was the worst thing to do, for a person prone to migraines. But Jenny had to have what she called her 'java fix.' "

"Please forgive my bluntness," Flynn said with a glance at Benson, "but all you've told me, Mrs. Hollander, does point to your daughter committing suicide. One does not, it seems to me, swallow five such powerful pills by mistake."

Pursing lips, the woman looked even more like a bird, ready to warble. "That was also Dr. Granick's opinion," she said with a nod. "And it was one that I accepted. Until Sebastian related his near-death experience, that is."

"I gather from what you seem to know about the phenomenon that you're a believer in near-death experiences?"

"I've seen people talking about them on television. But I never gave them any credence until Sebastian told me he had died and seen his mother. You see, there was no question that for a time one day a few weeks ago, when he was pulled from Crane Lake after diving from a big rock, Sebastian had shown no signs of life. Paramedics working on him had to use electrical shocks to revive the poor boy."

"When did he report having spoken with his mother? Did he wake up and blurt it out?"

"No. He said he had told no one about it but me. He said Jenny expressly told him to tell *me*. He was emphatic on the point. He did not do so until yesterday. I've come down from my home in Rochester to bring him a few back-to-school gifts."

"Did you ever consider that a bad dream or hallucination brought on by Sebastian's brush with death is a more plausible explanation for what he told you?"

"I'm not a ninny, Miss Flynn. Of course I considered it. But I have also considered another source of Sebastian's story. Isn't it possible that the shock of what happened to him brought back a memory of something he knew but had buried in his mind because it was too awful?"

"Concerning what?"

"The fact that his good-for-nothing whoring father murdered my Jennifer."

4

Exchange of Vows

"THAT'S A SERIOUS allegation, Elizabeth," said Benson. "It's *the* most serious one there is."

The woman's birdlike lips trembled a moment, then parted to emit a gust of breath. "Don't lecture me, Aaron," she said with an edge of impatience she might have directed at a stupid child. "I want to know if are you going to look into this or not."

"Assuming for the moment that your daughter was murdered," Flynn replied calmly, "why do you think James did it?"

"Isn't it usually the philandering husband?"

"Obviously, husbands have killed their wives. But it's been my experience that when most men exchange vows with their brides, they do mean it when they pledge to honor and cherish them."

"Well, who else could have murdered Jenny?"

"You said there were houseguests, business associates of your daughter. Why not one of them?"

"None of them stood to inherit seven million dollars in cash and stock in Jenny's business, plus real estate. The lake house is worth at least a million. There's a condominium apartment in the city. *Park Avenue.* And he now has total control of a million in trust funds set up in Jenny's will for the two kids. That's a million *each.* And growing by the minute. If that's not a motive for murder, tell me what is."

"I assume your daughter didn't become wealthy overnight a year ago."

"Of course not. It took her years and hard work to build on the inheritance from her father."

23

"How much of an inheritance?"

"A million and a half dollars. That's why James married her. To get his hands on that money."

"How long had they been married at the time of her death?"

"Twelve years."

"During which time Jenny's fortune had increased?"

"Certainly. She had a brilliant mind for business."

"My point is, if James had married her for money, why did he wait twelve years to kill her so as to inherit it? And then have to share it with children?"

"I don't know, Miss Flynn. When you arrest him, ask him! What about it, Aaron? Are you going to take action?"

"I appreciate how you feel, Elizabeth," he said, "but there is no evidence your daughter was murdered."

"But Sebastian said she was."

"I have no doubt that your grandson believes he went up to heaven and spoke to his mother. But he'd gone through a traumatic experience. What a boy thinks happened to him while he was being revived from a near drowning provides no sufficient cause for me to get involved. I can't open a homicide investigation based on a boy's claim of having had a near-death experience in which murder was alleged, especially in a case in which the death has been declared self-inflicted, intentionally or not."

"No! I cannot accept that verdict. I'm certain that somehow or other, that wicked man got those pills into Jenny. If it means that I have to sign a paper with your office or the state police to get at the truth, I am prepared to do so. If I have to go to the newspaper with my accusation, I'll do so. Let James sue me for defamation if he wishes to. The defense against slander is truth. I know that man killed my Jenny."

As Benson's pleading eyes turned in Flynn's direction, he sighed. "I'll tell you what we'll do, Elizabeth. Arlene will look into the matter of your daughter's death *informally*. Very, very discreetly. There's no better homicide investigator, believe me. If she finds a smidgen of evidence to warrant opening a full-scale murder investigation, I'll do so. But should Arlene come back and report she has found no evidence of foul play in your daughter's untimely death, you must promise me you will forget about what Sebastian said. Agreed?"

"If there's one thing I've learned about you over the past fifteen years, Aaron Benson, it's that you're a politician who keeps his promises, so I'll do this your way," she said. Rising so gracefully that she seemed to take wing out of the deep chair, she extended a hand toward him and wagged an admonishing finger. "But I have one condition I must insist on. I do not want anyone talking to Sebastian. The child's been through enough already."

"I don't think that will be necessary," he said, reaching across the desk and taking the hand between both of his. "In spite of the circumstances, Elizabeth, it's been grand to see you. I'll be in touch with you as soon as Arlene has something to report."

"I'm in Newtown for a week, staying at the George Washington Inn." With eyes as probing as an eagle's, she turned and offered the hand to Flynn. "I'm delighted to see that a woman can become a detective. Unheard of in my day, of course. Is it fun?"

"Most of the time, I enjoy it."

"You are *Miss* Flynn. Why aren't you married?"

"I am. To my work."

"Wise," she said, walking spritely to the door. "Very wise of you indeed."

When she was gone and out of earshot, Flynn glared across the desk. "Thank you very much, boss," she said brusquely. "How do you propose I handle this new investigation? Tarot cards? Dial up one of those psychic phone numbers? Maybe organize a séance?"

Benson resumed sitting in his imposing chair. "Far be it from me to tell the best detective in the game how to do her job! Now, what was it you wanted to see me about?"

"The old lady at Crane Lake. There's been a major break."

5

On Traitor's Lair Road

S HADED BY FLANKING woods, the road climbed steeply, then
crested at an estate that had been central to one of Arlene Flynn's
most celebrated cases. The clue that had unraveled the murder of one
famous author of best-selling thrillers by another mystery writer had
been an out-of-place mud-caked Oriental carpet in the library of one
of the county's venerated historic sites and once upon a time the home
of Ilona Troy. A theatrical and motion-picture star in the giddy era between the World War I and the Depression, she had acquired the property and spearheaded a 1930s invasion of Stone County by rich and
celebrated New Yorkers whose weathering of the Wall Street crash un-
scathed permitted them to scoop up river-view properties at bargain
prices. Three decades later, they had been marketed to a flood of
post–World War II refugees from the noisy city downriver. But Troy
had resisted the subdividers, becoming more and more reclusive as her
beautiful old fieldstone house and land had drifted into decay and her
finances declined into bankruptcy, until she was found in the library
one day, dead from being forgotten about.

Dated by the Stone County historians to the Revolutionary War,
the house was said to have been occupied for a few days by the British
spy Major André during his conspiracy with Benedict Arnold for surrender of nearby West Point. Tradition had bestowed upon it and the
winding, narrow blacktop road that bypassed it a most romantic name:
Traitor's Lair.

Half a serpentine mile beyond, Peter Sloan peered through the
trees and glimpsed the chimneys of the Tudor-style house at the address

of the woman whose dead body had been discovered by weekend hikers beside Ichabod Crane Lake, more than three miles farther on. Swinging left off the road, he entered a curving gravel driveway and proceeded slowly until he reached a macadam parking area. Directly in front of the entrance to the house, he encountered a battered 1970s vintage green Chevrolet station wagon. Left at an odd angle, with the driver's side door flung open, it appeared to have been hurriedly abandoned. Its muddy tires had treads worn down to the cording.

Although he felt confident no one would be found inside the house, he used a cellular telephone to call the dispatcher at the state police headquarters at Stone Light for troopers to respond as backup and to ask for a crime-scene team to be sent. Next, to a puzzlingly curt Arlene Flynn, he declared, "Better come on up to the address on Traitor's Lair. I think I've located the car that was used in the Ichabod Crane Lake homicide."

Arriving half an hour later, she stepped from her car into a a mixture of the strange and the familiar. The location of the investigation might be new to her, but she recognized everyone there. Waiting for her were experts in the implements of sudden and violent death: a photographer to record anything holding promise of solving the riddle, fingerprint seekers and bloodstain lifters and the other grim-faced and white-gloved men and women criminalists who seemed as coolly detached as she to the detritus of the unexplained and, consequently, the suspicious death of a stranger about whose life they all would soon know every intimate detail. "To know thy murderer," she had been taught in theory and had confirmed in practice, "thou shalt first know thy victim."

"As I expected," declared Sloan, hurrying across the parking area to her car, "there's nobody inside. Once the troopers and I ascertained that, I kept everybody out until you could get here."

With a nod, she said, "Okay. Let's go in and have a look."

He opened the front door, which led to a small foyer with dark wood-paneled walls. To the left, the bottom two steps of a narrow enclosed stairway were red-carpeted. A double doorway on the right opened on the living room. "I think you should look at the rug in here," Sloan said, standing next to it. "It's blue shag and looks to me like the same shade as the fibers found on the body. It's the only blue carpet that I saw on my quick walk through the house."

Without entering the room, she studied the rug. "Sloan, you get the Sherlock Holmes award for not only seeing but *observing*. What's upstairs?"

"Three bedrooms. The largest one, at the front of the house, appears to have been hers," he said as they climbed the narrow stairs single file. "There's one bathroom, adjoining her room."

Studying the tiny, narrow room from the doorway, she observed the tub filled with water. Rumpled next it, as though it had been kicked, lay a yellow bath mat. Lingerie consisting of pink panties and bra and a white slip had been placed neatly on a small table. With a sigh, she said, "This is where she died. I'd say she was either about to have her bath or had just gotten out of it. An analysis of the water for soap will tell which. Do you see any stockings?"

Sloan shook his head slowly.

"Show me her bedroom next," Flynn said.

On a nightstand stood a silver-framed photo of a teenaged boy and girl being hugged by a far younger Matilda Allen. On the bed, a plain blue dress had been laid out. Next to it was a straw wide-brimmed hat. Adjacent to it lay a Bible.

"The poor dear," she said with a long sigh. "She was getting ready to go to church." Turning away, she spoke angrily. "I've seen enough up here."

"If she was strangled in the bathroom," Sloan said as they went downstairs, "what's the explanation for the blue rug fibers on the body? The only blue rug is in the living room."

"He carried her down and put her there."

"Why would he do that?"

"To rest? Catch his breath? He may have left her while he brought his car closer to the house. Maybe he heard something to distract him. Only he can tell us why. If the bathroom is where he killed her, the CSU people will soon know. Let's get out of the way and let them do their jobs."

Outside, Sloan poked a tire of the station wagon with a toe. "How do you figure the owner of this jalopy got away?"

"He probably took Matilda's car. Have the state troopers get on the horn to Albany and find out what the Department of Motor Vehicles has registered to her and what they have on the Chevy. I can't imagine it still being in the vicinity."

"Unless the guy who took it is the stupidest creature on God's earth."

Looking around, she said, "Do we know how close the nearest neighbor is?"

"To the south is the old Troy place. The next house to the north is about two miles. It's owned by a man named Azerier. He's a radio and television announcer. He does commercials and voice-overs. Apparently, he comes up from the city only on weekends."

"Matilda was murdered on Sunday."

"What was the boss's reaction when you told him we'd identified her?"

"Before I got a chance to tell him," she said, getting into her car, "he dropped another murder in my lap."

Sloan's eyes widened. "I haven't heard of a new homicide."

"That's because it was either a suicide or an accident."

Blinking, he said, "I'm afraid you've lost me."

"There's more. The victim reported it to her son—after he died. But he came back to life. Only his grandmother says I'm not allowed to talk to him about it."

Sloan scratched his head. "Oh, *now* I understand!"

"After you wrap up here, meet me at the Scales of Justice," she said with a chuckle. "I'll buy you a beer and burger and explain everything."

6

Scales of Justice

IF ASKED TO choose addresses found in the best literature in the English language—which to her meant detective fiction—that she would most like to visit, Arlene Flynn would unhesitatingly list them: The digs of Inspector Morse of the Oxford Constabulary in England, where a phonograph was likely to be playing Mozart; Sherlock Holmes's consulting room at 221B Baker Street; Nero Wolfe's brownstone on West Thirty-fifth Street somewhere between Tenth and Eleventh avenues; No. 9 Bywater Street, Chelsea, London, home of George Smiley, whose espionage work was actually sleuthing; Flat No. 203, Whitehaven Mansions, the domicile of the persnickity Belgian detective with the egg-shaped head, Hercule Poirot; Cabot Cove, Maine, the home of Jessica Fletcher before her television writers moved her to New York City, took away her typewriter, and gave her a computer; and Pomeroy's Wine Bar, near London's Old Bailey, where barrister Horace Rumpole planned defensive strategies while imbibing Château Thames Embankment.

In real life, the closest she could come to the romance of these hallowed shrines stood across Jail Street, opposite the Stone County Courthouse. A shadowy, noisy, and smoke-infused old saloon that had opened as a Prohibition speakeasy, it was owned by a rehabilitated burglar and second-story man with a dubious claim that his true name was James Moriarty. For as far back as anyone could recall, the Scales of Justice had been a hangout used by denizens of the sedate structure opposite it to kill time as they waited for cases to be called: prosecutors, the defendants and their lawyers, witnesses, jurors, occasionally a judge, cops, and Martin Katz, representative of the *Stone County Clarion.*

Bald except for a grizzled gray band of hair as tight and wiry as steel wool, pink-faced from years of neat scotch, and too pudgy from hamburgers and french fries ever to look good in the white double-breasted suits he considered his sartorial signature in all seasons, Katz had been covering police and courts for the *Clarion* and other newspapers "since Cain killed his goody-two-shoes brother," as he phrased it. Inside Scales of Justice, he occupied a booth adjacent to the front door, the better to note who entered.

"There you are, Flynn," he blared, beckoning to her with a wiggling pudgy finger as she paused by the door a few minutes past six o'clock. "I got something I need confirmed."

Standing next to his table, she frowned down and said, "Ever hear of the telephone?"

"People have a way of dodging calls. Sometimes they go so far as to hang up on me," he said, feigning woundedness. "Word is, you got an ID on the old lady at the lake and she lived on Traitor's Lair Road. What say you to the readers of the *Clarion*?"

She drew a finger across her lips as if zipping them.

"Aw, c'mon, Arlene," he huffed. "A highly reliable source told me the deceased was a rich old recluse of a dame, name of Matilda Allen."

Flynn smiled. "Who's the source? As if I didn't know."

"Darling, you know better than to ask me that. If I named my sources, I'd never get anything from them again."

"What else did Ted Zeligman tell you?"

"Wrong, Little Miss Know It All! I probed Dr. Plodder. He stiffed me. No pun intended."

"The computer guy at the hospital!"

Massive white-suited shoulders shrugged. "Was it Matilda?"

"Marty, you know I can't give out information regarding the identity of a victim until we've notified next of kin. How would you feel if you found out your wife was dead by reading it in the *Clarion*?"

"You'll pardon me," he said, toying with a glass of scotch, "if I choose not to incriminate myself by not answering that one. When do you think you'll be able to give me a confirmation?"

"You'll get it straight from my boss when he's ready to make an announcement."

31

"I could go with what I've got, you know."

"Of course. But please wait. For the sake of the old lady's relatives, if any. We're working on finding her folks. Okay?" Looking up as a waitress suddenly loomed next to her, she ordered, a 7UP with a slice of lemon.

"For God sake," Katz grumbled, "have a real drink for once."

"Now I have a question for you," she said. "Do you believe in life after death? Heaven? Hell?"

"I know there is a hell. I worked there once. It's a weekly paper in Syracuse."

"What's your position on the phenomenon called 'near-death experience'? That is, if you have a position."

After a sip of scotch, he rubbed his jowly jaw with a large hand. "The paper did a feature on the leading guru on the subject in the Sunday edition a couple of years ago. His name is Kevin Albert. He's written books. He's got a big Victorian house over in Larktown where he does his so-called research. In my opinion, these stories are a lot of bullshit from a bunch of people like Albert with vivid imaginations. Hallucinations. Mind tricks. Same as those stories you hear from other loonies who say they were abducted by aliens from another galaxy. These near-death space cadets have been cut from the same cloth as the flying saucer and little gray men from Mars crowd. Why do you ask?"

"Someone I know claims that a relative had one."

"For a moment there, I was afraid you were going to tell me you'd zoomed down that long, dark tunnel and into some blinding, embracing, and eternal light."

"Not yet."

"Well, if it ever happens to you, and you get a chance to have a chin-wag with Jesus, will you ask him something for me?"

"This should be good!"

He swirled his dwindling scotch. "I'd like to know how the water at the wedding at Cana got changed into alcohol. If I could do that, I could cut way back on my liquor bill."

"The Lord changed water into *wine,* Marty. Not a fifth of Johnnie Walker Red." Looking up, she saw Peter Sloan barge through the door. "Now, if the *Clarion* will excuse me?"

Katz's alert brown eyes shifted toward the figure hovering near the door, his eyes scanning the room. "Your trusty young protégé has on his bloodhound's face. Where's he been? Poking around up on Traitor's Lair Road, perhaps? Shall he join us? Or will you two be meeting privately?"

"It's Thursday, Marty," she said, waving at Sloan. "This is the day the Lord has set aside for me to instruct young Peter in the catechism of the one true faith."

The reporter's mouth gaped in astonishment. "Sloan's turning Catholic?"

"I refer to the house of worship across the street—our own cathedral of Law, Order, and Justice for All, before whose altar we daily genuflect."

"Droll, Arlene. Very droll. However, I belong to the Fourth Estate. So, when you see the high priest of your church—namely, Aaron Benson—be sure to tell him that he must not keep the press waiting on the subject of the identity of the lady at the lake. The people's right to know? First Amendment and all that stuff?"

Leaving the booth, she encountered the waitress, took her 7UP, linked arms with Sloan, and led him past the crowd at the bar to a table for two at the rear of the room. Seated, she asked, "Did the DMV come up with anything on the station wagon and a car registered to Matilda?"

"Nothing on the wagon itself. Its license tags were stolen from a Toyota in Yonkers a few weeks ago. But get this! Matilda owned a maroon 1990 BMW convertible. The old lady was not only rich but quite a sport, apparently! Now, the way I picture this homicide having gone down is this. Matilda is spotted tooling along in the BMW by this guy with the beat-up Chevy with the bad tires. He trails her home with the idea of relieving her of the car. He lurked around till she was in the house, snuck in and up the stairs, and strangled her. The car was the motive."

Flynn tugged her lower lip. "Why didn't he just leave her where she was?"

"I thought about that. How about this? The woman is dead and he doesn't know if and how quickly the body might be discovered. Naturally, he is very eager to get a long jump on his escape—in the BMW. He bundles the old lady into his jalopy because there was no way that he was going to haul a corpse away in a car as noticeable as that BMW. He dumped her at the lake, returned to her house, left his heap there, and took off in Matilda's flashy wheels. Whatcha think?"

"Very plausible. Except . . ."

His beaming face sagged. "Except what?"

"She was killed in the bathroom, preparing for church. That puts the time of death in the morning."

"Granted."

"What was she doing out in her car *before* going to church?"

"She had an errand to run. Maybe she needed milk, bread. She went out for the Sunday paper."

"Possible. However, isn't it reasonable to assume that if she needed all the things you mentioned, she'd pick them up on her way back from church? She's elderly. She had a hip replacement. I think that's a woman who would not leave the house twice in a day if she didn't have to."

"The guy could have been passing by and spotted the car from out on Traitor's Lair Road, saw his chance, and grabbed it."

"But the only part of the house visible from the road is the rooftop and chimneys."

"He could have followed her at another time, remembered the car, and decided to go for it later."

"In the daytime, when somebody in the house was bound to be up and about? I think a car thief would prefer to have cover of darkness."

"Obviously," he said, poutingly, "you do not buy the car as the guy's motive."

"I think the car was important to him. It certainly was a big step up from his. And it would certainly be more reliable in getting away from a murder. But I'd be surprised if the BMW was his reason for killing her."

"Well, anyway, the state police have an alert out for it."

"Excellent. Tomorrow we'll see what we can find out about Matilda's relatives. They may have the answers that we can only guess at. Such as motive, and suspects. We may get some help from the public after we release her identity to the press." Her eyes shifted toward the front of the restaurant. "By the way, Marty Katz already knows. He was trying to get me to confirm it before you showed up. I put him off. But our beloved boss is going to have to issue a statement. In the morning, probably. What you should do then is go downstairs to the county records and dig out Matilda's file. If she had children, there will be certificates of birth. The recorder of deeds office will have the particulars on who owns the house. It may be in someone else's name—a daughter, a son. While you're doing that, I'll canvass Catholic churches in the county to see if I can learn which one she was getting ready to attend."

"How do you know she was a Catholic?"

"Her Bible was not the King James. It was a Douay. Being a papist, I can spot a Catholic Bible a mile away."

Slowly shaking his head, he muttered, "Amazing, Holmes!"

She smiled. "Elementary, my dear Watson."

"Now tell me about this new case the boss handed us."

"Ah, Peter," she said, whispering as she leaned toward him across the table, "this story is *really* going to amaze you!

7

—— ❖ ——

An Exchange of Questions

J ENNIFER DUNCAN," SAID Sloan thoughtfully as he bit into a
cheeseburger and Flynn suddenly turned her attention to the one
she had ordered but forgotten while she had related the story of Mrs.
Hollander's visit. "How come I don't remember the case?"

"You were on vacation," she said, lifting the top of the roll and
studying the meat. "But it never became a *case* for us. The husband first
called the family physician and Dr. Granick then brought in the sheriff. Because there'd been no suicide note and there was no reason for
anybody to suspect it had been foul play, Zeligman's inquest certified
an accidental drug overdose. In a review of Ted's report, Benson saw
no reason to contest the finding."

"So why is he now giving credence to this kid's ludicrous story
about a murder?"

"When *this kid* happens to be the only grandson of *the* Mrs. Hollander," she replied, shaking catsup onto the cheeseburger, "who happens to be one of the staunchest and most generous contributors
to the Benson reelection campaign war chests every four years, you
humor her."

"He humors. You get to the job of going through the motions of
an investigation."

"Exactly. I'll write him a report that validates Zeligman's verdict of
accidental death. Benson will show the report to Mrs. Hollander. She
goes away satisfied. Next year, she makes another contribution to the
coffers."

Reaching for his glass of beer, Sloan sneered. "Politics! Bah humbug. For the sake of politics, you have to run around in a circle, faking an investigation. All because a kid had a dream about his dead mother. Bizarre!"

"If it was a dream, it must have been awfully vivid," she said, forgetting the burger again. "He felt strongly enough about it to carry out his mother's instructions to tell it to his grandmother. And only to her."

"How do you know he didn't tell it to lots of people?"

She shook her head. "Sebastian Duncan is nine years old. It seems to me that a kid that age is not going to risk the ridicule he'd get from his pals by telling a story like that. If you were nine and had such an experience, would you rush out and tell your buddies?"

"Probably not," he replied, dabbing a paper napkin to his upper lip and blotting away a thin mustache of beer foam.

"Would you tell your father?"

"*My* old man," he said, crumpling the napkin, "was an ironclad atheist."

"What about telling a sister?"

"*Absolutely* not."

"But if you had a granny," she said, remembering the cheeseburger and holding it before her mouth as if it were a harmonica, "a doting grandma who brought you gifts, a granny whom your mom specifically told you to tell—and only her—wouldn't you do it?"

"I see your point."

"There is no question this boy nearly died," she said as she chewed the burger. "Did he see his mother?" She swallowed and shrugged. "But is it too far-fetched to assume something went on in his head during the traumatic experience of drowning and being jolted back to life with a couple of electric paddles?"

"However, he knew that Zeligman had ruled out suicide and found her death was the result of an accidental overdose. What's the difficulty in accepting that?"

"Suicide or a stupid accident—either way, to an eight-year-old it looked like his mother had abandoned him. That's something that any child would find hard to accept. Sebastian's brain may have concocted a story that it *could* accept. That somebody took her away from him. That somebody murdered her. If that is what happened, we are left with the fascinating dilemma of why it took more than a year for the story to surface."

As she gazed at him quizzically, he blurted. "Don't look at me. I'm no psychiatrist."

"Neither am I. But what if, deep within his nine-year-old mind as he jumped off that rock, Sebastian Duncan *knew* his mother had been murdered? What if he had somehow *witnessed* it but buried what he had seen so deep in his subconscious that it took nearly dying himself to shake the memory loose and bring it back to the surface?"

"Flynn, my friend and mentor," he replied as she nibbled her cold burger, "Either *you've* gone off the deep end or you have finally read one too many of those mystery novels that cram every nook and cranny of your house."

Part Two

Morse's Maxim

"Judge not—at least until the evidence is unequivocal."

—Inspector Morse, in *Service of All the Dead*

8

❖

The Companionship of Death

A LIGHT IN the living room window signified that a timer had done its work, switching on the lamp to make it appear that her house was occupied. But at the hour it went on, she was miles distant, jousting with Marty Katz in the Scales of Justice about the manner in which Matilda Allen's terrible fate might become grist for him and his newspaper to feed into the mill of the public's limitless fascination with violent death, and the more mysterious the circumstances, the better.

When official police could not satiate the hunger, there were the fictional detectives, whether employed by agencies of government or working as private eyes to crack cases, from Sam Spade in novels by Dashiell Hammett and the scores of other detectives in the volumes filling her own bookcases to sleuths of radio, movies, and television. These ephemeral gumshoes had been the components of her college senior thesis. In researching it, she had calculated that since the first program with crime as a theme went on the air in 1930, there had been no less than five hundred series, amounting to tens of thousands of hours. Television alone had offered more than three hundred series since 1948. Into America's living rooms and hearts had come Charlie Chan; the Thin Man; the Shadow; Martin Kane, Jack Webb's *Dragnet;* Columbo in his rumpled raincoat; the uniformed cops of the Hill Street precinct and the plainclothes detectives working the streets of San Francisco; the New York faces and accents of *Naked City, Kojack,* and *Law and Order;* and detectives roaming Baltimore on *Homicide: Life on the Street.*

Should American-style crime and punishment not satisfy, the British filled the menu, from Sherlock Holmes in Victorian times to the brutal realities of 1990s Scotland Yard's Detective Chief Inspector Jane Tennison or the civilized understatement of Inspector Morse, whose mind, love of classical music, and doggedness she admired greatly and tried to emulate, though not the passion instilled in Morse by his creator, Colin Dexter, for the solving of crossword puzzles.

Removing the brown houndstooth jacket with its big pockets that she had changed into after attending Mass for Alice Carew, she found it difficult to believe it had been just that morning that she had heard the entrance antiphon. "The Lord will open to them the gate of paradise, and they will return to that homeland where there is no death, but only lasting joy."

In the course of the ten hours since leaving her house, death had been her constant companion: pausing at her parents' graves behind the church; the Mass for the Dead; Dr. Zeligman's morgue; identifying the dead woman at Crane Lake as Matilda Allen; giving marching orders to Peter Sloan to go to the house on Traitor's Lair Road and look around, then being summoned there herself; venturing into Marty Katz's boozy bailiwick to do battle over when Matilda Allen's murder might become the subject for public consumption. Most intriguing of all had been Elizabeth Hollander's astonishing account of her grandson's claim to have had a near-death experience and an encounter with his dead mother and his returning to life with an accusation of murder.

Draping the jacket on the back of a chair, she thought she heard the clipped accent of Sherlock Holmes. "This agency stands flat footed upon the ground," he had said to Dr. John H. Watson in "The Adventure of the Sussex Vampire." "No ghosts need apply."

She placed on the stereo a recording that Inspector Morse would have enjoyed, Wolfgang Amadeus Mozart's Symphony No. 39 in E-flat Major, performed by the New York Philharmonic under the baton of Leonard Bernstein. As it began, she let her eyes scan the titles of books in floor-to-ceiling shelves that were the overwhelming feature of the overly furnished living room. The majority, by a wide margin, were mysteries. Scanning them, she noticed for the first time how many contained *Death* or *Murder* in their titles. Most evident among them were those by her lifelong favorite, the formidable and prolific Dame Agatha Christie. Running her hand across the spines of the hardcover books, all with their jackets, though not everyone as pristine and intact as when she had bought them, she found and fondly remembered herself reading *Murder on the Orient Express, Death on the Nile* and *Death in the Clouds, The Murder of Roger Ackroyd, Murder Is Easy,* and an old, often revisited favorite, *Murder at the Vicarage.*

Taking it down and leafing through it, she thought of the young priest of that morning and wondered whether Father Brennan enjoyed thrillers. Carefully sliding the book back into its spot on the shelf, she wondered if priests were allowed to read them.

None of the cases in her collection, as best as she could recall as she turned away from the bookshelves, had ever been solved on the basis of testimony from the victim crying out from what William Shakespeare had called "the undiscovered country from whose bourn no traveller returns." "Yet Sebastian claims to have come back," she muttered.

Settling herself near the stereo, she reviewed her memory of Elizabeth Hollander's visit to Benson's office, culminating in the accusation of murder against her son-in-law, James Duncan.

"I'm certain that somehow or other, that wicked man got those pills into Jenny."

With a smile she pictured the woman, a bluebird perched upon a big leather chair.

" . . . Seven million dollars in cash and stock in Jenny's business, plus real estate. The lake house is worth at least a million. There's a condominium apartment in the city. *Park Avenue.* And he now has total control of a million in trust funds set up in Jenny's will for the two kids. That's a million *each.* And growing by the minute. If that's not a motive for murder, tell me what is."

Motive? Yes. Evidence? None. Except a child's tale of having had a near-death experience.

Now Marty Katz spoke: ". . . a lot of bullshit from a bunch of people like Albert with vivid imaginations. Hallucinations. Mind tricks."

Yet there was no question that Sebastian had nearly died. Was it too far-fetched to assume something went on in his head during the traumatic experience of drowning and being jolted back to life? Had the electrical shocks that had revived him also brought back to life a buried memory of something he had witnessed? Might he have seen his mother murdered?

The Mozart ended.

"Ridiculous," she muttered, but then she heard the measured voice of Inspector Morse. It whispered to her from the pages of *Service of All the Dead* with a world-weary maxim for those accustomed to the companionship of death: "Judge not—at least until the evidence is unequivocal."

9

Data Bank

A S SHE WAITED in a parlor of dim wall lamps and dark wall panels, the rich aromas of waxed wood, candles, and incense drew her back to nights of memorizing catechism and late afternoons reciting it for a priest who seemed to her as old as the parish house of Sacred Heart Church itself but who probably had been no older than the one whom Mrs. Barron, the housekeeper, had hurried away to fetch.

"What a terrific surprise, Miss Flynn," boomed the voice of Father Brennan as he strode in a few moments later. The cassock and surplice of the day's Mass schedule had been replaced by a pale blue short-sleeved shirt and faded blue jeans. "It's not Christmas Eve yet, is it?" he asked, stretching out a big hand in greeting. "So what is it that brings you back to church so soon? Is this going to be one of those glorious moments that sets off a chorus of the heavenly angels singing hymns of praise upon the return of a wayward lamb to the sheepfold?"

"I'm sorry, Father," she said, taking his hand. "It's wordly business, I'm afraid."

"But all God's business is earthly, Miss Flynn. And please call me Bob."

Noticing a blush to her cheeks, he squeezed her hand.

"I'm so sorry. The familiarity embarrasses you. I understand. But, you see, whenever someone says 'Father' to me, I find myself looking around to see whom it is they're talking to. And what must you be thinking about the way I'm dressed!"

"Not at all. It suits you. Besides, I learned that a priest is human from seeing Bing Crosby as Father O'Malley in *Going My Way* and *The*

Bells of St. Mary's years ago, although I found it very difficult to accept Ingrid Bergman as a nun. She certainly wasn't like any of the sisters in my experience."

"Ah yes," he said, grinning boyishly. "I felt the same way regarding Julie Andrews in *The Sound of Music.* Now, what can I do to help you with this earthly business of yours?"

"I have reason to believe that the old woman who was found murdered last Sunday was Roman Catholic. I'm trying to confirm it and, hopefully, locate members of her family. Her name is Matilda Allen. Do you know if she attended Scared Heart?"

"If you will come with me into the office, I'll run her name through the computer. It's in the next room."

Entering it, she felt as though she had stepped into a different world. Sun poured through undraped windows. Modern furniture adorned the room. A desk in a corner held a computer.

"Sometimes when I'm fiddling with this thing," he said as he sat and switched it on, "I wonder what greater work old St. Paul might have done if he had had one of these babies to write on. Instead of reading from the Epistles of St. Paul each Sunday, we'd have passages from St. Paul's E-mail."

As the screen lit up and his fingers deftly manipulated the keyboard, she watched from behind him.

"Ah, yes. Here we are," he said, scrolling through a file of names. "The faithful of our beloved Sacred Heart Church."

A moment later, the cursor winked next to the woman's name.

"It seems Mrs. Matilda Allen has been a regular at Sacred Heart for more than thirty years," he said, reading the screen. "Her late husband, Jonathan, is buried out back. Also a daughter, Emily. Deceased a little over three years ago."

He let out a thin whistle.

"Matilda Allen was also quite a generous contributer to the church. Look at this! The record shows that the good woman named Sacred Heart as a beneficiary in her will. Whoa! A quarter of a million to be in the form of an endowment of a perpetual fund for financial assistance to needy widows. I hope that doesn't make me a suspect!"

Peering across the priest's shoulder, she asked, "Does the file contain any information on surviving next of kin?"

Moving slowly down through the woman's file, he shook his head.

"If she had any other relatives, they do not appear here. But that doesn't mean she didn't."

He scrolled quickly on and came to the letter *F.*

"Don't worry," he said with a chuckle, "we list only the names and address and other pertinent data of our flock. The keeping of the record of sins we leave to a Higher Authority."

"Do you suppose God keeps it in a computer?"

"One with an infinite memory bank, as we shall all discover one day," he said, scrolling again. "Judgment Day. When Our Lord says which souls go into the 'save' file and who gets deleted."

"This has nothing to do with Matilda Allen," she said. "But since we're on the topic of the hereafter, do you have an opinion on the phenomenon of the so-called near-death experience?"

"Do I have an opinion? Or does the Church?"

"Both."

"The Church teaches, and I believe, that death is an unknowing sleep until the Resurrection, when we shall all come face-to-face with Christ and our Heavenly Father. And not a moment before. Nor have I found anything in the Scripture about a round-trip ticket. Except, of course, for the one that was used on the first Easter."

The cursor rested next to "Flynn, Arlene."

"Baptism, confirmation," he muttered as he read the entry. "I'd say you have nothing to worry about in the afterlife. But I'd feel even better if I saw you at Mass more often. Address in this life: Gribetz Road."

She sighed. "I moved out of that apartment ten years ago."

"I promise you, the Lord's file has been updated. But as long as you're here, I'll catch this one up. If you wish me to."

She gave him her address and watched as he entered it. When he was finished she asked, "Can you go back to Matilda's file?"

"No problem," he said, commanding the computer to search for and find her name. "What are you looking for?"

"I thought the name of the executor of her estate might be listed."

"Let's see," he said, opening the file again. "Yep. There's the name. Timothy J. Flynn. Say! There's a coincidence!"

"No, it isn't. He's my kid brother."

10

❈

Legacies

Across the street behind the Stone County Courthouse, a four-story gray block of a building with LAW OFFICES engraved in the keystone of an arched entrance had been designed in the same year with the same architect's vision of the perpetual solidity of the American system of justice. That its suites had never been vacant during the eight decades since the building's large bronze doors first swung open attested to the enduring need of the citizens of Stone County for counsel in coping with it.

For ten years, those who found themselves in such a strait, whether civilly or criminally, had anxiously ascended the broad marble staircase from the building's austere and unadorned lobby to the second floor and, directly opposite the steps, opened a door with translucent glass bearing the title:

TIMOTHY J. FLYNN

ATTORNEY

PUBLIC DEFENDER

More than likely to be greeted from an inner office with a bellowed "My secretary's on an errand, so come right on in," a prospective client would discover a slender thirty-four-year-old man who looked ten years younger. Medium in height and build, with a mop of tousled auburn hair, he sat behind a desk that could be described, if one wished to be generous, as untidy. Framed on the wall behind it, one looked upon a black-and-white photograph of a personal and professional

48

hero, Clarence Darrow, taken in 1924 as he entered a Chicago court to argue against the death penalty for child killers Nathan Leopold and Richard Loeb. To the left of the picture of the most famous defense attorney in American history hung a needlepoint in red, white, and blue that posed the question asked by nineteenth-century philosopher Ralph Waldo Emerson:

> Can anybody remember when the times
> were not hard and the money scarce?

Finding the secretary's desk unoccupied, Flynn saw the door to her brother's private office ajar and listened for his voice. Hearing nothing, she called, "Tim! Are you there? It's me. Are you busy?"

"Yes, I'm here," blared the familiar voice. "Of course I'm busy." A moment later, he leaned through the doorway with a smile. "But when did that ever deter anyone from the DA's office?"

"Nice to see you, too, little brother," she said, brushing past him into the office. "I've come about a client of yours. The news is not good."

Following her, he crossed the room to his desk. Frowning, he asked, "Which one?"

"A woman by the name of Matilda Allen."

"What could Matilda Allen possibly have done that could be of interest to you and your boss?"

"I'm sorry, Tim," she replied softly. "She was the woman who was found dead up at the lake on Sunday."

He sank dejectedly into his chair. "That sweet old lady! I never made the connection."

"I understand you are the executor of her estate."

"That's right."

"Can you tell me the particulars of the will?"

"It's a very complicated document. She was a wealthy woman. Most of the estate goes to various charities. There's a bequest to the church, including specific instructions for establishment of an endowment to benefit—"

"I know. Needy widows. The new priest told me. That's how I learned about you being her lawyer. What about individuals who stand to benefit? Any relatives?"

"Her daughter was killed in a boating accident on the lake some years ago. She would have gotten all the jewelry. There is also a bequest to a ne'er-do-well son. No others that I know of."

"Where's the son?"

"Matilda said she'd lost touch with him. Rather, he hadn't been in touch with her for years. She didn't provide much in the way of a reason. I assumed there had been a row over money. His last known address was in the city. But not one of New York's finer addresses. That was five, maybe ten years ago. Closer to ten, probably. She came to me about the will shortly after I hung out my shingle. At that time, she must have been pretty angry with the son. She made no provision for him in the will. But after she fell down a flight of stairs a few years ago and had surgery to repair her shattered hip, she called me up and told me to put him in. I did so and took the will up to her house on Traitor's Lair Road to be signed."

"What's the son's name?"

"Oliver."

"Did you ever meet him?"

"Not that I recall."

"How much does Ollie stand to inherit?"

"Considering the extent of her wealth, not much. She leaves him twenty thousand in cash. The balance of one hundred thousand goes into a trust fund from which he's to receive a modest weekly allowance, adjusted for inflation, until he turns forty. Then he gets all of it, plus the proceeds accruing from the trust's investment portfolio."

"Do you know how old he is now?"

"Somewhere in his middle or late thirties, I believe. She had him rather late in her life. She was in her forties at the time. My impression was that Oliver's arrival came as quite a shocking surprise in Matilda's middle age."

"How will you go about trying to locate him?"

"I'll place advertisements in the New York newspapers. It's all I can do at this point."

"You said he was a ne'er-do-well. In what way?"

"Matilda didn't say. Except once she let it slip that he'd had a couple of scrapes with the law. Exactly what kind, she did not say."

"Well, that's a beginning, isn't it?"

"Beginning of what?"

"My search for him, of course. But if you locate him first, I trust you'll let me know. I do have to talk to him."

"About what?"

"Timothy, I can't believe you're that naïve. I am investigating the murder of his very wealthy mother. And you know what they say. Where there's a will, there's a motive."

"Sister of mine," he said, shaking his head slowly, "what a suspicious mind you have. No wonder you're so good at your work."

"How soon can you provide me with a copy of the last will and testament in question?"

"As soon as I receive official confirmation of her death."

"Since there are no relatives available, I'm afraid you'll have to identify her. She's in the county morgue. Shall I call Ted Zeligman to arrange it?"

"No," he said morosely. "I'll take care of it."

"There's something else I'd like to ask you to do for me, having nothing to do with Matilda Allen. When you bring me a copy of Matilda's will, can you also bring me a copy of the final testament of the late Mrs. Jennifer Duncan?"

He flinched. "Why's the DA's office interested in her?"

"I'm not at liberty to say. Don't press me, Timothy."

Bristling as she had seen him do many times as a boy who had felt somehow offended, he retorted, "Her will is in the county records, one floor below your office."

"I know where it's filed, darling."

"Now the plot thickens," he said, tilting back in his chair. "The DA's chief snooper does not care to be noticed looking up the will of a woman who died under mysterious circumstances. Is that it?" A smirk, the only trait of his she never liked, curled his lips. "Do I detect in all the secrecy the odor of—dare I say it?—a *suspicion of homicide?*"

"When you've got copies of both the wills, bring them to my house." Turning to leave, she blew him a kiss. "Meantime, mum's the word."

"When I bring them over," he called after her, "shall I wear a disguise?"

11

Web of the Spider

A S SHE ENTERED her office, Peter Sloan stirred and rose from the soft embrace of a comfortably stuffed armchair.

"Do you have any concept," he grumbled, "of what a morning rooting around in the birth and death records downstairs can do to a person with my allergies? Apparently, they never dust that place. I thought I'd never stop sneezing. However, my runny nose and watery eyes are pleased to report that Matilda Allen was the mother of—"

"A daughter," she said, cutting him off as she went to her desk. "Emily. Died in a boat accident on Crane Lake about three years ago. And a son, Oliver. He is still among the living, as far as I know. But present whereabouts unknown."

Wide-eyed and slack-jawed, Sloan sank poutingly into the chair. "How in hell do you know that?"

"I assure you, hell had nothing to do with it," she said as she removed a blue blazer and sat at the desk. "The Scripture lesson for today, Sloan, is taken from the Books of DOS and RAM. The Sacred Heart Church is now a stop on the information superhighway, by the way. Unfortunately, its computer was not on-line with the FBI's data banks. So that's your new assignment."

"Exactly what am I looking for?"

"As you know from your crime catechism, murder is a spiderweb with three strands: motive, means, and opportunity. We know the means of Matilda's death."

"Her stockings."

"It now appears that son Oliver had a motive. The same old story:

money. The question is whether Ollie had the opportunity. Might he have been around to do it? Since he's had a couple of brushes with the law, and assuming he hasn't changed stripes—"

Bounding up, he interjected, "He may still have an active file with the FBI or the state police up in Albany. If so, they might give us a lead on where he is these days."

"It's a long shot. Nothing more than a hunch."

"I'll get right on it."

"You know, Peter," she said as he strode purposefully toward the door, "at times like this, I almost feel sorry for criminals today. And even for people like us, the cops. All the new science and technology that you're so enthusiastic about may take all the mystery out of crime. There are times when it is not the fun it used to be. One of these days in the not-too-distant future, because of these computer you love so much, I might have to take my cue from Sherlock Holmes and retire to Sussex and keep bees."

"Fat chance of that happening," he said from the doorway. "You'll still be sleuthing when Gabriel blows his horn."

She grunted a laugh. "I wonder if cops get into heaven."

"They must. I can't imagine Satan wanting 'em around."

"But if there are police in heaven," she said thoughtfully, "what could there possibly be for them to do?"

"There's no mystery in that," he said, his cheeks dimpling and eyes twinkling merrily as he slowly closed the door behind him. "They'll catch up on their paperwork."

Laughing, she turned her eyes to a stack of pending cases that had piled up on her desk. Four prosecutions in the early stages of preparation included two grand larcenies, one burglary in the second degree, and a possession of cocaine with intent to sell. A vehicular manslaughter had already been calendared for trial. Three homicides required her review in preparation for Benson's presentations to grand juries, none of which offered even a hint of mystery. A Saturday-night knifing in a saloon had been observed by no less than six eyewitnesses. Two had resulted from domestic disputes and amounted to open-and-shut cases, the protestations of guiltlessness by virtue of temporary insanity by the accused notwithstanding. In all likelihood, they all would be plea-bargained, thereby saving the county's taxpayers the expense of trials.

Certainly, none of the files before her afforded challenges of the magnitude of the murder of Matilda Allen and the strange case—if that was what it could be called—of the death of Sebastian Duncan's mother.

Had Sebastian's experience been vivid imagining?

"Now, it is true that Sebastian has been gifted with intelligence and has an insatiable curiosity," the boy's grandmother had said. "but why should a boy of nine invent such a story?"

Why indeed?

Sebastian had been eight years old that evening in July when Peter Sloan had been on his vacation and Jenny Duncan had invited business associates up from the city for a weekend on Crane Lake. Swimming, boating, the cookout on the deck at sunset, interrupted by Jenny's migraine headache. To bed early. Discovered dead in it in the morning. Dr. Zeligman's autopsy showing the presence of a massive dose of a sedative.

The husband had seen five pills in the bottle on Saturday. When he found it in the kitchen on Sunday morning, the bottle was empty.

One does not swallow five such powerful pills by mistake.

Whenever Jenny took a pill of any kind, even an aspirin, her mother had said, she did so with coffee.

There could be only one logical explanation.

"Suicide," she said aloud.

Shuddering at the sound of the word, she recalled a line from a furious Sherlock Holmes.

"Your life is not your own," he stormed to Eugenia Ronder. "Keep your hands off it."

But Jenny had told her son she had not taken her own life.

Bolting up from her desk, she muttered, "Ludicrous!"

" . . . why should a boy of nine invent such a story?"

If she had killed herself, why hadn't there been a note? If not suicide, it had to have been an accidental overdose.

One does not swallow five such powerful pills by mistake.

If not suicide or accident . . .

Seated again, she lifted her telephone and buzzed Benson's secretary. The ever-cheerful Constance Hardwick responded, "Yes, Miss Flynn?"

"Connie, do you know what time the public library closes?"

"I believe it's at six o'clock, Miss Flynn. Shall I get the librarian on the phone for you?"

"No thank you. I'll just walk on over. If the boss needs me, tell him I'll be back in a few shakes of that proverbial lamb's tail. There's something I need to look up."

12

❖

God and Mr. Carnegie

L IKE THOUSANDS OF American towns, the seat of Stone County
owed its small square fieldstone library to the philanthropy of Andrew Carnegie. Built when Newtown had been little more than a rest
stop for sojourners on their way north to the U.S. Military Academy
at West Point and other sites of interest on the west bank of the Hudson, it and the courthouse opposite constituted anchors of the town
square and attested to the conviction of the people of the town and the
nation that civilization rested upon the bedrock of justice and education.

Immediately inside its dim entrance foyer stood a marble bust of the
President of the United States on the date of its dedication, Theodore
Roosevelt. To his left, a large bronze tablet had been engraved with
names of other benefactors, the citizens of Stone County who had
contributed the cost of stocking the shelves. Above these had been in-
scribed the sentiment of the eighteenth-century English poet Christopher Smart:

> For I bless God in the libraries of the learned
> and for all the booksellers in the world.

A card holder since her seventh birthday, Arlene Flynn had discovered during her first plunge into the seemingly boundless stacks of
books, in a row designated D–F, a slender blue volume that fell open
in her small hand, revealing a page containing the thrilling exclamation,
"Mr. Holmes, they were the footprints of a gigantic hound."

That same year, she had tingled from head to toe as housemaid Mary broke into Dolly Bantry's delightful dream and gave it "a very odd turn" by waking her with the breathlessly hysterical cry, "Oh ma'am, oh ma'am, there's a body in the library!"

In the J–L stack, she had met Carolyn Keene's Nancy Drew.

Not long after, her life brimmed with such mysterious introductions as "My name is Hercule Poriot"; "Samuel Spade's jaw was long and bony"; "Good evening, Inspector," chirped by the little old lady from St. Mary Meade who explained a corpse in the library and the riddle of the 4:50 from Paddington, Miss Jane Marple; Raymond Chandler's hard-boiled Philip Marlowe, earning $25 a day, with a guarantee of $250, and grumbling, "Murder is my business"; Rex Stout putting into Nero Wolfe's mouth the detective's favorite saying, "Any spoke will lead an ant to the hub"; and Wilkie Collins's Sergeant Cuff informing her as she read *The Moonstone*, "I don't suspect—I know."

As she had grown, so had the library. Taking over what had been a parking lot at its back, it had expanded rearward into a two-story glass and steel box with nothing to recommend it in the way of charm, save the contents of its unappealing but practical metal shelves. Thousands of books had been added, many of them on subjects that Andrew Carnegie, Theodore Roosevelt, the benefactors of the foyer's commemorative plaque, and seven-year-old Arlene Flynn—or even Sherlock Holmes—could not have imagined: the new age of computers and high-tech criminology inhabited by the brash young wizards such as Sgt. Johnny Bogdanovic of the New York City Police, who had been her partner in the Traitor's Lair case, and her earnest and eager young acolyte, Peter Sloan.

Housed in the basement of the new wing was every copy of the *Stone County Clarion* since it began publishing in the year Teddy Roosevelt had found himself catapulted into the White House by the bullet that assassinated William McKinley: 1901. Except for the current year, the daily doings of Stone County as preserved by Marty Katz and other reporters had been transferred to microfilm, with the hope burning in the ample breast of the librarian, the venerable Ida Singleton, that everything would someday be available on an information retrieval system known as CD-ROM.

Presenting the *Clarion* microfilm of the previous year, the librarian asked in a tone of voice that suggested the Arlene Flynn before her was still seven, "Working on a case, Arlene? Or is that none of my business?"

She replied as respectfully as she had at age seven. "Just hoping to jog my memory, Miss Singelton."

Seated at a viewer, she spun the reel forward to the first of July, then slowly ahead until she found the story.

MYSTERY DEATH AT CRANE LAKE
Businesswoman Succumbs
from Pill Overdose
Autopsy Results Awaited
by Martin Katz

An autopsy ordered by Stone County Sheriff Todd Himes will determine the exact cause of death of Jennifer Hollander Duncan, 32, at her lakeside home on Saturday night. However, Dr. Theodore Zeligman, county coroner, told the *Clarion* that the noted businesswoman appeared to have died in her sleep from an accidental overdose of a prescription drug for treatment of chronic migraine headaches. This opinion was also offered by Duncan's personal physician, Dr. Melvin Granick of Newtown.

"She has been under treatment for the condition for at least a year," said James Duncan, 35, her husband of twelve years. "Jenny had been feeling fine at a party we were giving for friends and her business associates who had come up from the city. But shortly after dinner, she had complained of a severe headache and left the guests to take her medication and go to bed. I found her dead on Sunday morning."

The only child of Mrs. Elizabeth W. Hollander, widow of the late financier and noted Stone County resident, William C. Hollander, Mrs. Duncan was the mother of Jessica, 11, and Sebastian, 8. The family lives in a magnificent home recently built on the west shore of Ichabod Crane Lake. Mrs. Hollander, who had settled in Rochester, New York, following the death of her husband, rushed to her daughter's home on Sunday morning. "Jenny was a brilliant young woman who had just completed an enormously successful business transaction," she said.

It was this multimillion-dollar deal that Mrs. Duncan had been celebrating.

"Given her apparently carefree state of mind, her recent business success, and the fact that no note was found, I do not believe this was a suicide," said Sheriff Himes, who had been summoned to the house by Dr. Granick, in compliance with state and county laws covering unexplained and unattended deaths.

"This tragedy has devastated all of us," said a guest at the affair, Felix T. Watson, vice president for development, Stone County National Bank.

Others present at the gala gathering included Lester Troy, president of Troy Chemicals, Mountain View Industrial Park, Newtown; Darlene Devonshire, chief executive officer of a Manhattan marketing firm; Elaine and Sidney Ruderman, Phoenix, Arizona, partners in a consumer products development company; Michael Borrero, CEO of Borrero Import-Export, New York City; Howard Schack, chairman, Schack Worldwide Enterprises, New York City; and Alexander Umlauf, Orchard Estates, chief of product development, Troy Chemicals.

"Jenny will be sorely missed. She was a wonderful woman to work for. I feel so sorry for the children," said Cornelia Stewart, a neighbor who frequently cared for Jessica and Sebastian when their parents traveled on business and who had been serving as a maid for the evening's festivities.

In addition to Mrs. Stewart, friends of the Duncans who were their weekend guests included Dominic Perillo of New York City; Madeline Trainor, a fashion model; Stanley Gordon, the renowned portrait painter; and T. Franklin Pierce, whose column "Cracker Barrel" appears weekly in the *Clarion*.

Funeral arrangements are pending, awaiting completion of the autopsy. "Unless Dr. Zeligman finds something totally unexpected," said Sheriff Himes, "my office finds no cause to believe this was not simply a terribly tragic accident."

"An opinion with which the DA's office concurred," Flynn muttered sourly.

Until *that woman* showed up with young Sebastian's bizarre tale of his alleged brush with death.

With the drop of a quarter into a slot, she commanded the viewer to provide a photocopy of the article.

"Well, that didn't take long, Arlene," said the librarian as the reel went into a return box on the checkout desk. "I hope you found what you needed."

"I did, thank you."

"May we be of any other assistance?"

"I believe that's all I need."

"As I recall, you never left here without an armload of detective novels. But I suppose that in your present work, the reading of fictional crime would be carrying coals to Newcastle."

"No, I'm still devouring them like peanuts. But I do have the luxury I did not enjoy as a child, the thrill of owning the books I read. I've accumulated rather a nice collection of my own, actually."

"Still, there's no substitute for a library when there's a particular book you wish or need to read but don't care to buy, is there? Or for just looking something up. As Richard Brinsley Sheridan, creator of Mrs. Malaprop, said 'A circulating library in a town is as an evergreen tree of diabolical knowledge.' And we *are* just across the square from your office."

"Now that you mention it, Miss Singleton," she said, "there is a topic on which you may be able to advise me."

The librarian beamed delight. "That is our raison d'être."

"It's the phenomenon known as 'near-death experience.' "

"On my dear, yes. There has been a great deal published on the subject. Some of the books have been best-sellers. Indeed, one of the leading authors on the topic lives right here in the county. His name is Kevin Albert."

"As a matter of fact," she said, recalling the conversation with Marty Katz, "someone mentioned him to me the other day."

"He lives in Larktown. He conducted much of the research there for his book *Be Not Afraid*. He presented the library with several copies of it. I'm not an expert on the subject, but I've been told by those who have read extensively on it that it's by far the best overall study. Shall I find you a copy?"

"Just point the way for me."

"You'll find it in the annex," she said, pointing in the direction of the new wing. "On your left, third row."

"As long as I'm into the realm of the extraordinary, can you also recommend a book—not too technical a one—on the phenomenon of repressed or recovered memory?"

"That will be the fifth row, right. Look for *Healing Your Past,* by Dr. Eric Lyle."

Having found the books, she presented them with her card.

"My, it has been a long time since you checked something out, hasn't it?" said the librarian. "We replaced these old cards three years ago with plastic ones. They have a coded strip on the back. So much more efficient. But never you mind. I can have one for you in no time."

Carrying the books and clutching the new card, she stepped into the bright outdoors and walked across the lush green square with its towering oaks, feeling as self-conscious and inadequate as she had as a schoolgirl, and just as antiquated.

13

Flynn's Laws

WELL, WELL, AREN'T you the bookworm?" declared Peter Sloan as Flynn entered her office. With a glance at the titles of the books, he arched his eyebrows. "You have got to be kidding!"

"Ignorance, Peter Sloan, is the Achilles' heel of the cop," she replied, setting the books on her desk. "That's Flynn's Law, precept two."

"Will there be a quiz?"

Removing her jacket, she sat. "What have you done for yours truly today to justify your very existence, not to mention your paycheck?"

"I have been traveling through cyberspace," he said, sitting on the corner of the desk. "I was on-line, conferring with our brothers and sisters in righteousness in Washington and Albany."

"On the subject of the ne'er-do-well Oliver Allen?"

"Ne'er-do-well is right," he replied, drawing a folded sheet of computer printer paper from a side pocket. "Once I got a look at what's on record for him as an adult, I decided to run a check to see what sort of a child he'd been. According to what I found in the county files downstairs, this character was no good from the get-go. Ollie's follies began at the ripe old age of ten. That year, he set fire to a classroom wastebasket, a prank that ended in half the school being burned to the ground. He said he did it because he hadn't done his homework and he didn't want the teacher calling up his mother and telling her about it. Juvenile court ordered psychological counseling. When next heard from, at age twelve, he stole another kid's bike and, when he was done with it, tossed it into Crane Lake. Mother paid for a replacement. At fifteen, it was a car. That landed him in the County School for Boys.'"

"In less sensitive times, it was called a reformatory. My father used to threaten my wayward brother, Tim, with being sent to what Daddy called 'the bad boys' place' whenever Tim got out of line. That was back when children actually took the commandment 'Honor thy parents' as gospel. Funny, though. I never heard a word about a 'bad girls' place.' "

"Now we get into Ollie's adulthood," Sloan said, unfolding the computer printout. "Lots of arrests but no convictions. He always had an alibi, usually some fellow hoodlum he'd met in a gay bar on Riverfront Road called Major André's. He wasn't gay, apparently, but he hung out in that bar in order to fleece or roll men who took a fancy to him. Four years ago, he was nabbed for an armed robbery. That case was dismissed when the victim failed to show up to testify. No one knows why."

"That also rings a bell," she said, drumming fingertips on the desk. "Speculation was rampant that he skipped town in fear of retribution from Oliver or one of his like-minded pals. Do any of your cyber pals know where he's been lately?"

"Up in Attica."

"For what?"

"Assault with a deadly weapon. A couple of months after the armed robbery case fell through, he got five to ten years. He was eligible for parole after three. That would have been January."

"Did he get one?"

"I'm waiting for a callback from the parole board."

Hands folded as if in prayer, she asked, "Anything on Matilda's BMW?"

Shaking his head slowly, he picked up the two books. "Do you actually intend to read these?"

"Certainly. They're my weekend project."

"What on earth for?"

"Credibility, Sloan," she said, taking the books from him. "Precept five of Flynn's Law: A detective is nothing if he, or she, is not credible. My report to the boss and the lady with the deep pockets has got to leave no doubt I have thoroughly explored all possibilities. Besides, I expect to learn something. The day on which you have learned nothing is a wasted day that will weigh heavily against you when the scales are balanced on that day of reckoning that we all must face, sooner or later. Even our wee band of detectives. *Especially detectives.*"

"Is that another precept of Flynn's Law?"

She nodded. "Precept six."

"How many precepts are there?"

"Many. But have patience. You'll come to know them all. And you'll be the better man for it, too," she said with mock gravity as her direct phone to Benson rang. "Make note of precept one," she whispered, picking it up. "Always answer your boss's calls on the first ring."

Making walking motions in the air with two fingers, Sloan mouthed, "Shall I go?"

Shaking her head and pointing him to the overstuffed chair, she spoke into the phone. "Yes, boss?"

"Hi, Arlene," Benson said politely. "Katz is bugging me for an identification of that woman at the lake. Where's the search for next of kin stand?"

"There's one, a son. We haven't located him yet, but I don't think there'll be any problem in giving Marty Katz her name. He's known it at least since yesterday."

Benson grunted. "Is there anything happening on the matter we talked to Mrs. Hollander about?"

"I'm making inquiries."

"Discreetly? You're staying away from the kid?"

"I'm being as quiet as a . . ." Her eyes fell on the books. "A librarian. I think you can count on a report from me early in the week that will satisfy Mrs. H."

"You're being great about this. I really appreciate it. You have a good weekend."

Putting down the phone, she made the sign of the cross above it and muttered, *"Pax vobiscum."* Noticing Sloan's quizzical look, she said, "Latin. From the Mass. It means 'Go in peace.' In the parlance of today's RC generation, 'Have a nice day.' "

Part Three

Groping Toward the Light

"There are no limits to which the human mind
cannot soar in that unique, god-like instant before
the end of life."

—Frederic Dannay and Manfred B. Lee,
writing as Barnaby Ross,
The Tragedy of X

14

Saturday's Child

RANKED HIGH IN the qualities that had persuaded her to leave the Gribetz Road address that Father Brennan had discovered in Sacred Heart's computerized file of the faithful and purchase the split-level ranch at 9 Lark Avenue on Newtown's west side had been the vanity lights arranged like a horseshoe around the bathroom mirror. Switched on, they afforded a brutal daily confrontation with mortality that far surpassed anything about living and dying she encountered at the scene of a homicide, for there was in the forensic regarding of someone's else's dead body only the investigator's intellectual confrontation with death, in which the only question was, Who did this?

Infinitely more troublesome was the challenge posed by her image in the big mirror. The older she got, the more her reflection asked, So, how much time do *you* have left before some cool-eyed stranger, whether it be a Dr. Plodder or a Peter Sloan, pokes around to survey and analyze the cause of your demise?

At what point in nearly five decades of life she had first asked the question, she could not recall, though she was certain it had been posited long before the day in the training of all recruits when they were marched up from the Police Academy on Twentieth Street to New York City's morgue at First Avenue and Twenty-ninth to observe an autopsy. The more likely moment was the death of her father, Michael Flynn, during her first year in college.

Of her mother dying, her most vivid memory was her father telling Tim, "Mommy has gone to see Jesus in heaven."

Barely a week before, knowing her mother's death was near, she had watched her nearly smothering Tim with kisses and telling him, "I had you on a Monday, Timmy. There is a poem that goes, 'Monday's child is fair of face.' And oh, darling Timmy, it is so true."

Looking past the boy at her daughter, she smiled and said, "And you were born on Saturday, Arlene. 'Saturday's child . . .' "

"I know, Mom," she said, choking back tears. " 'Saturday's child has to work for its living.' "

Poet Robert Browning had put it differently:

> In God's good time,
> Which does not always fall on Saturday . . .

Yet she liked the day of the week on which she had emerged into the world. While growing up, it had been the best day of the week, spent with her parents and Tim amid the glories of life in a small town in the 1950s, the last years of America's innocence. Shopping the food stores in the morning with her mother—butcher, baker, the farmers' market on Old West Point Road, the open-air stalls along Riverfront Road where the fishermen sold catches of Hudson River striped bass and clams and oysters they had brought up from Long Island.

Between the shopping and taking Tim to matinee movies at the Roxy on Main Street, she squeezed in the confession box at Sacred Heart.

"Bless me, Father, for I have sinned. . . ."

Then being enthralled when the second film of the double feature at the Roxy proved to be Basil Rathbone in a Sherlock Holmes film, aided by Nigel Bruce as a befuddled Dr. Watson, who was nothing like the able companion created by Sir Arthur Conan Doyle.

Supper was always out, usually overlooking the old railroad cars that formed a museum behind the Depot, a restaurant that once upon a time had been Newtown's railway station, and after eating, to the Roxy again with her parents for a big musical or a drama. A TV in the parlor was yet to arrive.

Now, Saturday was her day for all the domestic things she had no time to do during the week. Because it was the Jewish Sabbath and Aaron Benson observed it strictly, rare had been the Saturday when she answered the phone and found him on the line, breaking the law of his religion by working.

Had she not lapsed in the observance of her own religion, she thought as she leaned toward the mirror, she would have stepped into a Sacred Heart confessional in preparation for Sunday Mass and Holy Communion.

What sins have I to atone for? she asked herself as she studied the unforgiving mirror and looked for new gray strands among sleep-mussed red hair and examined un-made-up skin for lines that had not been there the last time she looked into the glass.

Did sins manifest themselves so as to be seen in a mirror, like those of Dorian Gray in that loathsome painting locked away in his attic room? Is that what aging was? Were one's sins etched in the flesh? Did you get the face you deserved?

Resigned to, rather than satisfied with, the reflection revealed by the glaring horseshoe of vanity lights, she returned to her bedroom to dress. Donning sensible shoes and slacks immediately upon arising, even on weekends, had become as natural to her as the weight of the .38-caliber Police Special she carried in a handbag, color-coordinated with her outfit. On this Saturday morning, it would go into one of tan leather to complement beige trousers. Her shoes were old and soft as slippers. Should she have to go out to work on what was a gray and drizzly day, she would put on her favorite brown-and-white houndstooth jacket and change the shoes for the same pair of rubber-soled brown half boots she had worn to the spot where hikers stumbled upon Matilda Allen's body, one day shy of a week ago.

"Poor Matilda," she muttered as she put on the clothing and thought of Matilda's worthless son and her terrible death, "she must have been born on a Wednesday."

Descending stairs and striding into her kitchen to see about breakfast, she recited the line from the poem. "Wednesday's child is full of woe."

Carrying a buttered toasted bagel and a cup of black coffee, she entered the living room, switched on the stereo, pressed the play button, and watched as the long, slender arm floated down to Mozart's Mass in C Minor. Selected for its appropriateness to the previous evening, the record had repeated continually while she sprawled in what she affectionately called her reading chair and plowed deeply into Kevin Albert's exploration of the near-death experience, *Be Not Afraid.*

Fascinated, she had read the tales of men and women who had told the author:

"An incredible feeling of peace swept through me."

"I was floating in the air. Detached. I looked down. I was above it all."

"All of a sudden, it was very dark."

"Have you ever been on a train that goes into a tunnel that you didn't know was coming? That's how it was for me. Like going into a railroad tunnel."

"Everything was black. But I wasn't scared. And then a very bright light came on. Just as if somebody turned a switch."

"The light was more intense than any I'd ever seen. Brighter than a camera's flash. Only it did not hurt my eyes or blind me."

"The light was filled with a tremendous happiness."

"I couldn't believe my eyes. My father was standing there with his hands on his hips, the way he did when I was a kid and he was going to scold me. But this time, he smiled and said to me, 'I really missed you, Bobby. Now I'm going to help you.' "

"This will probably sound silly, but you know the saying, My whole life passed before my eyes? Well, it *did.* It was sort of like when you run a videotape on fast forward. It goes quickly. But you see all the action. It was *weird.* "

"I watched everything I had done in my life, the good and the bad. But I didn't feel any guilt about the bad. It felt a little sad. Foolish, too. But I somehow knew that it was *okay.* "

"I met this . . . *being.* And it asked me if I wanted to stay. I did. But I also didn't. And the next thing I knew, I was back in my body and a doctor who was next to my bed in the hospital had this look on his face and was saying, 'We thought we lost you.' "

Presently, she had come to the chapter on the experiences of children, some of whom had been younger than Sebastian Duncan.

"Everything got real dark," said seven-year-old Kevin. "And then I talked to an angel. She said I had to come back."

David had been eight and in intensive care for a kidney problem at the time. "I knew I was going somewhere," he said, "but I didn't know where. It wasn't scary at all. Just interesting. Then I was in the middle of a fantastic light show. That's when I saw Jesus. He told me I was going to be fine. Then I woke up. The next day, they found a kidney for transplant."

"I knew the light wouldn't hurt me," said a six-year-old girl who, like Sebastian, had had a close call while swimming.

She read of a young girl named Virginia, suddenly afloat in her bedroom and looking down and seeing herself asleep. Just as abruptly, she rejoined her body. "When the girl told her parents what had happened," Albert had written, "they rushed her to the family doctor, who hooked her up to an electrocardiogram. The ECG revealed evidence of an intermittent heartbeat. She was immediately scheduled for corrective surgery. Had Ginny been dead for just a split second?"

A boy whose vital signs could no longer be detected by the surgery team operating on him for a ruptured appendix had told Albert, "My grandmom, who died when I was six, took my hand and asked me how old I was. I told her I was fourteen. She said that was too young and if I wanted to go back, I could. I said, 'Yes, I want to,' and I went back."

Awash in the music of Mozart as she picked up Albert's book, she recited another childish poem in a singsong voice:

> Solomon Grundy,
> Born on a Monday,
> Christened on Tuesday,
> Married on Wednesday,
> Took ill on Thursday,
> Worse on Friday,
> Died on Saturday,
> Buried on Sunday.
> This is the end
> Of Solomon Grundy.

"Was it, Solomon?" she asked, putting down the book. "Or did you just go through the tunnel and into the light, too?"

Had Matilda Allen?

Jennifer Duncan?

Did Sebastian truly have a near-death experience?

She picked up her telephone and punched the numbers for what

71

used to be information but now identified itself in the cheery voice of a young man.

"Directory assistance. How may I help you?"

"A number in Larktown, please. Last name Albert. First name, Kevin."

"Here's your number," he said.

An androgynous, computer-generated monotone voice provided it.

15

The Boy Who Died

S LATE GRAY CLOUDS and the mist of what her Irish ancestors called a "soft day" contributed an appropriate mood as she drove past the black iron gates of the back entrance to the cemetery where her mother and father lay behind Sacred Heart Church. With a slight smile, she heard again the conviction of Father Brennan responding to her question about the first moments of the afterlife as described by those who claimed to have had an after-death experience.

"The Church teaches, and I believe, that death is an unknowing sleep until the Resurrection, when we shall all come face-to-face with Christ and our Heavenly Father. And not a moment before," he had said firmly. "Nor have I found anything in the Scripture about a round-trip ticket. Except, of course, for the one that was used on the first Easter."

In that moment, if she had thought of it, she might have replied in the words of Inspector Minardi to Leonard Wibberley's fictional priest and sleuth, Father Joseph Bredder. In *The Saint Maker* the policeman said to the priest, "Your profession is based on faith. Mine, on doubt."

Exactly when the doubt had insinuated itself into her mind, she could not say. But she was certain it had happened before she had become a police officer. Wearing a cop's uniform and then the plain-clothes attire of the detective had merely reinforced it.

Yet the paradigm of doubtful reasoners, Mr. Sherlock Holmes of 221B Baker Street, had held open the door to something beyond the life of earth. "There is nothing in which deduction is so necessary as in religion," he said as he leaned his back against shutters and contemplated a dainty blend of crimson and green in the form of a rose. "Our highest assurance of the goodness of Providence seems to me to rest in the flowers. All other things, our powers, our desires, our food, all are really necessary for our existence in the first instance. But this rose is an extra. Its smell and colour are an embellishment of life, not a condition of it. It is only goodness which gives extras, and so I say again that we have much to hope from the flowers."

A mound of them marked a fresh grave site in the Sacred Heart cemetery as she accelerated her car.

Crossing Town Line Road, she pondered Holmes on the extra of flowers and supposed that Inspector Morse would suggest classical music was also such a bonus.

During her father's wake, she had insisted that the funeral director omit the music he normally played on the funeral home's sound system and put on cassettes of Mozart that she supplied.

Had Mozart been sent by God? Might Wolfgang Amadeus Mozart have been an angel? If she went through the dark tunnel and into the light attested to by so many people in Kevin Albert's book, might she be greeted by her father and mother, accompanied by the music of Mozart?

"Death is a lonely business," whispered a voice from the novel of that title by an author who was best-known for science fiction, Ray Bradbury, in his first detective novel, published when he was sixty-five. "Death is as pointless as having a key for an open door that you are going to walk through once," declared Michael Vallone in *Meanwhile Back at the Morgue*. Author of *The Voice of the Corpse,* Max Murray, chimed in, "Death is not necessarily the heaviest sentence that can be imposed on man. There are times when it can seem the lightest."

"The idea of death was enormous," wrote North Patterson in *The Lasko Tangent,* "like infinity made personal."

Even William Shakespeare's melancholic Dane, Prince Hamlet, had pondered the afterlife. "To sleep—perchance to dream: ay, there's the rub, / For in that sleep of death what dreams may come / When we have shuffled off this mortal coil / Must give us pause."

The master mystery writer Cornell Woolrich had put it a bit differently, perhaps putting his finger on the real explanation for the tunnel, the light, and those who had returned. "It's not taking on death that's tough," he wrote, "it's taking off life."

Proceeding northwesterly from the boundary of Newtown, the Larktown Road that had been flanked by fields of corn in summer, their dried remains in the autumn, and blankets of snow in winter when she was a girl were bounded now by houses with manicured lawns and two-car garages. Whether they might one day be incorporated into the town, as proposed by the officials who held sway in the offices in Municipal Hall and worried about increasing budgets and a static tax base, had been heatedly argued for as long as she had been investigating murder cases, which fed her doubts on the subject of Providence. Should the plan ever be adopted, the northern extent of the town would be pushed three miles to Valley Road, bringing not only the homes onto the town's bottom line but also the rich revenue harvest of the sprawling Newtown Mall, which had spelled the end to the Saturday shopping sprees amid Newtown's downtown shops.

Two more miles and she passed an even newer development of homes, Orchard Estates. Stradling Larktown Road, the tract had been hacked out of groves of apple trees that each autumn had afforded the ingredients of innumerable home-baked pies and fat jugs of cider, sold from ramshackle roadside stands. Straight ahead for four miles brought her into the village of Larktown, barely changed since she had gone down to the City to college and her life's work.

Turning right off Main Street at the only traffic light, she delighted in three blocks of gingerbread facades of the Victorian houses that were Larktown's abiding hallmark. Reaching the end of Ulysses S. Grant avenue, she noticed a small sign:

KEVIN ALBERT
PSYCHOLOGIST

Turning right again, she followed a long driveway, gently ascending to a chilling reminder of the mysterious hilltop house in the movie *Psycho*. But the creepy feeling quickly dispelled. When she left the car, went up the wooden steps to a broad porch, and knocked on the door, she heard the happy squeals of children at play in a side yard.

Flinging open the door, Kevin Albert bore no resemblance to the gawky, skeletonlike Norman Bates of Alfred Hitchcock's horror film. A foot taller than she, broad and with a trim brown beard, he looked down at her with sparkling hazel eyes. "Ah good! You're here! You look

75

exactly as I imagined you did when we spoke on the phone. Most people don't match their voices at all. I know that I don't. Most people get the impression that I'm small and mousy, an academic Woody Allen. Come in. I'm fascinated by your reason for calling me up on this gloomy morning."

He led her into a large parlor that had been turned into his office.

"If the kids are too noisy for you to concentrate, say so," he said, removing a pile of stuffed file folders from a chair. "I'll boot 'em off the premises."

"They're not your children?"

"One. The gang's leader. And by far the biggest mouth," he said, inviting her to take the armchair as he sat in a creaky swivel desk chair. "He shows alarming signs of growing up to be a politician. His name is Richard. It's he who got me started in the research work that resulted in the book you read last night. Rich is fourteen. And that is quite remarkable, for he died when he was ten. He's in the book with a fictional name. I changed the names of all the kids in the book. Although those I interviewed about their near-death episodes were eager to tell me about them, I have found that they were extremely reluctant about discussing what happened with other kids. They did not want to appear odd. Children are terribly afraid of not fitting in, as sales accounts of makers of childrens' clothing and athletic shoes attest. Now, what is it you wish to know?"

"You've just answered one of my questions. The boy I'm going to tell you about has related to only one person the near-death experience he says he had."

"Whom did he tell?"

"His grandmother."

Albert nodded. "It was she who related the story to you?"

"That's right."

"Why to you? Are you a relative?"

"No. She came to me—that is, she came to my boss, District Attorney Benson—because of a concern about what Sebastian had said to her. That Sebastian claimed to have had a near-death encounter with his deceased mother and that she sent him back to this life in order to report that she had been murdered."

"Oh, Miss Flynn," he said, leaning forward eagerly. "As far as I know, this is a first. No wonder you're here! Murdered! This is astonishing. Therefore, the burning question of moment for you is whether Sebastian is to be believed. But there are two questions you need answered first, aren't there? One: Is there really such a thing as the near-death experience? In seeking that answer, you have read my book. I'm flattered."

With a glancing memory of Ida Singleton pointing her toward the lovely old library's unlovable new annex, she said, "It was highly recommended."

"Having read it, is it your feeling that the experience of this boy was in accord with those related in my book, especially those of children?"

"It was. But with a notable exception—that is, in what it was that Sebastian's mother said to him, why she sent him back."

"Therefore, your second question. Did Sebastian truly have an NDE?"

"Exactly."

Leaning back, he lifted his hands in a questioning gesture. "I can not tell you without having interviewed the boy. When can you bring him to see me?"

"I'm afraid I can't. His grandmother would never permit it. I had to promise her I'd keep my distance from him."

"Outrageous! If this boy's story is true, he has gone through the most profound experience possible. How old is he?"

"Nine."

"Damn! This child must not be kept from talking about this. Perhaps if I talk to the grandmother, I can persuade her to see how foolhardy she is. What is more, there is an allegation of a murder. It is utterly outrageous that he's being kept silent!"

"Forgive me for saying what I know will sound terribly insensitive on my part, Mr. Albert, but the only thing I really care about at this time is whether to lend any credence to the boy's story of a murder having been committed. Once I've satisfied myself on that score, I'll be happy to do all that I can to bring you and Sebastian together. Whether Sebastian died and was revived is immaterial to me, except to the extent that he came back to life and talked about a possible murder. Your book was extremely persuasive, but . . ."

"But you closed *Be Not Afraid* dubiously."

"I've got another book to read. It's Dr. Eric Lyle's study of repressed and recovered memory."

"Yes. It's a superb work. Lyle and I have debated both our books a number of times. In your capacity as a criminal investigator, you are quite right to explore repressed and recovered memory as an alternative explanation for the boy's remarkable tale. But if I am to shed a definitive light on its veracity, I should talk to the boy. Since I can not at this time, can you tell me, from what you know of Sebastian's event, if it coincides with the cases you read in my book?"

"It does in every aspect, except for his being sent back by his mother with specific instructions to tell his grandmother, and only her, that the mother's death about a year ago was not a suicide or the result of an accidental overdose of a drug. That's what had been believed at the time."

"As a consequence, you've got a fancy little problem on your hands. If it was murder, how do you prove it when your witness is dead and the only evidence is the word of a nine-year-old kid who reported having had a near-death experience? If he did have one, what court would accept his testimony? I expect almost any defense lawyer worth his salt would contend Sebastian is crazy, has a colorful imagination, or just made up the story."

"Have you dealt with people who tried to fool you into believing they'd had a near-death experience?"

"Two. Both were reporters, one for a magazine, one from a TV show of some kind. I saw right through them."

"What about people who thought they'd had such an experience but actually fell in Dr. Lyle's realm of suppressed memory?"

Albert shrugged. "That is possible. But not, I think, very probable. My interviews probe quite deeply and extensively into a subject's entire life experience."

"As a psychologist yourself, do you accept suppressed and recovered memory?"

"Definitely. But I reject the argument that it has anything to do with NDE. That's what makes my debates with Eric Lyle so popular on the college lecture circuit and the occasional television talk show. I'll be fascinated to hear which side of our debate you finally come down on at the conclusion of your investigation. Whichever it may be,

I certainly wish you good luck in finding the murderer of Jennifer Duncan. I knew her, by the way."

She smiled. "It occurred to me when I let Sebastian's name slip that it might ring a bell for you. It did not occur to me that you might have known someone in the Duncan family."

"Strictly casually. I met her and her husband socially on a few occasions after they built their magnificent house on Crane Lake. Of course, there was always the possibility you were talking about some other Sebastian. But your mention of how the boy's mother died was the clincher."

"I'm sure you'll appreciate that I must ask you to keep our conversation confidential."

"You have my professional word on it, Miss Flynn."

"What was your impression of the Duncans?"

"Personal or professional?"

"Both."

"I found James charming and shallow. He struck me as being uncomplicated and lazy. Jenny had an edge to her—tough, driven. I felt very glad I neither worked for her nor had to do business with her."

"Were you surprised by her death?"

"I was astounded."

"In your opinion as a psychologist, was she someone you would expect to take her own life?"

"Definitely not."

"Why not?"

"Suicide is a cry for help. Jennifer Duncan appeared to be anything but helpless. When I read of her death in the *Clarion,* I assumed she had died as the autopsy suggested—accidentally. The idea of her being murdered never crossed my mind."

"Well, I've taken up enough of your Saturday. Thanks for your insights."

"If there is any other way I can be of help to you, I'm at your disposal anytime."

"Thank you. I'll take you up on the offer right now. May I have Eric Lyle's telephone number?"

"Of course you may," he said, turning around to the desk to jot it down. "He lives on Long Island but has an office in the city. I'm giving you both the home and office phone numbers."

A moment later, standing on the porch, she looked around a corner to a knot of boisterous boys playing football and asked, "Which one is Richard?"

"The one carrying the ball," he said, smiling proudly.

The boy plowed through the others.

"He's a fine player," she said.

"That he is. It's because he's so fearless."

16

Country Houses

RAIN HAD STOPPED and breaks in scudding gray clouds held out the promise of light as the village's only traffic signal turned green and she made a right turn northward onto Main Street, three blocks of stores and shops doing a lackluster rainy-day business. Two minutes later, she crossed the town line, increasing speed to the forty-mile-an-hour limit on a road now identified by a sign as county route 11N. Seven miles farther, a fish-hook swing right led to a dead-end intersection with Lake Road. By wheeling right again and proceeding for four miles, she came to the start of a low fieldstone wall marking the south side of the Duncan property.

Slowing, the car glided past gracefully arched wrought-iron gates affording a glimpse of the house. Nestled into a grove of old oaks, its skilled intermingling of wood, stone, and glass in the walls gave the feeling that the low, rambling front had grown up naturally from the earth, while the fullness of the foliage of the trees obscured the second story. A short stone driveway led to a pebbled parking area. In it stood a sleek gray vintage Jaguar and a boxy black four-wheel-drive minivan.

Leaving the property behind, she came to a gentle curve in the road and gaps in the foliage revealing a spectacular view on the left of Ichabod Crane Lake and the foreboding rock known as Horseman's Head. From its far side, Sebastian had dared the leap that had almost put an end to his young life, and, if he was to be believed, resulted in a startling conversation with his dead mother.

Stopping the car, she studied the face of the rock that, she had been told when she had been Sebastian's age, contained the grin of a man. Now, as then, she could not quite see it.

Yet others had. And continued to. Or imagined they did.

"Without imagination," she muttered, quoting Sherlock Holmes as she drove onward, "there is no horror."

Yet for strange effects and extraordinary combinations, he had lectured the good Dr. Watson in "The Red-Headed League," one must always go to life itself, which is always far more daring than any effort of the imagination.

What would Holmes make of Sebastian's story?

" 'No ghosts need apply,' " she said aloud, entering another turning of the lakeside road that left behind Horseman's Head Rock. " 'When you have eliminated the impossible, whatever remains, however improbable, must be the truth.' "

In the words of Sgt. Joe Friday of *Dragnet* fame, "Just the facts, ma'am."

Fact: Sebastian Duncan had jumped off Horseman's Head Rock and electric shocks had been required to get his heart beating again.

Fact: Jennifer Duncan was dead.

Was it possible, however improbable it seemed, that on the cusp of Will Shakespeare's "bourn," from which "no traveller returns," these two had met? In however many moments it had been between a boy's plunge into forbidden depths of a lake and his jolting back to consciousness, had Sebastian hurtled down that dark tunnel she had read about in Kevin Albert's book, into a brilliant but not blinding light, and been urged back to life by his dead mother? Had she, like the ghost of Hamlet's father, told him of murder? Or had Sebastian's near-death experience been one of the dreams that Prince Hamlet had dreaded in his immortal soliloquy?

If neither, had the boy's vision on the dividing line of life and death been a *memory* too horrible for his consciousness to confront?

Suddenly aware of darkness around the car, she realized she had entered a covered bridge spanning the continuation of the creek that fed Crane Lake on the west and flowed from it on the east. Quickly emerging into the light, she followed the twisting, narrow, tree-arched blacktop to another crossroads. If she went straight, she would come to the state police barracks and then Stone Light and the Hudson

River. A right turn on Traitor's Lair Road would carry her past the old Ilona Troy property with its memories of a murder case solved by the chance observation of a carpet that looked out of place. Left would bring her almost immediately to Matilda Allen's house with its significant blue area rug in the living room. There, for an inexplicable reason, Matilda's killer had put down the body.

"Why would he do that?" Peter Sloan had asked, and rightly so.

"To rest? Catch his breath? He may have left her while he brought his car closer to the house. Maybe he heard something to distract him," she had replied, guessing.

"I never guess," Sherlock Holmes had said with all his towering arrogance to Watson in *The Sign of the Four*. "It is a shocking habit—destructive to the logical faculty."

Startled by the blare of a car horn from behind, urging her impatiently to proceed one way or the other, she looked into the rearview mirror and found the reflection of the Jaguar that had been parked in front of the Duncan house, although she could not see who was at the wheel. Edging forward and turning left toward Matilda Allen's house, she managed a glimpse of a man in the Jaguar, presumably James Duncan.

Never guess!

Pulling into the driveway of the Allen property, she found the roadway blocked by yellow tape marked CRIME SCENE DO NOT ENTER, left by Capt. Sam Mason's troopers. Getting out of the car and leaving it, she ducked beneath the tape and walked to the house. Parked in front was a state police car and in its front seat the familiar figure of trooper Norm Miller.

Seeing her, he bounded out, clapped on a flat-brimmed gray Smokey the Bear hat, and saluted smartly. "Hello, Miss Flynn. I didn't figure I'd see you here on a Saturday." He smiled. "Fact is, I didn't figure I'd see anyone."

"I happened to be passing and thought I'd have another look around the house."

"I've got the keys right here. Shall I come with you?"

"No need," she said, taking a ring of three keys. "I'll only be in there a couple of minutes. Which is the front-door key?"

"The brass Yale."

Turning the lock, she read another warning in the form of a yellow rectangular sign:

CRIME SCENE
SEARCH AREA
STOP
NO ADMITTANCE BEYOND THIS POINT
UNTIL SEARCH IS COMPLETED
BY ORDER OF STATE POLICE

In the tiny foyer, she looked right into the living room and saw that, like the abandoned station wagon, the blue rug had been taken away by the CSU. Turning her eyes to the left, she considered the stairway. At the top of the narrow passage, she saw a dim shaft of light coming through the opened door of the bathroom where Matilda had died. Standing at the foot of the red-carpeted steps, she pondered the logistics of bringing her body down the steep and confining stairwell.

In her going up and down with Sloan they had had to climb single file. Therefore, how did the killer bring Matilda down? Clearly, it was too narrow for her to be carried in his arms. And the space seemed inadequate, as well, for him to have slung her over his shoulders.

Had he grasped arms or feet and dragged her down?

That would have left abrasions or contusions, even upon a corpse. It also would have left red fibers on the body. Only blue had been found.

Gazing upward, she tugged her lower lip.

Then, with a slap of her thigh, she blurted, "Of course!"

17

Going into Overtime

D O I GET paid time and a half for coming in on a day off?"
Peter Sloan leaned against the doorjamb. He had on a red-and-white-striped polo shirt, khaki slacks, white sneakers with a blue boomerang trademark of the manufacturer, and, looped around his neck, a white tennis sweater.

"We who labor in this cop shop do not work overtime. We just work," she said, glancing up from a stack of reports accumulated from the state police crime laboratory and Dr. Zeligman's autopsy notes of Matilda Allen. "Isn't a sweater a tad warm for the weather?"

"Yeah, but ain't it dashing?" he said, stepping in. "On the phone, you were, to say the least, cryptic."

"Pull up your chair, Sloan, and I'll be uncryptic. I've been up to Matilda Allen's house again."

He sat in the deep armchair with his left leg on his right knee, its sneakered foot jiggling in a manner she had long since recognized as an unconscious signal of impatience, usually with her. "Looking for what?"

"Nothing in particular. I just happened to be nearby."

"Ha! All the time I've known you, you never *just happened* to do anything. So what did you see that got missed before?"

"I didn't find a thing we didn't see before. But this time, I took the trouble to *observe* that stairway. Remember how you and I had to go up and down single file?"

The foot stopped jiggling and his brow furrowed. "Okay. We went up single file," he said, thinking aloud. "Why? Because the steps were narrow. What's the significance in that?"

"You tell me."

The foot did a little jerk. "The body was carried down the steps and set down in the living room. I wondered about that. How come the murderer parked the corpse? Why not just carry it right out to the car? Did he need to rest?"

"Hell, that old lady must have been as light as a feather. Zeligman said she'd lost at least fifty pounds over the past year."

"So why do the pause at the bottom of the stairs?"

"Narrow stairs," she reminded.

The foot jiggled again, excitedly.

He muttered, "Narrow steps, narrow steps."

The furrow deepened.

"He's got the body."

Rising from the chair, he held his arms before him in the form of a cradle.

"He holds it like this and goes down the steps."

The arms fell to his sides.

"He couldn't have! There wasn't enough room. And I can't see him sidestepping down them."

"And I don't believe he slung her over his shoulders," said Flynn. "Or on his back like a bag of potatoes."

Sloan resumed his position in the chair, his foot jiggling. "Maybe she was dragged."

"Impossible," she said, slapping the stacked reports. "From Dr. Plodder's autopsy report, we *know* the body showed no signs of postmortem mistreatment. Matilda *was carried* down those steps."

As the furrow disappeared from his brow, a little smile of understanding twitched his lips. "He had to have had help. Two people carried her down the stairs single file. They come to the bottom and have to put her down so they can open the front door, or to do whatever they thought they had to do. That's how Matilda winds up in the living room."

"If we have a pair of killers," she said, "the complexion of the case changes. This was not an opportunistic homicide. Nobody drove in from Traitor's Lair Road to steal a fancy car, or even to pull a burglary or a robbery. The presence of these two, if we're right about there being a pair, means that Matilda knew who they were and let them in. Maybe she *invited* them in as her houseguests. And that's why your Saturday off is out the window."

He made a sour face. "I hate murderers."

"You and I, Peter Sloan, are going to go over every piece of paper in this pile. It's all here. Everything we need, from an inventory of the contents of Matilda's house down to the tiniest possession. Captain Sam Mason's team is thorough, if anything. We have the crime-scene photographs, plus the fingerprint reports. We'll be looking for proof there were two other people in that house while Matilda was taking her bath. She had already had it, by the way. Mason's team found dissolved soap in the tub and blessed Doc Plodder turned up fresh soap scum on the body. Ivory, in case you're wondering the brand." She sniffed the air. "What do you use, by the way?"

"I haven't the faintest idea. My wife does the shopping."

"Tut-tut, Sloan. These days, husbands are expected to share in domestic chores!"

"In this job, with the boss I have, when would I ever get the time to go to the Newtown Mall?"

"The boss is a tough taskmaster, eh?"

"You said it. Both of 'em."

"Who's worse?"

"The male is a sweetie. The latter is a . . ."

"A bitch?" she said, smiling and picking up a batch of the crime-scene pictures and holding them out toward him. "Poor you, Peter Sloan!"

When she spoke again, it was in response to a yawn. Looking up, she observed him rubbing his eyes. As his hand came down, he caught her gaze and shrugged. "Those hotshot crime detectors up at Stone Light need to take a good look at the ribbons in their dot matrix printer. You could go blind reading this stuff. Better yet, Mason should break down and hook their computers to a good laser to crank out their reports. And while he's at it, he ought to bring in someone to teach them how to write."

Setting aside a report, she asked, "What time is it?"

He glanced at his wristwatch. "Half past five."

"So what's your considered opinion on our 'there had to be two of them' theory?"

"Except for the problem of the stairs," he said, standing and stretching his arms, "I find nothing to support it. If two people were staying with Matilda, they did not spend the night in the other rooms. The photos show the beds weren't slept in."

"Matilda probably made them."

"At eight in the morning?"

"Making the bed is the first thing I do in the morning. I bet your wife does, as well." She smiled. "Presuming you don't. What do you make of the photo of Matilda's kitchen?"

He thought, remembering an unexceptional picture. "A kitchen is a kitchen is a kitchen."

"Dig it out of the pile and look again, paying attention to the dish rack on the sink drain board."

Finding the photo, he studied it. "Okay. I'm looking at it."

"How many cups?"

"Three."

"Saucers?"

"Three."

"Plates?"

"I get your point. But who's to say they don't represent three meals that Matilda ate alone?"

"*I* say. That's a kitchen of an old-fashioned and meticulous housekeeper. And no lady I have ever known like that would ever not put away the dishes after washing and drying. No. Those three cups, saucers, and plates and the knives, forks, and spoons were washed and put in that rack after breakfast the morning Matilda died. She had houseguests, Peter. Two of them. As sure as God made little green apples. Therefore, first thing Monday morning, I want you to get together with Sam Mason's fingerprint analyst up at Stone Light and see what you can discern among the latents lifted from the house that might help us find out who the guests might've been."

"You did say Monday morning?"

"Yes. You may have tomorrow off. *Pax vobiscum.*"

With a slight genuflection and a sign of the cross, he said, "Thank you very much."

"Please take note, Peter Sloan," she said as he left the office. "I am not a bitch on the Lord's day."

18

A Stilly Night

WITH A MUG of root beer at hand, Mozart's Symphony No. 25 in G Minor by the New Philharmonia Orchestra conducted by Maestro Riccardo Muti on the stereo, and Dr. Eric Lyle's weighty book in her lap, Saturday night began in a swirling exploration of the one trait found in humans that distinguishes them from all other creatures—their ability to recall their history and, therefore, to grasp that one day each and every individual of their kind will die. Sooner or later, every man, woman, and child who walks the earth has to come to terms with the innate capacity that the jurist Benjamin Cardozo had termed "archives" and Abraham Lincoln had called the "mystic chords" of memory.

From the preface of *Healing Your Past* leapt the plaintive plea to a physician by Shakespeare's Scottish king, Macbeth:

> Canst thou not minister to a mind diseas'd,
> Pluck from memory a rooted sorrow,
> Raze out the written troubles of the brain,
> And with some sweet oblivious antidote,
> Cleanse the stuff'd bosom of the perilous stuff
> Which weighs upon the heart?

And Lyle's introduction had offered her in the contemplation of the case of Sebastian Duncan's experience a stanza by a cleric whose earthly existence reached the dimensions of a Shakespearean tragedy, Sir Thomas Moore:

Oft in the stilly night,
Ere slumber's chain has bound me;
Fond memory brings the light
Of other days around me;
    The smiles, the tears,
    Of boyhood's years,
The words of love then spoken;
    The eyes that shone
    Now dimmed and gone,
The cheerful hearts now broken.

Reading the poem and thinking of the nine-year-old boy who had lost his mother, apparently by her own hand, her own eyes had dimmed with tears.

Proceeding into the heart of Lyle's work and thesis, she plunged into the psychologist's years of exploration into the concept of repressed and recovered memory. Into a small notebook resting on the arm of her chair, she jotted telling phrases:

"Repression is the avoidance in one's conscious awareness of unpleasant experiences."

"Recovered memory is a sudden unblocking of the trauma. This may occur through therapy. Or it can be the result of yet another trauma."

"I have found that there are no limits to how long a memory can lie buried. Some individuals have unknowingly carried their dark secrets all their lives. In others, it may be a few years."

"Children, especially the very young ones, may experience recollection in the form of dreams and nightmares."

"Indications of repression are depression, anxiety, loss of appetite or eating disorders, sexual problems, and difficulty with intimacy. Children may act recklessly."

"The phenomenon may take the form of multiple-personality disorder."

"Not uncommon in the anecdotes of those who abruptly recover repressed memory are assertions of having been victims of satanic rituals, multiple rape, incest, and conspiracies against them that involved pillars of their communities, such as the mayor, police chief, teachers, or the school principal."

"Some people, and in a growing number, related horrifying tales of abduction by aliens from space who performed painful experimentation upon them, usually of the sexual and reproductive organs. In my studies, I classify these people 'experiencers.' "

"Are these otherwordly episodes the mind's way of coping with terrifying incidents of this world—namely, sexual abuse and exploitation? I believe so."

Looking up from this paragraph, she smiled slightly and softly said, "At least Sebastian hasn't claimed that he met his mother during a trip on a flying saucer."

Realizing the Mozart had finished and the root beer grown warm and flat, she replenished both and resumed reading and taking pertinent notes.

One lengthy passage she underlined:

"Hypnosis can be extremely effective in eliciting the roots of the recovered memory. I have found that my use of the technique has been particularly helpful in treatment and counseling of individuals who exhibit characteristics of a loose sense of self. Many such individuals report paranormal experiences, including seeing ghosts. In two cases, encounters with heavenly angels were reported. All of these people were found through psychological testing to be highly suggestible. They are highly functioning, intelligent, and wholly convinced of what they report. I try not to believe or disbelieve. I listen, observe, and record what they tell me."

Scanning the many case histories in the book, she found them to fall into the categories of repressed and recovered memories of painful and degrading sexual experiences as children.

"There is no limit to the kind of traumatic events that can be repressed," Lyle wrote. But in none of those he recounted had she read of an abruptly resurrected memory of someone who met a loved one who had claimed to be the victim of a murder. Deciding that in the morning she must telephone the author to ask him if he had ever encountered such a thing, she closed the book.

Placing it aside, she had not made up her mind whether she believed in the thesis of Lyle's studies. Rather, she recalled another quotation he had cited in the introduction that spoke to the wisdom of maintaining open-mindedness on the subject of repression and recovery of things past. Long before men like Lyle had begun probing horrendous events that might have been buried by the conscious mind, the poet Oliver Goldsmith had warned, "O Memory! Thou fond deceiver."

As she turned off the stereo, which had long since ceased playing, she looked at her watch and realized that three hours had passed since Saturday turned into Sunday while she had gone on reading, oblivious to the stillness.

19

On the Seventh Day Even God Rested

DREAMLESS, SHE AWOKE looking at a combination radio, clock, and calender that had been a Christmas gift from her brother. Its glowing green digital face asserted: 6:00 A.M. SUN.

When the radio came on at that time on a weekday, she found herself greeted by the voice of a newscaster on Newtown's own station, WRSC, whose mellifluous tones were nonetheless stern in advising her that remaining in bed was impermissible. Nor on the sixth day of the week, when she need not concern herself with her boss and could go about doing Saturday chores. Unless she felt a compelling reason to do so, she would not set the alarm for the seventh day. However, after so many years of waking up at six o'clock the other six, she had found her inner biological clock commanding her eyes to pop open at that hour on Sundays, as well.

Were she to turn on the radio at six on Sunday, she would not hear news, but a recorded sermonette by the venerable pastor of the First Street Baptist Church, the Reverend Winston Parker, followed by fifty-five minutes of sacred music leading up to a live broadcast of the seven o'clock Mass for the benefit of shut-ins and others who could not or chose not to show up at Sacred Heart to fulfill the Catholic's obligation to partake weekly of the Blessed Sacrament.

At Mass on this Sunday, she wondered, might Father Brennan look out upon the faithful for her?

Ordinarily, should she decide not to go back to sleep, she would shuffle downstairs in robe and slippers to the kitchen and switch on another radio. Tuned to an FM station in New York City, it offered classical music. Instead, when seven o'clock came this overcast morning, she switched it to the local station to hear if, by chance, the Mass was being celebrated by Brennan.

Disappointed at hearing another priest's voice intoning the welcome to the faithful early worshipers within the church or listening via the airwaves, she returned to the FM band and the Water Music of George Frideric Handel for accompaniment to a leisurely breakfast of ham, two scrambled eggs, dry rye toast, orange juice, and two cups of coffee while scanning the *Clarion,* a luxury of unlimited time not available during the workweek.

Picking up the heavy Sunday edition of the newspaper from her doorstep, she read a banner front page headline:

CRANE LAKE MURDER VICTIM NAMED
Matilda Allen Was Local Benefactress
DA Benson Appeals for Public's Help
in Hunt for Strangler

Bearing Marty Katz's byline, the story below began, "Almost a week after the nude and brutally strangled body of an elderly woman was discovered by hikers at Crane Lake, authorities have identified the victim as Mrs. Matilda Allen, a benefactress of numerous Stone County institutions and groups who, since the death of her daughter three years ago in a tragic boating accident, had lived a reclusive life at her Traitor's Lair Road home. Identification was confirmed by District Attorney Aaron Benson late on Saturday night in a telephone interview from his home."

She imagined Katz crouched over his telephone, waiting for the moment when the Jewish Sabbath ended and Benson would be free to answer a call.

"Although the *Clarion* had independently learned the identity earlier in the week," the article continued, "confirmation could not be obtained at that time."

A quote from DA Benson explained why. " 'The policy of this office is to withhold the identity of every homicide victim until next of kin have been notified. Because Mrs. Allen's only known surviving relative, a son, Oliver, could not be located, it was decided not to delay further releasing the name. Far more important at this time is to appeal to members of the public who might have information about this atrocious crime.' "

"As to the son," Katz wrote, "Benson would state only that Oliver Allen had been recently paroled from prison and that his whereabouts are unknown. Meanwhile, Mrs. Allen's attorney, and the executor of her will, Timothy Flynn, announced that he was making funeral arrangements and that they would include a Mass at Sacred Heart Church, with interment in the adjoining cemetery, but that no date had been set."

Finally, Katz gibed, "Regarding the search for the killer, neither the state police nor the person in the DA's office who is supervising the investigation appears to have any leads."

Interpreting the words as Katz's retaliation for her refusal to give him Matilda's name in the Scales of Justice, she plopped into her reading chair and answered him aloud. "Not true, Marty."

They had an abandoned station wagon, a missing maroon BMW, three coffee cups, three saucers, three plates, and three sets of silverware that had been washed but not put away.

Setting aside the news section of the paper, she gleefully turned to the comics. As she had since her girlhood discovery that she liked detective stories, she started with Dick Tracy and proceeded methodically and without variation to Blondie, Peanuts, Garfield, and a consistently amusing and often bitingly satirical strip inhabited by a flock of birds working for a treetop newspaper. Her favorite character, the Professor, was a grumpy, overweight, cynical reporter engaged in a constant struggle to tame a computer and a rolltop desk heaped with paper. He reminded her of Marty Katz. Despite the jab at her in his story, she smiled fondly at the thought of his curmudgeonly style, as much an affectation as his white suits. They were part of why she liked him.

Next in her routine came the entertainment pages and the ads for the new movies at the cineplex in the Newtown Mall, which had spelled doom for the old downtown theater of her youth, the Roxy. Like the old brewery north of town, the Roxy was a shuttered hulk of a building that was too big for anyone to think of a fresh use for it. Consequently, the Roxy's marquee, which once had heralded the exciting arrival of Hollywood's choicest family pictures, had become a ghostly white blank. Scanning the offerings at the twin mall theaters, she found nothing appealing and hardly any names of actors and actresses that she recognized, or, if she did, had any interest in watching while submitting her eyes to relentless violence and her ears to assault by a sound track offering rock and roll that was always too loud and dialogue punctuated by profanity and obscenity not required by plot or character.

Whimsically, as she glanced at an ad for a movie in which drug use appeared to be integral to the story, she recalled that the release of Basil Rathbone's first Sherlock Holmes movie, *The Hound of the Baskervilles,* had been held up in 1939 because the final words of the greatest fictional detective of all had been a reference to Holmes's taking a 7 percent solution of cocaine. Ultimately, "Come, Watson, the needle" had been excised from the film and had remained absent until the film's rerelease in the decade that ushered in unabashed use of recreational narcotics, the lamentable 1960s.

Turning to the Sunday-night television listings, she looked in vain for a worthwhile mystery program, save for stalwart Angela Lansbury as mystery novelist Jessica Fletcher in *Murder, She Wrote.* Unfortunately, she noted "(r)" adjacent to the listing, indicating a repeat broadcast and an evening Arlene Flynn would pass in her reading chair with a mystery book in her lap.

Several new ones were stacked on the adjacent table. But on top of them lay last night's reading, Dr. Eric Lyle's study of repressed and recovered memory. Glancing at an ornate Victorian grandfather clock in a corner, she wondered if Lyle might be up and about at half past seven on a Sunday morning. Choosing to phone him later to seek his opinion on the experience of young Sebastian Duncan, she turned in the *Clarion* to slick, colorful advertising inserts and studied them for coupons that might offer attractive savings on products she customarily picked up at the supermarket.

Fruitless in her search, she set aside the newspaper and settled back in the chair, focusing on the music on the radio as violins of Vivaldi's "Summer" reached a scintillating conclusion. But when the strings were followed by Bach on a harpsichord, she all but bolted out of the chair. Turning it off, she muttered, "God forgive me, but I do hate the sound of a harpsichord."

Returning upstairs, she would shower and dress for a Sunday that might easily turn into a day like the previous one, with a phone call from the sheriff's office to Benson's roomy home in the upscale neighborhood known as the Heights. It had drawn them to a bank of Ichabod Crane Lake and the body of a woman she had come to know as Matilda Allen.

Stepping into the tub, she drew the shower curtain closed with a memory of the shower scene in Hitchcock's *Psycho* and the murderous attack on Janet Leigh. She had been twelve years old when she saw it and had cowered in her seat at the Roxy, her eyes squeezed tightly shut and her hands covering her ears so as to shut out a horribly screeching sound track. Opening her eyes, she had watched blood mixed with water swirling down the drain. Years later, she had learned that the black-and-white film's blood had been chocolate syrup. She had seen numerous murders in movies since then, shot in color, but not a drop of the blood in them had been as convincing. But in the bathroom of Matilda Allen's house on Traitor's Lair Road, there had not been a single drop of blood shed. Nor had Matilda stood in a shower. She had filled an old-fashioned white porcelained iron tub with claw feet and had met her death after getting out of it.

Stepping from her shower, she wondered which was the worse way to die—hacked like the young woman in *Psycho* or garroted like old Matilda Allen? Peering at her fogged reflection in the steam-clouded mirror, she tried to recall whether Matilda's bathroom had a looking glass that might have provided her a glimpse of her killer before he looped knotted nylons around her frail neck. How long had she fought for air? Not long, surely. The only sign of a possible struggle had been the yellow bath mat on the floor by the tub. Had it been kicked askew during her fight for life? Or had it been moved underfoot as she stepped from the tub?

Clothed for work, should she receive a summons to do so, she went down to the kitchen to clean up the dishes and pans from breakfast. Satisfied with the absence of a harpsichord's jangling on the radio as she washed, dried, and put them in a cupboard, she considered again the triple sets of cups, saucers, and plates and the silverware in Matilda Allen's fastidious kitchen, certain that she was correct in her deduction that two people had shared the old lady's meal on the last morning of her life. Unfortunately, Matilda's dedication in the cleaning up had washed away any chance of finding her murderous guests' fingerprints. Now all she could hope for was that Peter Sloan's scrutiny of prints for any other than Matilda's would provide them with a break in the case.

Hope also thrived regarding the two automobiles. Although the license tags of the Chevrolet station wagon had proved useless, other identifying numbers on the car itself might afford a lead. The serial number of the engine and the digits etched into other components could be traced from the manufacturer to a dealer and to the individual who had bought it new. That could then lead to a search for subsequent owners. Yet none of this would be of use if the Chevy had ever shared the fate of Matilda's BMW and been stolen. And there remained a glimmer of hope that the state police bulletin for the missing BMW would yield it, though she doubted it would.

Finally, there was always the possibility of the murderers walking into the Stone County Courthouse and up to the top floor to turn themselves in. Or even one of them doing so. However, except for those recorded in the Holy Bible, she had not heard of miracles. Confessing a murder, after all, was not the easy thing that kneeling in a confession box and admitting one's sins to a priest had been when she still practiced her faith. Admitting a murder did not culminate in the assignment of Hail Marys and Our Fathers as penance and a priest admonishing, "Go and sin no more."

In fictional detective stories the murderer's confession was an indispensable element of the story, the icing on the cake for the sleuth. It was recognition by the culprit of the brilliance of the deductive reasoning that made it inevitable. Tying up the loose ends. The moment at which the killer snarled at the unraveler of the crime, "Damn you, Poirot!" Or Miss Marple. Or Morse. Or Sherlock Holmes. Or to Sam Spade and all his successors and imitators. That wonderful experience of feeling utterly stupid as a reader, looking up from the page and exclaiming, "But of course! The clues were right there in front of me! How could I not have recognized them?" And almost as thrilling, saying to the detective as the last page was turned, "Why, I spotted the murderer right away. What on earth took you so long?"

Confessions in real life were rather harder to come by. In the first instance, a suspect had to be a fool not to heed the Miranda warning, advising that nothing need be said without the presence of a lawyer. Should a confession be forthcoming, more often than not it followed negotiations on the subject of a plea bargain between a lawyer and a prosecutor feeling the pressure of the costs of going to trial and judges grousing about overloaded court dockets.

Admission of guilt hardly ever resulted from the pangs of a troubled conscience. It came from an accumulation of evidence, ideally an eyewitness to the crime, but usually circumstantial: a fingerprint, blood type, the exciting development of the technology of biological fingerprinting from DNA, a smoking gun in the hand of someone standing over the corpse, or, as Sherlock Holmes had put it, quoting Ralph Waldo Emerson, something as convincing as finding a trout in the milk. The case that DA Aaron Benson would one day bring against the murderers of Matilda Allen—she was sure she and Peter Sloan were looking for a pair of killers—would have to be a circumstantial one.

Although Benson would not be required to produce a motive for homicide in court, the jury that would try the case would be like all juries and expect to hear one, the evidence notwithstanding. Juries looked for hate, rage, revenge, love, jealousy, sex, and money, or combinations of these. But what had been the motive for killing a lonely old woman while she got out of her bathtub on a Sunday morning? Surely not one of hate. Rage? Not likely. Revenge, love, and jealousy in the life of a woman in her seventies? Dr. Zeligman had found no indication of sexual molestation. That left money.

Of that, Matilda Allen appeared to have had plenty. But it was safely tucked into the Stone County National Bank. Had she a cache of currency in her house? The state police criminalists had discovered no sign of the house having been disturbed in a search for hidden cash. The only thing known to be missing had been the automobile, the explanation for which seemed obvious. It had been the killers' getaway car.

Furthermore, if theft had been the objective, she thought as she left the kitchen and entered the living room, why murder her? And why then remove the body from the property and dump it by the lake, at the risk of being noticed doing so?

Glancing at the clock, she decided nine o'clock was still too early to telephone Dr. Lyle on the subject of her other case, if that term could be applied to the matter of Sebastian Duncan and what he claimed his dead mother had said to him in the course of his near-death experience. As she settled into her chair to review notes of her reading of Lyle's book, the doorbell rang.

"I figured you'd be up," declared Timothy as she let him in. "I've got the wills you asked for. And I bring you greetings from Sacred

Heart. I've been to the eight o'clock Mass. Father Brennan expressed the hope that he'd be seeing you there. Foolish man."

"The Lord knows that I'm on call on Sundays."

"Yes, but does God approve?" he said, handing her the wills. "On the seventh day even he rested."

20

***

Never Buy a Car Built on a Monday

S LOUCHING INTO FLYNN'S office and into the big armchair at 8:30 the next morning, Peter Sloan grunted, "G'morning, chief. Sorry I'm a bit late."

Setting aside the morning's second can of diet root beer, she frowned. "You do look kind of used. Domestic difficulties? Are the wife and kids okay?"

"They're fine," he said, stretching long legs before him and crossing them at the ankles. "Everything in the Sloan household is just hunky-dory."

"Glad to hear it. So what's troubling you?"

"Did you know medical researchers have proved that there are more deaths from heart attacks on Monday than on any other day of the week?"

"Fascinating. Is that the explanation for your tardiness? You suffered a coronary? Don't tell me you died and came back! One near-death experience on my agenda is more than sufficient, thank you."

"It's also a fact," he said, "that on the first working day of the week, people make more mistakes on the job. That's why you should never buy a car that was built on Monday. Or a Friday, for that matter. Mondays, people are worn out from their weekend. On Fridays, all they're thinking about is the weekend ahead."

"I guess my trusty Plymouth must have been put together on a Wednesday. It's been running just fine for five years."

"Is it still under warranty?"

"I believe so."

"The minute it expires," he said, grouchily as his right foot began twitching, "you'll start having problems with it."

She took a sip of root beer. "Am I right in deducing that your pride and joy, that German-made *Wunderwagen* of the autobahn of yours, has gone on the fritz? And that's why you're late and in a grumpy mood?"

Both feet jiggled rapidly. "Nothing went wrong with the actual running of the car. But somebody creamed the right front in the parking lot at the mall yesterday."

"I'm sorry. No one hurt, I hope."

"We were in the mall at the time. Now I am looking at a two-grand repair job. It's in for an estimate. So I had to walk over to the office this morning."

"Poor Peter Sloan. Three whole blocks."

"It's not the distance. It's the principle of the thing. And to make matters worse, whoever slammed into it just took off. No note giving his address. Didn't call a state trooper or one of the sheriff's deputies to file a report. No phone number for an insurance company stuck under the windshield wiper, which means mine pays the freight. And then my premiums will probably go up. I was on the phone with my agent at eight o'clock on the dot this morning. That's what held me up."

"A friend and colleague, Chief of Detectives Harvey Goldstein of the New York City Police Department, told me that it is settled law that there are four things that will ruin anyone's life: a house, a spouse—kids included in that category—a pet, a car. You, poor soul, possess them all."

"If I find the bastard who wrecked my car and I murder him, would it be justifiable homicide?"

"Not if Benson prosecutes. As to your lack of wheels, I'm sure the boss will let you use one of the office cars till yours is fixed."

"I think I'd prefer to walk. I'll bet you that if we checked the records of the maker of those heaps, we'd find out that every one of them was slapped together on a Monday."

"Since you've brought up the subject of automakers, where do we stand on the state police report on the ownership history of the station wagon that was abandoned at the Allen house?"

"Captain Mason said this week. Maybe."

"When you go up to Stone Light to go over the latent prints recovered in the house, goose them on the Chevy."

He scowled. "It's Monday there, too, you know."

"I'm sure I can count on you to do your best in spite of the calendar, Peter."

"I know how your Saturday went," he said with a vague tone of accusation as he rose from the chair. "How was yesterday?"

"Some progress has been made. I called Dr. Eric Lyle in the city to pose a couple of questions on his favorite subject. He's on vacation, but his secretary promised to get in touch with him. I'm hoping he'll find time it to talk to me. And I got copies of the wills of Matilda Allen and Jennifer Duncan."

Opening a drawer, she pulled them out and slapped them on the desk.

"Anything helpful?" he asked.

"Each was in accord with what I'd been told. These were *very* well-to-do women. Of course, Matilda was not in Jennifer's league by a long shot. But people have been killed for a lot less in the way of an inheritance. However, I did find one item in Matilda's will that surprised and puzzled me. There is a bequest to Matilda's daughter of a jewelry collection."

"I thought the daughter was dead."

"After she was killed in the boating accident, a codicil was added that leaves the collection to the Stone County Historical Society for its museum. Trouble is, first thing this morning I checked the state police inventory of the contents of the house and did not find the jewels listed."

"The old lady probably stashed them in a bank vault," he said from the door. "Shall I look into it?"

"No. I'll take care of that as soon as Stone County National opens at nine o'clock. You head on up to Stone Light to work on the fingerprints and the station wagon."

"I'll let you know if I come up with anything on both counts as soon as possible."

"After the bank, I'm likely to be out for much of the day. With luck, before I go home tonight, I shall put to rest Sebastian's story about his mother being murdered. I intend to talk to as many people as I can locate who, on that fateful and fatal night in July of last year, were Jennifer's houseguests."

Part Four

RSVP

"Murders do break up a house party."

—G. D. H. and Margaret Cole,
The Blatchington Tangle

21

The Banker's Account

I F THE COURTHOUSE on the town square and the law offices of the building directly behind it exemplified justice in the eyes of the people of Stone County, the stolid gray structure standing one block to their south at the northeast corner of Jail Street and Third Avenue symbolized faith in the soundness and durability of American capitalism. Erected on the eve of the financial panic of 1893, the Stone County National Bank had withstood that brief upheaval and the periodic economic temblors of the next century, including the crash of 1929 and the savings-and-loan scandal of the 1980s. That it had remained relatively unbuffeted by those sudden shifts of the monetary tides had been credited to the fact that throughout its history it had at its helm at least one direct descendant of the bank's founder, Thadeus Felix Watson, known to everyone in his time as T.F.W.

Bearing a strong resemblance to his ancestor, Felix T. Watson more than equaled the stereotypical figure of a banker. As tall and elegant in movement as a nineteenth-century clipper ship, he presented steel gray hair, a formidably high brow, direct, ice blue eyes, impressive jowls, and a full but not fat physique in an exquisitely tailored navy blue three-button pinstriped suit and a vest draped with a heavy gold chain with a rakish fob in the shape of a baseball catcher's mitt. If asked about it, he seemed delighted to explain that as a member of a Yale University team, he had participated in America's pastime with George Herbert Walker Bush when no one had any inkling that the lanky, gawky kid would go on to be President of the United States. But it was the banker's handshake that more than anything about Felix Watson conveyed a reassuring sense that his word was his bond.

"What a terrible tragedy," he declared, concerning the murder of Matilda Allen, as Flynn sat opposite the expansive desk that had been T.F.W.'s. "She was a charmingly unassuming woman. I was proud to regard her as a friend, as well as a client of our bank. How may I help you in your investigation, Miss Flynn?"

"Can you tell me if she maintained a safe-deposit box?"

"She did at one time. I arranged for it myself. However, she came in a few years ago, shortly after the death of her daughter, and emptied it. She said she felt she no longer needed it. I have a clear memory of the day because I was quite surprised. Indeed, I did my best to persuade her against it. But she could be a most hardheaded woman when she put her mind to it."

"Did she offer an explanation?"

"She said only that it had nothing to do with any dissatisfaction with the bank. Indeed, she continued her accounts with us—personal checking, savings, and two accounts from which she drew for her various philanthropic interests. She was a generous woman when it came to them. She'll be sorely missed. I can not fathom who would want to kill her."

"I know it's been awhile since she closed the safe-deposit box, but can you recall if it ever contained her jewelry collection?"

"No, I'm sorry, I don't. And we would have no record of the contents. I do remember that it was not a large box. It was the kind usually used for keeping papers and documents. That's not to say jewelry could not be accommodated. Was the collection a substantial one?"

"I don't know. Her will bequeathed it to the museum of the Stone County Historical Society. I infer from that fact that it must have been more than a couple of pieces."

"That's interesting. I don't remember ever seeing her decked out in jewels. Perhaps someone at the historical society can be of assistance. I'm a member of the broad of directors, should that be of any assistance to you in inquiring."

"That's kind of you. I'm sure I'll have no problem. Now, if I may have just a moment more of your time?"

"Take all the time you wish, Miss Flynn."

"I have to ask you to keep the rest of our conversation in strictest confidence. It's nothing to do with Mrs. Allen. Nor is it to be considered an official investigation. It concerns the death a year ago of Jennifer Hollander Duncan. I understand that you were a guest in her home the night she died."

"That's correct. The occasion was one of both business and pleasure. The business aspect involved plans to launch a venture into cosmetics, based here in the county. The bank was involved in financing her takeover of Troy Chemicals. She was about to go into the development and manufacture of a wide range of upscale women's cosmetics. The principals and a few friends were invited to the house on Saturday for swimming and boating during the day and an informal cookout on the deck. The papers were to be signed on Sunday."

He paused and the blue eyes brimmed with tears.

"Then, just like that," he said, snapping his fingers, "she died in her sleep."

"Did you know her well personally?"

"Since she was a little girl," he said, struggling against a choking in his throat. "Her parents banked with us. Elizabeth Hollander still does business here, even though she lives now in Rochester. I saw her on Friday. She's in town all week."

A momentary glint in his eyes and a slight flicker of lips suggested to her that his banker's mind had made a connection between having seen Elizabeth Hollander and the presence of an investigator from the district attorney's office. Relieved that he did not verbalize whatever conclusion he may have formed, she asked, "What was the mood during that weekend at the lake?"

"I found everything quite festive. We were all having fun. The Duncan children, Jessica and Sebastian, were romping with a neighborhood youngster. The weather was fine. The companionship was amiable. The drinks were plentiful. The food was delicious. It was a grand time. That is, until Sunday morning when James came down to the sundeck, where we were all having our breakfast, and broke the horrible news of his having found Jennifer dead. Then Doctor Granick came. And then the sheriff, of course. The speculation was rampant that Jenny had committed suicide. But I never thought it for a second."

"Why not?"

"It made no sense whatever. She was on the verge of a huge success. But it wasn't the money to be made that excited her. It was the adventure. The last words she spoke to me before going to bed were, 'Felix, this is going to be so much fun.' "

"Obviously, she was feeling quite good."

"I never saw her more upbeat."

"Yet she left her guests early to go to bed."

"She did say something about having a headache. And I believe she asked the maid to bring one of her pills and a fresh glass of iced coffee to take it with. When I said I never saw her more upbeat, I was referring to her state of mind. Not how she was physically. She looked radiant. Of course, I knew of her history of sudden headaches, prompted by stressful situations."

"But you observed nothing stressful that night?"

"No. I expected to see her bright and chipper in the morning and to enjoy the moment when she signed the papers I'd brought to close the financing of her project."

"Was the deal ever consummated?"

"Unfortunately, no. It would have been a real moneymaker. I'm sorry. That must have sounded terribly cold-blooded of me."

"Not at all. I gather that her husband was not interested in pursuing the project?"

"You gather correctly."

"Did he explain why?"

"It has been my experience that James Duncan never explains. He simply notified me by telephone the following Monday that the deal was off, that he was not interested."

"Were you surprised?"

"Not really. James had never been enthusiastic about it."

"I thank you for your time, Mr. Watson," she said. "Again, I ask that the subject of our meeting be kept strictly between us."

Accompanying her to the office door, he said, "You have my solemn word, Miss Flynn."

22

❊

The Gossip's Story

A TELEPHONE CALL from a pay phone in the echoing marbled lobby of the bank found T. Franklin Pierce at his home overlooking an inlet called "the cove."

Once a scene of thriving fishermen who drew a modest living from Hudson River striped bass, the waterfront area had rebounded from hardscrabble times in the two decades after the World War II. The rebirth took the form of a colony of artists and writers attracted from the big city downstream to a quiet and picturesque neighborhood financed with 1960s urban-renewal funds solicited by Newtown officials and provided by President Lyndon B. Johnson's Great Society. The project had been encouraged by Lady Bird's campaign to beautify America.

Among the first to purchase property, Pierce had chosen a former tackle shop on a low bluff above the cove and turned it into a showcase. The house had been featured in an architectural and interior-design magazine, and he had been photographed perched on a porch swing in white tie and tails, with the cove and river at his back. Tall and only a little overweight then, he was described as "Hudson Valley's New Age Oscar Wilde."

Standing on the small porch of the pseudo-Victorian cottage as Flynn arrived, he presented a more portly figure dressed in a rumpled denim work shirt and jeans, shouting down a flight of red-painted wooden steps, "Am I about to be arrested?"

"Is there something to arrest you for?" she retorted as she reached the top.

"If you let me off, I'll never put anything but good stuff about the DA's office in my column," he said beggingly as he entwined puffy fingers as if in prayer. "There will be more fluff than a goose-down pillow. Will you grill me here or inside?"

"The porch is fine," she said, taking in its splendid view of the river. "You get a wonderful breeze, Mr. Pierce."

"Sit here," he said, drawing up a white rattan chair with huge daffodils on the pillows. Choosing a more commodious settee, he went on, "My friends call me Tom. Please do the same. The initial stands for Thomas. I have been called that all my life. But my first editor when I went into the newspaper business told me that readers would remember my byline better with a more distinctive name. Then it was a year before he let me have a bylined story. Go figure. How may I be of assistance to you? Assuming I won't be incriminating myself!"

"First, I can't emphasize too strongly that I am not here on an official investigation. Secondly, I have to ask you to regard this meeting as off the record, professionally and personally."

"It shall be so," he said, crossing his heart.

"I'm going to take you back to July last year—to the Duncan house up at the lake."

He gasped. "The night that Jennifer Duncan died! Thank God someone's finally looking into it. I simply could not understand why there was not a more thorough investigation of the death by the sheriff's office at the time. Obviously, it was not a case of a suicide. She had everything to live for. Accidental overdose? Ridiculous. Jennifer Hollander never had a moment of carelessness in her life, Miss Flynn. Unless you count saying 'I do' when the minister asked her if she wished to take James Duncan as her husband. I was at the wedding. And when the preacher asked if there was anyone who had a reason why they should not be joined in holy matrimony, I was certain Jennifer's mother would jump to her feet shouting, 'Me. Me.' I was tempted to myself. But who was I to object? I was merely a scribbler, covering the event for my paper. As I'm sure you know, journalists are not supposed to get subjective about what they're covering. So I bit my tongue and kept silent. I wish to God I hadn't. Maybe Jennifer would be alive today. James is the one who deserved to be murdered, not Jennifer."

"Murdered? What an extraordinary thing to say."

"No matter what that half-witted Zeligman found, Jennifer was murdered. That Keystone Kop coroner ought to retire."

"What makes you think Jennifer Duncan was murdered?"

"She would never kill herself, and she was much too clever a woman to kill herself by mistake. I was convinced on that Sunday morning that she'd been murdered and I remain so today. It galls me no end to know that James is living off her estate. I'm surprised he hasn't done in the children by now. When I heard that the boy nearly drowned, I was sure his father had had something to do with it."

"What's your basis for this dark opinion of James Duncan?"

"I have known James Duncan since we were in the same class in Newtown High School, as it was known before the county consolidated all the districts. James always was, is now, and forever will be a moneygrubbing cad. He married Jennifer Hollander for her fortune. And now he's got it. Whatever it may be that brings you here to see me today, I hope it results in your arresting him for murdering her."

"Because you feel so strongly about this accusation, what's the basis for it?"

"Do you mean how did he do it?"

"Yes."

"I have no idea. Since she was supposedly poisoned with her own medicine, he must have managed some way to slip it into her coffee."

"It seems to me that if he intended to put pills into her coffee and make it appear to be suicide or an accident, he would hardly have done it surrounded by so many houseguests."

"That is the point! Lots of guests. Lots of suspects. Fortunately for him, the dunces from the sheriff's office, Jenny's doctor, and the Keystone coroner bought the accident explanation. And the man you work for signed off on it. No one gave a thought to the possibility of it being a murder."

"Back up a second and explain to me how in James Duncan's mind the weekend houseguests translated into suspects."

"Because, except for the children and that housekeeper, a Mrs. Stewart, and yours truly, of course, there were plenty of people with motive. As charming as Jennifer Hollander Duncan was in a social situation, she could be a veritable piranha when it came to business. For a prime example, I propose the underlying purpose of that gathering at the lake. Her brutal takeover of Troy Chemicals. Old Lester Troy and his chief scientist and heir apparent, Alexander Umlauf, were furious about it, although helpless."

"As I recall from reading about the deal in the *Clarion,* they each would have gotten a whole lot of money and would still hold important positions in the company."

"Money isn't everything, Miss Flynn. The so-called positions were nothing but a fig leaf. My guess is they would have been out in a year. Imagine if you had spent your life building a company, as Troy had, and it was yanked from under you. Now consider Troy's position. He was a serious man. His interest lay in chemistry for the betterment of mankind. Suddenly, all that he's worked for is going to be jettisoned in the name of beauty cream and various powders and ointments for milady's *twah-let,* as the French say. But Troy and his chemist weren't the only ones who might have been suspected of poisoning Jennifer."

"Excluding yourself."

"I admired Jennifer Hollander enormously."

"Despite her being a piranha businesswoman."

"I'm not *in* business. I am a gossip columnist." His pudgy face puffed with his smile. "And that, as you know if you read my column in the *Clarion,* is a quite different kind of predator. I may nibble my prey. But I don't devour it."

"You said there were plenty of guests with a motive to do harm to Jennifer Duncan."

" 'Plenty' may be a slight exaggeration. I can think of at least two others. One was Madeline Trainor, a so-called fashion model. Somehow or other, James had persuaded Jennifer that Miss Trainor should be the embodiment of Jennifer's cosmetics firm, to be featured in all the ads and commercials. Everyone must have seen that something was going on between James and her."

"It's been more than a year since Jennifer died. If James and Madeline were such a hot item, why hasn't he married her?"

Pierce's brows arched. "Why buy when you get it free?"

"Getting back to that Saturday night. If everyone at the party saw what was going on between James and Trainor, what was Jennifer's attitude?"

"I felt so sorry for Jennifer. She must have seen it, too. She and James had a hell of a row down at the boat slip. Raised voices, lots of gesticulation going on. Shortly after, Jennifer excused herself from the festivities, saying she felt one of her headaches coming on."

"Did you hear what was said during their argument?"

"Only the tone of their voices. No words." He paused, thinking for a moment. "I do seem to recall noticing someone else who was closer. Give me a second." He closed his eyes tightly. "He had a soft brown tweed Alpine-type hat and a brown jacket that struck me as wholly out of whack for July." The eyes popped open. "I remember him now. He was a portrait painter. Mrs. Hollander had recommended him to Jennifer to do a painting of Jennifer with the children. He has a home and studio somewhere up on Arnold's Peak. But his name escapes me."

"Could it be Stanley Gordon?"

"That's him. How ever did you know?"

"The guests were listed in Marty Katz's story on Jennifer's death."

"How astute of you to have thought to look it up. What an awful shame it is that you didn't probe into all this last year. Had you, I'm certain James Duncan would be in jail for murder."

Drawing the photocopy of Katz's story from her big brown handbag, she said, "Tom, if I may take a few more minutes of your time, I'd appreciate a gossip columnist's thumbnail sketches of others listed as guests that night. I presume you did not check your reporter's hat at the door."

"A gossip columnist is like any writer, Miss Flynn. If you don't care to discover yourself in print, do not have one for a friend. And *never* invite one to your party."

"Begin with Felix Watson."

"Mr. Bankroll. Charming man. Old-fashioned in the best sense of the word. When he speaks, you look down to see if he's got on spats. He and Stone County National lost out on a lucrative deal when James canceled the project. I can see no reason whatever for him to kill the goose that was guaranteed to provide a trove of golden eggs. Whether he felt like killing James after the deal fell through is quite another matter."

Flynn consulted the list. "Marty Katz includes a woman named Darlene Devonshire, described as the chief executive officer of a Manhattan marketing firm."

"A lovely dinner companion. Very down-to-earth. She licked the barbecue sauce from her fingers. That's my kind of dame! If this were a mystery novel, she'd fall into the category of local color. The last person you'd suspect."

"Sometimes the last turns out to be the culprit."

His eyebrows arched. "Don't you just hate that?"

"The next name is Michael Borrero."

"Import-export man from the city. He was earmarked by Jennifer to handle the worldwide distribution."

"Not Howard Schack, chairman, Schack Worldwide Enterprises?"

"Oh, there's a character for a whodunit! This guy was the last person you'd ever expect to have been a spy. Yet he was. He used his international construction business to conceal years of espionage in the Arab world on behalf of Israel. I believe he's written a book about it. Old friend of the Hollanders. Jennifer adored him. And vice versa. Cross him off your list."

"Who is Dominic Perillo?"

"He brought Madeline Trainor up from the city," he replied with a shiver. "The word *mob* was etched into his face. I kept a discreet distance. Built like a walking fireplug. He was not the sort of person I'd expected to find in Jennifer's presence. But then I figured out James had invited him. The man was a beard."

"Excuse me?"

"He was a beard. Surely you know what a beard is? And I'm not talking about facial hair. I refer to someone who pretends to be in a relationship with another person as a cover for what is really going on. In this case, Perillo acted as if he had a close relationship with Madeline Trainor, when the relationship was between her and James. In a way, I felt sorry for Perillo because he was virtually ignored by everyone. He spent most of the evening teasing the children, especially Jessica, concerning her obvious crush on Cornelia Stewart's good-looking son, Rick. He also seemed to enjoy flirting with Mrs. Stewart. He seemed to spend as much time in the kitchen as she did."

"Marty Katz's article also mentions Elaine and Sid Ruderman. Who are they?"

"Only the true masterminds behind Jennifer's plans to invade the lucrative cosmetics business. It's my understanding that Sid and Elaine came up with the marketing plan that was to launch the line of products that Jennifer's firm would manufacture. I heard via the grapevine that the deal that was finally cut was not at all to the Rudermans' liking. To put it mildly, they were *irked.*"

"That sounds more like a motive for a lawsuit. Where's your basis for anyone suspecting them of murder?"

"All I know is that when the deal collapsed after Jennifer's death, the Rudermans managed to raise their own financing from a consortium of well-heeled Arizonians and are going ahead with the very plan Jennifer would have employed. But out of Phoenix. The Rudermans winter there. Of course, James Duncan could not have cared less about what happened to them or anyone else who might have been associated in the deal. He canceled it so fast, it took everyone's breath away."

Flynn stuffed the article into the bag. "You've been very helpful. Thanks. Remember! This chat was off the record."

"What chat?"

23

The Coroner's Report

As she drove straight west on Cove Road, passing the library on the right with a distinct impression that she could smell the ineffable aroma of old books even from the street, she glanced left through the trees of the town square to the gilt dome of the courthouse, asparkle in the morning sun. Catching a green light at Main Street, where Cove Road crossed and became Seventh Street, she passed the old George Washington Inn, Elizabeth Hollander's residence while she was in town. On the right, it occupied half the block between Main and Ina streets, a stretch of quaint shops offering antiques and local handicrafts. Two long blocks farther, with the tall spire of Sacred Heart Church looming at the end of Seventh, she swung left into appropriately named Diagonal Street and managed to catch the lights green all the way to Stone County Medical Center and the basement bailiwick of Theodore Zeligman.

Seated beneath his chilling mottoes, he peered at her over the rims of his half-moon reading glasses. "If you're looking for your brother, you just missed him," he said. "He arranged for the removal of Matilda Allen's body to Devlin's funeral home. He left not five minutes ago."

She placed her shoulder bag on a chair and sat next to it. "I'm not here about her," she said. "I need to have a look at a file on a different case."

Removing the glasses, he dangled and swung them like a pendulum beneath his jowlish chin. "I was not aware that Jennifer Duncan had become a case for the DA's office."

"She hasn't," she replied, attempting to mask surprise by adjusting the bag. "I've been tidying up our files and . . ."

"Oh, I see. That's it," he said, twirling the glasses. "For a minute, I thought you and Aaron Benson might actually be giving credence to that ridiculous tale Elizabeth Hollander's grandson made up and now has that silly woman believing. She was in here last Tuesday saying that you might be coming around. Please excuse my jumping at an obviously preposterous conclusion."

Abandoning pretense, she fixed him with a respectful look. "You sly fox. Has anything ever gotten past you?"

"The widow Hollander thinks so. She's wrong, of course. But if you choose to go over all that well-trod territory, you may be my guest." Swinging round to a cluttered table behind his desk, he removed a thin folder from atop a stack of papers. "This was an open-and-shut case a year ago," he went on, offering the file. "And I have no doubt your perusal of the reports will persuade you it remains so. They're all there in the folder—Dr. Granick's statement and the death certificate he signed, sheriff Himes's report, a statement from James Duncan, my official autopsy report and my contemporaneous notes while conducting it, if you can make out my handwriting. You will also find Granick's prescription for the pills she took, along with an affidavit from the pharmacist at the Newtown Mall, who specifically remembered filling it."

"Is that so?" she asked, taking the folder and placing it in her lap. "That druggist does a heck of a lot of business. Do you recall why he was so certain in his memory of that prescription?"

"He'd never filled one like it before. It was a relatively new drug. He had to special-order it each time because it was so expensive—too costly to keep in stock for just one customer. And it didn't have a long shelf life."

"Does it have a name?"

"Yes. But don't ask me to pronounce it. There are at least umpteen letters in it. It's contained in the file. If you want the Zeligman shorthand, it's a sedative and muscle relaxant with a base of curare. One pill spells relief. Two produces fatigue. More and the heart and lungs go into arrest."

"Would that occur immediately?"

119

"Obviously not. Jennifer Duncan had time to take the pills with a glass of iced coffee downstairs and get up to her bedroom without collapsing. But barely. I would say that she was dead a moment or two after she placed her head on the pillow."

"Given the lethality of a taking an overdose and the fact that she was aware of the danger, I find it hard to believe she swallowed those pills accidentally. It looks like suicide to me."

"Me, too. But there was no note."

"Plenty of people kill themselves without leaving notes."

"Absolutely. However, I must concern myself only with facts. I found none permitting a verdict of suicide. All the evidence at hand pointed to a woman with everything to live for. She was on the verge of closing an important business deal—the very next morning! She had been in an upbeat mood all that night. The girl, her daughter, Jessica, said her mother kissed her good night and said she'd see her in the morning and take her and the boy, Sebastian, for ice cream in the afternoon. Did something happen in the meantime to plunge her into a suicidal mood? Maybe. But I had no facts to support that hypothesis. That left accidental death."

"Didn't the possibility of homicide occur to you?"

"Immediately. But the possibility of homicide is not for me to declare. That's your office's job. Aaron reviewed the facts as they were presented in the documents you have in your possession. He chose not to open an investigation."

"And you agreed with his decision."

"My personal opinion was that she had committed suicide. But I had no cause to express my *professional* opinion to that effect, lacking compelling evidence. Frankly, I also considered the kids. It's one thing to grow up without a mother. How much worse would it be knowing their mother abandoned them by committing suicide? Death by accident seemed to me to be a more humane verdict, given the lack of evidence of suicide and none pointing to homicide. In those circumstances, your boss did exactly the right thing. As to the claims of Elizabeth Hollander based on her prejudice against her son-in-law, a wild story from a child claiming his deceased mother told him otherwise carried no weight in this office."

"You don't believe in the near-death experience."

Putting on his glasses, the coroner grunted a laugh.

"How about repressed and recovered memory?"

"Bunkum. It's pop psychology's latest fad. Nothing more."

"Are you familiar with the work of Dr. Eric Lyle?"

"The man's an opportunistic charlatan of the first rank. He has a best-selling book and a fat bank account to prove it. Call me old-fashioned, but he can keep all that nonsense about deeply buried memory manifesting itself in multiple personalities and jaunts via flying saucers to some big experimental laboratory in the sky run by alien beings. It's a manifestation of the modern world's utter need for a meaning to life, rationalized by those whose so-called science cannot accept the idea of God as found in the holy books of Judaism, Christianity, and Islam. That's why the men of Lyle's ilk attribute these stories of encounters with an afterlife to the surfacing of repressed memories. If scientists were to accept life after death, they would have to abandon Darwin and Freud and all the other underpinnings of their explanations for the existence of the human race. They'd have to jettison the big bang theory and take another look at the Book of Genesis. If humanity is the result of evolution and natural selection, there can be no room for dark tunnels and the embracing light of eternal life. Hence, the explanation for anyone claiming to have died and crossed over into a spiritual existence must be found in a brain trying desperately to cope with the shocking realization that it is dying. Or else it's a trick of the brain in deep trauma."

"What does Dr. Theodore Zeligman believe?"

"Only what he knows. I know we all die. If at the moment of death we discover within us the ability to find some comfort or even pleasure in the event, that's great. If it turns out that I find there is something after I stop breathing and that it's good, or the God of the faith I was taught in synagogue really does exist, wonderful. I hope so. But if it turns out that there is a God, I also hope I'll be permitted to express my opinion as a man who has had to deal with death in all its forms that he could have handled the creation a whole lot better. Why all this violence?"

Leafing through the file on the death of Jennifer Duncan, Flynn asked, "May I borrow this for a while?"

"Certainly. Keep it as long as you like, my dear."

Cursorily paging through the file as she sat in her car, she came upon the prescription for the long and unpronounceable name of Jennifer Duncan's pills and was astonished to read the name of their manufacturer.

24

❖

The Deadly Potion

L ESTER TROY STOOD in the center of a small laboratory on the second floor of Troy Chemicals.

A cluster of almost windowless redbrick buildings, the firm anchored the western edge of the sprawl of the Mountain View Industrial Park. It had mushroomed in the 1960s on boggy lowland that had attracted Arlene Flynn, her brother, and their childhood friends in wintertime for ice-skating.

"I'm sorry that my chief chemist, Alex Umlauf, is not here, Miss Flynn," Troy said. "He's on a business trip to Europe."

A long white laboratory coat exaggerated his tall, slender physique, while a slack blue paper mask dangled beneath a bony jaw and underscored his pale, gaunt face. Had he also presented a hawkish nose, been younger, and had lived in Victorian London, she thought, he might have provided inspiration for Sidney Paget's illustrations of Sherlock Holmes for *The Strand* magazine.

"I must admit I am surprised to be called upon by somebody from the police. I thought the matter of the death of Mrs. Duncan was settled a year ago."

"I'm not the police, Mr. Troy. I work for District Attorney Benson. In closing our file on the matter, I discovered a gap or two in the records that, just for statutory purposes, should be closed. One gap is the name of the fatal ingredient in the pills that she took that night." She paused to marvel at the ease with which she lied. "It's not noted in our file."

"The common name for it is curare. Most people think of it as the poison South American natives dipped arrowheads into for hunting, or tribal wars. It renders a quarry or an enemy helpless through its ability to paralyze respiratory muscles. It's an extract from a number of plants. *Strychnos toxifera.*"

"Is that also the source of strychnine?"

"It's a relative," he said, inviting her to sit on a metal stool next to the lab table where he had been working. "That old favorite of fictional poisoners and countless real-life ones is derived from a similar alkaloid plant found in India, *Strychnos nux-vomica.*" He paused and smiled wanly. "Mother Nature has been almost boundless in her ability to concoct deadly potions for us. Fortunately, the curare-type alkaloids also have medical uses as a muscle relaxant. They can be extremely helpful for the setting of fractures, for instance. Curare has been used for the relief of spastic paralysis in some mental disorders. But its employment in the treatment of the condition suffered by Jennifer Duncan, as combined with other ingredients, is still experimental. However, it's been fully authorized for use in certain cases by the Food and Drug Administration."

"Is it always prescribed in pill form?"

"That's the standard practice. But there's no reason why it could not be administered in a capsule or even as a powder."

"Does it have a noticeable taste?"

"Combined with the other components of the drug, it would be slightly sweet."

"So it could be mixed with sugar or an artificial sweetener and not be recognized?"

"Certainly."

"What about solubility?"

"As a powder, about the same as sugar."

"And if it was in pill form and dropped into a liquid?"

"I expect it would react in the same manner as an aspirin in liquid. It would crumble and slowly dissolve—faster if stirred."

"Would it have any effect on milk and cream? Curdle it? Turn it sour?"

He stroked his pointy chin. "I don't see why it should."

"After taking one pill, how rapidly would effects be felt?"

"About half an hour. The drug is always highly diluted."

"But if five pills were taken?"

"The reactive time would be the same, I think. Naturally, the effect would be deadly."

"Would there be convulsions?"

"The objective is to *relax* muscles. Breathing would stop. But because of the paralytic effect, I would not expect to note evidence of a struggle, such as thrashing about. Indeed, I was told that when Jennifer Duncan was found dead in bed, she looked as if she were in a deep and peaceful sleep."

"Do you have any of the pills in stock at the moment?"

"The drug is so rarely ordered that when we get a request for it, Dr. Umlauf produces it right away and we ship it out to the purchaser immediately. No one's requested it since we filled Mrs. Duncan's last prescription. I delivered it myself."

"Directly to her?"

"No. I took it to the Newtown Mall Pharmacy, run by a fine druggist by the name of Kim Myung Rho. We're not permitted to deal with individuals. Regulations require us to transact our business only with registered pharmacists. Even if she had taken over the company, she still would have been required to purchase the drug from a licensed pharmacist. She found that astonishing. Had she assumed control of Troy Chemicals, she would have had much more to learn about the law, rules and regulations, even in the area of manufacture that interested her. She showed little appreciation of the fact that the manufacture of cosmetics is more than making pretty-smelling perfumes and makeup. In all candor, Miss Flynn, I believe Jennifer Duncan would have been terribly frustrated and disappointed had she taken over. I tried to make her see it, but she turned a deaf ear."

"Then why did you go along with the deal?"

"Economic reality. Troy is a small firm, a little fish in a sea of sharks. Jennifer was not the only suitor for the company. But she had the advantage of being local. I thought that if she assumed control, there would no chance of the lab and plant being shut down and moved lock, stock, and barrel to the south or down to Mexico. I wanted Troy Chemicals to remain a Stone County enterprise. I began this company here with a one-thousand-dollar loan from my great-aunt Ilona Troy and here is where I intend to keep it."

"I had no idea you were related to Miss Ilona Troy. I just assumed a coincidence of names."

"I would have liked to have taken Traitor's Lair and made it my home and restored it to the way it was in her day. But circumstances did not permit it. I understand it may go on the market again, as soon as the current owner's affairs can be straightened out. I believe he's in prison."

"Indeed he is. For murder. I had the privilege of helping send him there. On the matter of your company remaining here in Stone County . . ."

"I believed that was Jennifer Duncan's intent. Then I found out at the last minute that some of her partners favored a shift of everything except the front office to Arizona."

"What do you mean when you say you found out at the last minute?"

"The night before the deal was to be closed, I was informed by Felix Watson during dinner at the house. Felix was as shocked as I was. After all, his bank expected the new operation to be a Newtown operation. Unfortunately, the money package had already been sewed up. Happily, so far we've managed to stave off being taken over, with signs that the crisis has passed."

"Did you know Jennifer Duncan very well—that is, beyond a business relationship?"

"I knew about her, of course. And we'd met before. But I did not know her well. That was the only time I visited her home."

"Did your chief chemist know her prior to her attempt to take over the business?"

"Not that I'm aware of. If you feel you should talk to Alex, I can provide his phone number in Europe."

"I don't think that's necessary at the moment. But if I may have a couple more minutes of your time, I'm interested in your impressions of that gathering at the Duncan home—especially of Jennifer Duncan."

"What do you mean by 'impressions?' "

"Was she happy? Was she thrilled about the big deal she was consummating?"

"I'd say her mood when Alex and I arrived was very amiable. She was quite gracious. She tried to make us feel at home. We met her children. And she introduced us to an artist whom she was in the process of engaging to paint a portrait of herself and the kids. Only late that evening did her conviviality flag."

"That was when she felt one of her headaches beginning?"

"It's been over a year. It's hard to recall. But I think I detected a change in her attitude before she excused herself to go to bed. I had the impression that she'd had a spat with someone. I have a vivid memory of her being sharp with the housekeeper. She even yelled at the woman's son, Rick, and told him to stay away from her daughter. When I found out in the morning that she'd died from an overdose of the pills, I very nearly became ill myself. I felt responsible in a way. They were my company's pills she chose to kill herself with."

"The coroner ruled it accidental."

"Absolute nonsense. Impossible. There is no way by which she could have taken them inadvertently."

"Yes, I see your point," she said, sliding down from the stool. "Thanks very much for your help in filling the gaps, Mr. Troy. And good luck with keeping your company in the county."

Escorting her to the front door, he said, "She comprehended the strength and the proper dosage of those pills, Miss Flynn. So it had to have been suicide."

Getting into her car, she muttered to herself, "Or murder."

25

The Artist's Sketch

MURDER! NOT TO be confused with homicide. The latter meant the taking of human life—excusable under some circumstances. But murder—the deliberate act of killing a human being—could never be forgiven. The problem lay in proving it to a jury.

"For murder, though it have no tongue, will speak / With most miraculous organ," Shakespeare warned in *Hamlet*. And "murder cannot be hid long," he wrote in *The Merchant of Venice*, well before Cervantes had allowed Don Quixote to declare, "Murder will out."

However, the Bard of Stratford-on-Avon had been dead wrong on one point when he penned in *Titus Andronicus*, "How easily murder is discovered!"

If someone, somehow, had laced Jennifer Duncan's iced coffee with a lethal dose of her headache pills, the murder had gone undiscovered for more than a year. Why?

As usual, Sherlock Holmes had a comment. "There is nothing like first hand evidence."

Flynn shrugged and asked aloud, "What evidence?"

Sebastian's NDE?

Granny Elizabeth's unsupported accusation against James?

Just about everyone's insistence that Jennifer Duncan could not have swallowed her entire supply of curare-based medicine by mistake? Their unanimous belief that suicide made no sense?

"Did she kill herself?" she asked as she sat in the car.

"Maybe," she replied, switching on the ignition.

Or had she made a stupid, fatal mistake?

"Possibly." She sighed. "But highly unlikely."

Therefore, she was left with murder.

Suspects?

Several intriguing possibilities.

Means of the murder? Established. The pills in the coffee.

Who had the opportunity?

Apparently, every guest in the house that night.

If she had been murdered, was the act done on the spur of the moment? Or had the murderer gone to Crane Lake with a plan?

"There will be time to murder and create," T. S. Eliot wrote in "The Love Song of J. Alfred Prufrock." "And indeed there will be time to wonder, 'Do I dare?' "

If someone had dared to murder Jennifer Duncan, why?

Motive? As many as she had potential suspects.

Evidence against any of them?

Not a shred.

"I can't make bricks without clay," she muttered, quoting a frustrated Sherlock in one of his cases as she drove from the industrial park.

Turning east, she pointed the Plymouth toward a loaf-shaped mountain peak named for the man whom county lore had placed upon it. Searching the river below for British agent Major André, so as to surrender West Point to the detested redcoats, he was a furtive figure whose name would be forever a synonym for betrayal. More than three hundred years later, the most treacherous things about Benedict Arnold's Peak were ski trails cut through its trees by the developer of a winter resort in the 1960s and the snaking, steeply climbing, and narrow roadway that had been there as long as anyone could remember, probably even in Arnold's day. Going slowly, she studied roadside mailboxes for names.

Near the summit, the eighth announced "S. Gordon" in elegant scarlet scroll. Following a tree-arched dirt lane, she reached an A-frame chalet. Peering through its ground-to-roof window to the second floor, she found a small portly man in a gray artist's smock in front of a towering wooden easel. Holding an immense oval palette in his left hand and a long brush in the right, he seemed to attack the large canvas before him as though he were a fencer. Hearing the beep of her car horn, he startled a little, then put down brush and palette, descended a spiral staircase, and opened the front door.

"Good morning," he said, wiping hands on the paint-smeared smock and looking at her quizzically. "Are you here to fix the television?"

"No, I'm not, Mr. Gordon. You are Stanley Gordon?"

"That's right. I didn't think you looked like a TV repairman." He chuckled. "If you were, I guess I'd have to call you a TV repair *person.*"

"I'm Arlene Flynn," she said, digging in her bag for her identification card. "I'm with the district attorney's office."

He studied the card. "Really? What's the DA want with me?"

"Nothing to be alarmed about, Mr. Gordon," she said blithely as the card went back into the bag. "I'm making a routine follow-up to the death of Mrs. Jennifer Duncan. I believe you were at her home when she died. Something about you painting a portrait of the Duncan family?"

"The painting had been commissioned by Mrs. Duncan's mother, Elizabeth Hollander. She wanted one of her daughter and the two children. Do come in, Miss Flynn. May I call you Miss?"

"That's what I am."

"I'll be happy to assist you," he said, standing aside as she entered the house. "But I don't know what I can tell you. I was sleeping when she died. So was she. I was told it had been an accidental overdose of medication. A terrible tragedy."

Indicating a soft brown leather armchair for her, he stood before the stone fireplace and beneath a portrait of a grouping of two young girls, a younger boy, and a younger Stanley Gordon.

"Jennifer Duncan was a beautiful young woman," he continued. "She had great bone structure. I saw that the little girl would be a real beauty, as well, when she grew up. A handsome son, too. But he looked more like the father."

"Your commission was a portrait of her and the kids only?"

"That's right. I formed a distinct impression from Elizabeth that the last thing she wanted was a painting of her son-in-law."

"What gave you that impression?"

"Frankly, it wasn't just an impression. Elizabeth told me straight out that she did not want the husband in the picture. I don't know if you've met Elizabeth Hollander, but she is a very blunt woman when she wants to be."

"I have met her. And she certainly is."

The artist moved from the fireplace and into a plain wooden armchair. "Excuse me if I'm out of line," he said, "but I know Elizabeth is behind your reason for visiting me. She came to you with Sebastian's story, didn't she? I was afraid she'd do something like that. I wish she hadn't. I warned her that she'd be stirring up trouble. But she got all huffy and said to me, 'Stan, that's exactly what I intend to do.'"

"Did she explain why she wanted to make trouble?"

"She didn't have to. Everytime I was with her over the past year, she kept coming back to her belief that her son-in-law had murdered Jennifer. Then, last week, she dropped in on me with the story Sebastian had told her and informed me she was going to see the DA and demand an investigation. Obviously, judging by your presence out here in the woods, she was pretty convincing. But I am surprised that Mr. Benson took that boy's tale seriously."

"Our office must take any allegation of a crime having been committed seriously. Mr. Benson takes friendship seriously, as well. He and Mrs. Hollander have known each other a long time. He felt that he could not dismiss her or her allegation, however preposterous it might have sounded, out of hand."

"Therefore," Gordon said, smiling impishly, "he stuck you with the sticky wicket."

She returned the smile. "I would not phrase it that way, Mr. Gordon."

"Everybody calls me Stan. Nonetheless, he stuck you with the job of finding some way to get him off the hook and let Elizabeth down easily. I don't see how I can help you. I was at the Duncan house that night. But I was pretty much like a picture on a wall. Once all the guests took a look at me, they ignored my presence. I spent most of the time sketching the two kids. They were really good about it and posed quite nicely, until their mother came around to pack 'em off to slumberland."

"Did she do that before or after the argument with James, which I've been led to understand you overheard?"

"You've been talking with Tom Pierce," he said with a look of displeasure, leaning forward in the chair, hands clasped between his knees. "He's been trying to get me to tell him about what he calls 'that big row' for over a year."

"Was it a big row?"

He sat back. "Miss Flynn, I have never been one to gossip. That's Tom Pierce's territory. And my parents taught me that if you can't say something good about somebody, don't say anything. They also taught me never to speak ill of the dead."

"Surely, Stan, those maxims do not extend to a possible case of murder?"

His head snapped back and hit the chair with a bump. "You can't be serious. Murder? Nonsense."

She did not reply.

He leaned forward again. "You *are* serious."

"Let's just agree that I have to keep an open mind until the time when I can assure Elizabeth Hollander that her daughter was not murdered. Anything you can provide by way of facts to bolster me will be very much appreciated. What was the big row about?"

Paint-stained fingers drummed the arms of the chair. "It was on the subject of another woman. She told him that if he did not stop seeing her, she would divorce him and that she would see to it that he didn't get a cent of her money and that she would use all of her influence and her mother's to get a court order to keep him from ever seeing the kids. I never felt more embarrassed in my life. I also felt very bad for the girl and boy, because they were there with me and heard all that was said, too."

"What did James say?"

The artist cocked his head and gazed at the painting over the fireplace. "What he said is what I might have said if I was ever threatened in that way."

Her eyes drifted to the painting of him and his children. "Which was what, Stan?"

His eyes held on the picture for a moment longer before fixing upon hers. He cleared his throat but still spoke huskily. "He told her, 'I'll see you dead first.' "

Part Five

Whoever You Are

"Whoever you are, God or anybody else,
you work with the materials at hand."

—Lawrence Block, *Eight Million Ways to Die*

26

Who's There?

CHERCHEZ LA FEMME? Is that what you're saying?"
District Attorney Aaron Benson paced his office.

"I expected you to come back to me with a logically ironclad explanation for the death of Jennifer Duncan," he said, rolling up the sleeves of his crisp white shirt. "You were supposed to find something that would get her mother out of my hair."

With hands clasped behind his back and his fingers wiggling, he stared out the window at wind-rippled foliage of the trees of the town square below.

"But there you sit," he said, turning around and returning to his desk, "telling me that perhaps murder is not such a wild idea. Now what am I to do?"

"The question, boss, is what do you want *me* to do?"

Hands steepled under his chin, he said, "Go over it for me again."

"I'll be glad to. 'Nothing clears up a case so much as stating it to another person.' Sherlock Holmes in 'Silver Blaze.' "

"Thank you very much. Now I don't have to go over to the library and look it up."

"Did Jennifer Duncan commit suicide? I don't believe it. Did she gulp down all those pills by mistake? Impossible. 'When you have excluded the impossible, whatever remains, however improbable, must be the truth'—from 'The Adventure of the Beryl Coronet.' "

"We are not at a meeting of the Baker Street Irregulars," he said sharply, unsteepling his hands and balling them into fists atop his desk. "You are the chief investigator for the district attorney of Stone

135

County. If you can make a case for murder, do it. I want to hear about suspects based on means, opportunity, and motive. Especially motive. Motive, motive, motive. Start with Elizabeth Hollander's nominee, the husband."

"Means? James knew about the pills. He had access to them. He had the two most tried-and-true of motives. Money. The other woman, Madeline Trainor. Elizabeth said last week that Duncan was a philanderer. The difference between her and me is that she suspected him of playing around, whereas I can prove it. I have at least one witness to testify that James was all over her that night."

"That's what bothers me about the randy husband as the chief suspect. He would have to be a fool to murder his wife on a night when the house was crammed to the rafters with people."

"Granted. But aren't all murderers fools? Also that night, Jennifer threatened him with the loss of his access to her money and his children. I have a witness. And what did he hear James say to her?"

"Yes, yes. He said, 'I'll see you dead first.' That does not add up to a verdict of guilty beyond a reasonable doubt. Go on to the next-most-likely suspect."

"That could be either Lester Troy or his chief chemist, Alex Umlauf. Possibly both. Their futures were at stake. They made the pills that killed her."

"Reasonable suspects. Who's next on the list?"

"The friendly banker."

"Arlene," he said, shaking his head, "I have known Felix my whole life. Every four years, he's my campaign's finance chairman. Don't tell me Felix is capable of murder."

"If he was capable of it, he had motive. He had committed millions in Stone County National's assets to a business venture that suddenly appeared to be about to pull up stakes and put down roots elsewhere. Would you care to explain that embarrassment to your bank's board of directors, not to mention the editorialists at the *Clarion* and who knows how many local businessmen who had their loans turned down?"

"Go on to someone else. Somebody I have not known all my life. How about the gangster who was in and out of the kitchen all night, wooing that Stewart woman? Have you considered the possibility that Dominic Perillo was in cahoots with the femme fatale of this melodrama? She hired him to bump off the wife so she could marry the widower and share his inheritance. Later, she gets Perillo to eliminate Duncan. Then the dame and Perillo link up as man and wife, which may have been their plan all along."

"I can see Trainor wanting Jennifer out of the way. But if that was her intent, she must be disappointed. James has shown no sign of marrying her. However, if she was in a conspiracy with Perillo and James does pop the question one day, and he winds up dead, with Madeline subsequently settling down with Perillo, I would not care to be underwriter of the life-insurance policy of either of the newlyweds."

"You have a wicked mind, Arlene. Which is why you are so good at your job. Who else qualifies as a suspect?"

"The couple from Arizona. The Rudermans certainly wasted no time after the death of their intended partner in setting up shop on their own."

"Your implication is that they might have already decided to do so and spiked the java to abort the deal they had with her?"

"Bingo, boss!"

"And what of Jennifer Duncan's other business associates? The import-export guy and the international tycoon?"

"At the moment, I can offer nothing in the way of motive for either Michael Borrero or Howard Schack, unless there's one to be found in the fact that a last-minute decision had been made that would locate the manufacturing plant in Arizona. Both Borrero and Schack have New York–based operations."

"Shall I assume you do not include on your list the writer and the artist? Or have you come up with motives for them, too?"

"I can't see the painter killing off the reason for his portrait commission. And T. Franklin Pierce is more likely to kill with a poison pen than lethal pills in a glass of iced coffee, I think. But, in the immortal words of the Shadow, 'Who knows what evil lurks in the hearts of men?' "

"How could any of those people have been sure of getting the pills into her drink and no one else's?"

"She was the only one drinking iced coffee."

"Why didn't she drop dead with her first glass?"

"The pills were put in her last glass at the time she took the one pill."

"Excuse me. That leads to the conclusion that whoever put the pills in her glass of coffee had to have dropped them in at the time she was taking one herself."

"That's right."

"How did he, or she, manage that trick?"

"I don't know how. All I can say for certain is that Jennifer complained of a headache coming on, that she excused herself from the guests, and that she said she was going to take a pill and go to bed. She did and she died. The pill bottle was found empty in the kitchen in the morning. Unfortunately, because no one investigated the possibility of murder, it was never looked at for fingerprints."

With an expression that may have registered criticism of his decision not to investigate the possibility of murder, he said, "Who else was in that house?"

"Mrs. Stewart, her son, and the two Duncan kids, Jessica and Sebastian. I haven't talked to any of them."

"Good. The last thing I want right now is for James Duncan to know that this office is taking a second look at the death of his wife. And I hate to think of what Elizabeth Hollander would do to me if we broke our pledge to stay away from the boy."

"Regarding Mrs. Hollander, I regret to inform you that she has not been discreet concerning her suspicion of James."

His eyes widened with alarm. "What?"

"She's talked to Ted Zeligman about it, for one."

He groaned and held his head.

"When I went over to see if I could finesse the Jennifer Duncan file out of him, he had it ready and waiting," she said. "He had been told by Elizabeth Hollander to expect me."

Benson banged a fist on the desk. "Damn it! Instead of those depressing mottoes that old fart has hanging on his wall, he ought to have one of those posters from the World War Two. 'Loose lips sink ships.' If word of this gets back to James Duncan . . ."

"If I'm to proceed with this investigation, I'm going to have to talk to him eventually."

"Yes. But not now."

"Sooner or later, I'll also need to sit down with Sebastian to talk about what the kid may know concerning how his mother died."

Vaulting out of his chair, Benson exclaimed, "No. Not on your tintype. I promised Elizabeth we'd keep hands off the kid."

"That pledge was made when neither of us took the kid's story seriously."

Turning abruptly, he said, "Don't tell me that now you *are*. Oh, come on, Arlene. If that ever got out, I'd be the laughingstock of the county. The state. The whole damned country. Every tabloid paper and television show in the nation would be camped out on the front steps. I can see the headline now. DEAD WOMAN CLAIMS MURDER AND HICK DA INVESTIGATES. No! How could you even consider talking to that kid?"

"Because it's possible he may hold the answer to what really happened to his mother. He might have seen the murderer put the pills in the coffee. He may have repressed the memory of it. I don't see how I can proceed without an interview with Sebastian."

Benson returned to his chair. "Then drop it."

She gasped. "You can't mean that."

"I certainly do. If that's your only way of proceeding, I'm not going to authorize you to go on with the investigation."

"Very well. You're the boss," she said, standing and lifting her bag from the chair and slinging it over her shoulder. "Save your face. Let the murderer of Jennifer Duncan get away with it."

As she strode toward the door, he pleaded, "Wait a minute."

She turned to face him.

Worry wrinkled his brow. "Are you absolutely *convinced* this was a murder?"

"If I'm wrong, I'll retire to Sussex and keep bees."

"You are *convinced* that Sebastian may hold the key?"

"Honestly, boss, I don't know. But what if he does? How can we ignore the possibility?"

He sighed deeply. "All right. Here's what I'm willing to do. Bring me something I can hang my hat on, and my reputation. Show me reasonable cause to authorize an interview with this kid. Can you do that?"

"I think I have a shot at it. But I'll have to go down to the city for a day."

"What's there?"

"It's not what's there," she said, leaving the office. "It's who's there."

27

The Fond Deceiver

"THANKS FOR INTERRUPTING your vacation to see me, Dr. Lyle," Flynn said, following him into his office. "I know little about psychology, and until I read your book, everything I knew about repressed and recovered memory came from two films."

He indicated a blue wingback chair for her as he sat behind a desk as Spartan and clean as Benson's. "No doubt the pictures you saw were *The Three Faces of Eve* and *Sybil.*"

"Of course, they dealt with the sudden emergence of multiple personalities in two women. As far as I know, the case I want to consult with you about does not fall into the category of multiple personalities. This was a boy's near-death experience, which I have reason to suspect may have been a repressed memory."

"Concerning what?"

"The purported murder of the boy's mother."

"Why do you call it a 'purported murder'?"

"The official explanation was that it had been an accidental overdose of a prescription sedative."

"When did it happen?"

"A year before the boy had his NDE."

"What caused it?"

"He drowned and was resuscitated after several minutes."

"When did he first relate the NDE?"

"Just a few days ago."

"To you?"

"To his grandmother."

"How soon after the drowning incident did he tell her?"

"A couple of days."

"He told no one else?"

"Not that I'm aware of."

"Has he exhibited a dramatic change in his personality and behavior? People who claim NDEs usually do. They report psychic powers they'd never had before. Many become extremely religious. How old is the boy, by the way?"

"He's nine now. His mother died in July of last year."

"As to change in behavior or personality since his purported NDE, I meant anything other than what you might expect in a growing boy."

"I'm afraid I'm not able to answer that. I've never met him."

"Really, Detective? Why is that?"

"I had no reason to before last week, and since then, I have not been permitted to see him."

"You're investigating his story of a possible murder and yet you haven't interviewed him? That strikes me as extraordinary."

She paused and drank in a view of the upper facades of Park Avenue beyond his window. "The circumstances are unusual."

"To even begin to help you, Detective Flynn, I would have to conduct an interview with him. If that process proved encouraging, I would then induce a state of hypnosis in order to determine if something had really happened to him, no matter what you choose to call it. Not to put too fine a point on it, through hypnosis I'll know if this was a typical NDE episode, a manifestation of recovered memory, or an exercise in a boy's invention."

"If he did not have an NDE or the burst of a recovered memory, why would he lie?"

"For the same reason kids cry, throw temper tantrums, and do all the other things that drive adults to distraction. To draw attention and affection. I'm not an expert on near-death experiences and I have grave doubts about those that have been reported. That's the department of a researcher named Kevin Albert."

"I've spoken to him. And I read his book."

He smiled. "I thought you might have. Then you know that individuals who claim to have had a near-death experience customarily relate that experience immediately, often within minutes of waking up. This boy did not do so for a couple of days, and then to his grandmother. I find that interesting."

"He says that in the NDE he was instructed by his mother to tell only his grandmother. He spoke to her only last week. She came to see him from her home upstate."

"Is the father deceased or otherwise unavailable?"

"He is alive and well. The boy lives with him and a sister."

"Do you know if he told the sister?"

"No. But if brothers and sisters are the same as they were when I was growing up with my brother, I doubt it."

"You're probably right. But his not confiding in his father could be meaningful. The father may have played a significant role in whatever it was that this child desperately felt a need to forget."

"Assuming this is a case of repressed and recovered memory."

He smiled again. "Do I detect a doubt on the subject?"

"In the introduction to your book, you recalled the words of the poet Goldsmith. 'O Memory! Thou fond deceiver.' "

He barked a laugh. "If he were alive today, I'd give him an *A* in poetry but an *F* in modern psychology."

"On the basis of the scant information I've provided you, does the boy in question qualify in the category of your area of expertise?"

"It appears that he might."

"It's your opinion that he did not have an NDE?"

"I'm sure he believes he did. I'm equally as certain that if I was given the opportunity to work with him, I'd find a dark and scary memory presenting itself in a manner he can cope with."

"I'm a cop. Therefore, this is a police question. Is it at all possible that the memory he is suppressing involves being a witness to the death of his mother?"

"It's more than possible. I'd say it's likely."

"Would hypnosis bring out the truth?"

"I believe so."

"Can people lie under hypnosis?"

"No technique is foolproof, Miss Flynn. People trick polygraphs, which is why they are not admissible as trial evidence. A psychopath might very well lie while under hypnosis with the same facility with which he deceives people in his everyday life. If you administer a lie detector to a psychopath, he's likely to pass it with flying colors. The test picks up telltale signs of what we term *the conscience*. A psychopath has none, in the ordinary sense. If this boy is a psychopath, not even deep hypnosis can be expected to break through."

"How does one recognize a psychopath?"

"One usually doesn't, unless you know what you're looking for. You can be sure only after he's caught. The proof is in the history of serial killers. The common reaction from those nearest and dearest to him is, 'Why, he was such a nice boy.' But if you examine his past, he wasn't a nice boy. He may have set some fires, tortured and killed animals. Look up the serial killers of recent years and you'll find an early pattern of antisocial behavior. One used to twist off dolls' heads as a boy. He grew up to behead women. Look at Jeffrey Dahmer. John Wayne Gacy. David Berkowitz, known as the Son of Sam."

"I don't have to look him up, Dr. Lyle. I worked on that case. You could say I cut my baby cop's teeth on it."

"I did digress. I'm sorry. As to your nine-year-old boy, I'd venture the opinion that if I was allowed to work with him, I'd soon be able to tell you exactly what he knows about the death of his mother. Incidentally, the official verdict notwithstanding, do you believe she was murdered?"

"You'll understand, I'm sure, that I can't answer that."

"Of course. It's a fascinating case. I hope circumstances change and I can help you."

"If I get to a point where I believe you can, I'll be in touch. Meanwhile, thanks for seeing me."

"I'm puzzled by something, Detective Flynn."

"What's that?"

"Don't get me wrong about this. It was fascinating meeting you. But there was nothing you asked that could not have been addressed on the phone. Why come all the way down here?"

"Why do you assume you were my only reason?"

"Touché! That's my ego showing off."

"Actually, you are the sole reason. But I've found during my years in this job that there's nothing as important in talking to someone as being able to look him square in the eye."

"And you said you know nothing about psychology!"

28

❈

Messages

FOR AN OUTSIDER to reach Aaron Benson's office, the visitor entered a bank of three elevators in the ornate rotunda of the courthouse and rode to the top floor, then exited into a small lobby adorned with DISTRICT ATTORNEY in black letters on the opposite white wall and a black arrow below that pointed right to double glass doors with golden lettering:

OFFICE OF THE DISTRICT ATTORNEY
AARON BENSON

GRAND JURY ROOM

Through these doors one found a surprisingly cozy reception room with a leather couch and four matching chairs, a rectangular walnut coffee table with scrupulously up-to-date magazines on it, and end tables with lamps casting soft light on maroon walls decorated with photographs of historic sites or scenic beauties throughout Stone County. Also illuminated was a row of portraits of previous prosecutors, one of whom had gone on to offices that political sages anticipated in Benson's future, New York State attorney general and governor.

Usually, a small desk opposite the glass doors and before the plain entrance to the grand jury chamber was occupied by the latest in a series of earnest young men or women working their way through law school, watched over with eagle eyes by a short, stout gray-haired woman. Benson's executive assistant, she knew more about the law than many of the attorneys she encountered as buffer between Aaron Benson and those claiming to have business with him or against him.

Soon after becoming his chief investigator, Arlene Flynn had recognized that to gauge the climate in the DA's office, there was no more reliable barometer than Constance Hardwick. Since the day Benson first raised his right hand to swear the oath as Stone County's prosecutor, she had held sway over his domain as surely as Ida Singleton reigned over the town library.

Although Flynn ordinarily turned left from the elevators to a wooden door without lettering and then along three small hallways to her corner office, upon her return from New York City, she followed the arrow through the glass doors, noted the absence of a receptionist, and proceeded directly into Hardwick's adjoining office. Glancing through Benson's open door and finding his chair unoccupied, she asked, "Is he around, Connie?"

"He's down in court," she said, explaining without having to that the law student serving as receptionist had been pressed into duty to carry the case file for him. "It's closing arguments in the Davis arson today." With an urgency of tone signaling unusual weather, she continued. "Peter Sloan is looking for you. Very excited. He said he had to see you the minute you got back from the city. I think it has to do with the Allen case. He's been climbing the walls of his office for about an hour and bothering me every two minutes, asking if you were back yet."

"Let me know the very *second* the boss comes back," she said, striding away. "I have to see him right away, too."

Sandwiched between a supply room and equipment storage on the back side of the building and affording a single window with an uninteresting vista of the roof of the Law Offices Building, Sloan's office looked more like the workroom of a computer technician than a detective's. Tables topped by screens, drive units, keyboards, and printers cluttered three of its four sides. A pair of tall bookshelves crammed with operating manuals stood against the wall with the window, flanking the desk as Sloan scanned the green screen before him. Deft fingers flitted over a keyboard.

"Hurrah, hurrah! You're finally back," he exclaimed without looking up. "I'm on-line with our most esteemed colleagues at the Washington, D.C., headquarters of the Eff! Bee! Eye! Pull up a seat. I'll be only a nanosecond more."

Choosing an armless chair with separated back and seat pads supported by a pedestal with splayed feet that rolled on eight wheels, she said, "Take all the nanoseconds you need. The boss is in court and there's not a thing for me to do till he's done. Except my paperwork, of course. And to the devil with that for now. What are you asking of the feds?"

"Their computer analysis of two sets of unidentified latent prints lifted from Matilda Allen's house that I sent to them from the state police at Stone Light. A beautiful full thumb from the right side of the outside knob of the bathroom door and some not-so-terrific partials off the outside of the bottom drawers of Matilda's bedroom bureau."

Flynn looked down at her hands. "If the good print was on the right side," she said, curling them as if turning doorknobs, "it's got to be a left thumb. What about size?"

"Definitely a man's."

"And the ones in the bedroom?"

"Hard to say. They looked kind of small. Those are the hard ones. The thumb, I have reason to hope, may be that of the ne'er-do-well Oliver Allen. Did I tell you that we heard from the parole board this morning?"

"You did not."

"Right. You were in the city. Well, I did. Ollie was sprung in January and was supposed to report to his parole officer here in Newtown. In keeping with his character, he didn't. There's a warrant outstanding, issued by Her Honor Marian Copeland back in February. I also received a DMV file on both the Chevy wagon and Matilda's BMW."

"You've had a productive day."

"Alas, the Chevy was stolen two months ago from in front of a bar on Hudson Street in Greenwich Village and duly reported to the NYPD."

"Damn. It would have to turn out to be untraceable."

"It was the paper concerning the BMW that surprised. That nifty set of wheels originally belonged to Matilda's daughter. The title was transferred upon her death. Unfortunately, there's been no sign of the car since it went missing."

Flynn tugged her lower lip. "It's probably been dumped by now, the license plates changed, maybe even repainted. Or else it's hundreds, or thousands, of miles away. If it was sold in the city, it could have been shipped down to South America or anywhere in Asia. The Middle East. Maybe Africa."

While Sloan's hands rested at the edge of the keyboard, his attentive eyes studied the screen. "How did the chat go with the Park Avenue shrink?"

"He wants to hypnotize Sebastian."

"Oh great! Imagine what some defense attorney could do with that in front of a jury."

"Imagine what Elizabeth Hollander would do if I approached her about it. Not to mention James Duncan. And there certainly is no way we could compel a nine-year-old to be hypnotized."

Sloan's eyes darted away from the screen. "If you could get a subpoena, would you go for one?"

"If it was entirely my decision, yes, I would."

"What if you could get Sebastian hypnotized and it came out that he really did die for a while and that he met his mother?"

"Much more likely, I think, he'd have something to say about seeing something, perhaps the murderer in the act, but that he buried what he knows or saw deeply inside his child's mind. It stayed there more than a year, only to be shaken loose during his brush with death. But in a manner that his mind could handle."

"Assuming that's what happened, assuming the only way his mind could cope with what it remembered was by forming a vision of his mother telling him to go back to life and tell his granny that she'd been murdered, and assuming Sebastian knew who did it, why wouldn't his mother have given him a name to pass on to Elizabeth Hollander?"

Flynn's eyes narrowed and she tugged hard on her lip. "Oh, Peter Sloan, what a wonderful question!" The eyes went full and the hand snapped tight into a fist that pounded his desk. "Now here's one for you. What if he *did* tell her?"

"She would have told you."

147

The fist pounded again. "Perhaps she did, sending me a message in a backhanded kind of way."

Sloan looked at her sidelong. "Huh?"

"What did she tell me? She started with a question. The very one I've been asking myself and the one I put to Kevin Albert and Dr. Lyle. Isn't it possible that the shock of what happened to Sebastian brought back a memory of something so awful that he'd buried it? Then what did she say? This is almost an exact quote. She told me that 'his good-for-nothing father murdered my Jennifer.'"

"Which was her way of telling you indirectly that Sebastian had named his father?"

"When Benson warned her against going public with such an accusation, she replied, 'Let James sue me for defamation if he wishes to. The defense against slander is truth. I know that man killed my Jenny.' She did not say, 'I think,' or 'I believe,' or 'I suspect.' She said, 'I know.' That is a very smart lady, Sloan. She understood perfectly the difference between what she knew and what could be proven in a trial. She also knew Benson well enough to count on him trying to soft-soap her by assigning someone to go through the motions of an investigation. She counted on that person coming up with the *possibility* that Jennifer Duncan had been murdered after all. She was so sure of what Benson would do that she visited Ted Zeligman to alert him that someone from the DA's office would be dropping in on him to have a look at his files on the Duncan case. And when did she go see Zeligman? The significance of that date went right over my head till now. She saw him on a Tuesday. That was two days *before* her chat with me."

"Why, then, wouldn't she let you interview the kid?"

"She was afraid Sebastian would deny everything, which he would do, I think. If I were a nine-year-old and some detective came around asking questions about a terrible secret of mine, I'd certainly clam up. Plus, and more importantly, Elizabeth Hollander wanted our investigation to result in turning up evidence to arrest James Duncan without having to involve Sebastian."

"Do you think you'll be able to?"

"Progress is being made."

As she spoke, Sloan jerked straight up in his chair. "Okay. Here's what we've been waiting for," he exclaimed, stabbing the computer screen with a finger. "The Federal Bureau of Investigation's considered opinion on the thumbprint on Matilda's door. Look at it and smile!"

Peering over Sloan's shoulder, she saw only the name.

ALLEN, OLIVER DAVID.

"No luck on the other prints, though," Sloan said, pointing to a second message. "They weren't sufficient for a definitive identification at this time. Our friends have a query."

She read:

Do you authorize further analysis?
Y/N.

She nudged Sloan's shoulder. "Tell them, 'Hell yes.' "
Sloan tapped the keyboard's *Y.*

29

❖

Strategies

W HAT A GLORIOUS invention the jury system is," declared the district attorney of Stone County, draping his jacket on the back of his chair. "Twelve good and true citizens sit quietly during the course of a trial, absorbing the evidence, and then go into a room all by themselves to weigh, analyze, discuss, debate, and vote on it. And here is the majesty of the thing! They hardly ever screw it up. Except once in a million, if that, they do the right thing. They serve justice."

As he sat in the big chair behind the immaculate desk, Flynn responded with a smirk and said, "I take that speech to mean that you anticipate a quick verdict of guilty."

"I gave a terrific summation of the people's evidence." He grinned proudly. "I figure they will find Harlan Davis guilty of arson in the first degree on their first show of hands. But they won't let the Honorable Judge Melissa Ludlum know they've reached a verdict until around seven tonight. *After* they have had a nice dinner at the county's expense at the Depot restaurant."

"That's pretty cynical of good-and-true citizens."

He shrugged. "How did your trip to the big city go?"

"Before I get to that, there's an interesting development in the Matilda Allen murder. A thumbprint lifted from the bathroom door belongs to Oliver Allen."

"I thought he was in Attica."

"Paroled in January. There's a warrant out for breaking it."

"His print on the door doesn't prove he killed her."

"No. But it's mighty persuasive."

Benson's expression knotted. "Matricide. That slimy bastard! I knew he'd end up killing somebody. But his *mother?*"

"He appears to have had an accomplice. Unfortunately, prints that may be that accomplice's are so far useless. I've authorized further analysis by the FBI."

"What about the missing car?"

"It's still missing. It originally belonged to Matilda's daughter. Because it's the kind of buggy that's popular in the automobile international black-market trade, I believe you may safely assume it was sold in the city and shipped far across the bounding waves. The Chevrolet station wagon was stolen and is of no further importance. The prints appear to be our only hope."

"Find both these creeps and one of 'em will squeal. Give me one's confession and I'll work out a plea bargain with him that will nail the other one. I just hope it's Oliver."

"There's one other matter in the Allen case that may go to show motive. The old lady's jewelry collection is unaccounted for."

"Maybe she sold it."

"That is certainly something to be looked into. If she did, it wasn't because she needed the money. Also, she'd left them to the county museum in her will."

"I see your point. If she figured they were worthy of being in a museum, she probably wouldn't have sold them. And if she had gotten sick and tired of them, she'd more than likely have let the museum have them while she was alive. Now, if that's it on the Allen case, you can tell me what your jaunt down the river was all about."

As years of prosecuting criminal cases had perfected in him the art of assessing the receptivity of jurors, her experience in laying out the details and strategies of investigations for Aaron Benson had honed her ability to read him, allowing her to anticipate his reactions. Consequently, as she broached the subject of discerning the validity of repressed and recovered memory by way of hypnosis, she could not fail to notice a flicker of tension in his facial muscles, a squaring of shoulders, and a narrowing of eyelids until they became little more than slits.

As if someone had shoved the muzzle of a gun in his back and growled, "Stick 'em up, buddy," he lifted both hands and quietly said, "Not on your life. I gave my word that you'd stay away from that kid."

"I appreciate that, boss," she said pleadingly, "But unless I talk to Sebastian, I don't see how I can make any progress."

The hands lowered, palms down on the desk, fingers splayed. "I said no, Arlene. And that's that." A long sigh dispelled all the tension. "I must have been nuts to get us into this mess in the first place. The next time you see me about to do something stupid, whisper into my ear 'Elizabeth Hollander' and then give me a swift boot in the ass. For now, go down the hall to your office and write me a report that will satisfy her that you have looked into the matter thoroughly and have found no cause to believe her daughter was murdered."

"There's only one problem in doing that, boss." Her tone was strained. "It would be a bald-faced lie."

Tilting back in his chair, he faced the ceiling. Closing his eyes, he muttered, "Dear Lord in heaven, why me?"

She answered, "Because you wanted to be district attorney."

Opening his eyes a little, he looked down his nose at her. "What's that supposed to mean?"

"It means you should never have cut that deal. You knuckled under to her demands as if she weren't Jennifer's mother but your own and if you didn't do what mommy said, mommy would spank."

The eyes went wide open. "Now just a damn minute!"

"It also means that I think that you're afraid you might be embarrassed if it turns out Jennifer Duncan was murdered."

"You are way out of line, Arlene."

"You could have authorized an investigation into her death a year ago. But you signed off on the opinions of Zeligman and all the others. You let it slide, when what you should have done, for Jennifer's sake, at least—the victim's sake—was take another look at her death. In just a few days, you could have come up with all that I have. On that Saturday evening in July a year ago, there were plenty of people at that house on Crane Lake with reasons to want Jennifer dead. If this office had investigated at the time, we might have discovered on our own that she might well have been murdered. Instead, we've got a nine-year-old boy with a story of meeting his dead mother and coming back with a claim of murder. And we've got his grandmother going all over town, doing all she can to get James Duncan arrested for it. Well, if she ever says that to Marty Katz, look out!"

He sat stonily silent for a long moment. But when he spoke, it was with a startling question. "Do you think it is possible that God could be a woman?"

"Heavens no. A woman could ever have made such a botch of the job."

Benson smiled. Forgivingly, she decided.

"Furthermore, the proof's in the Book of Genesis," she said with relief. "It states God took six days to create the universe and rested on the seventh. A woman would have finished in five."

He frowned. "That would mean two Sabbath days."

"Oh no. On the sixth day, She, with a capital S, would have gone shopping at the mall."

He sat upright, his hands folded on the desk. "Find a way for me to open an investigation into the death of Jennifer Duncan that won't make me look like the fool of the year. And an election year at that! Give me one of those classic Arlene Flynn memorandums of 'information and belief' that a judge will not rip up and throw back at me like confetti if we ever have to go into a court. Give me everything you've come up with so far. But not a word about this cockamamy yarn about some near-death experience. Not a whisper of repressed and recovered memory. Leave out those head-shrinkers. *No hypnosis,* for God's sake."

"I'll start writing it now."

"And then draft me a press release that will announce what we're doing is simply a routine cleaning up of the files, tying up loose ends. Make it sound as routine as the sunrise."

She grinned. "In other words, bureaucratic busywork."

"*Anything* to get that woman out of my face and to keep me from having to defend myself and the county against slander. I do not want to be a laughingstock on the front page of the *Clarion.*"

"I'll put a picture of Marty Katz on my desk to remind me."

"After that, bring me sufficient evidence to prove Jennifer Duncan was murdered, without having to put her son on the stand as a witness for the prosecution."

Standing, she answered, "I'll do my best."

Adjusting a crooked gold cuff link in the shape of balanced scales of justice, he said, "You damn well better."

Going to the door, she said, "You'll have the memo and the draft of a press release first thing in the morning."

"One more thought on the Allen case. Regarding the missing jewelry. Since the items are apparently unique, and assuming that whoever snatched them may hope to peddle them, have you alerted pawnshops and jewelery dealers?"

"That's a problem. We have no descriptions of the items."

"Perhaps the museum does. I'll put Detective Richards on it in the morning. Now that the Davis case is in the hands of the jury, Ed's free. Matter of fact, he can team up with Pete Sloan on the Allen investigation full-time."

"That's great, boss. I'm sure Sloan will welcome all the help he can get."

30

Night Shift

"THE BOSS IS lending us Eddie Richards starting tomorrow," Flynn said, leaning in Peter Sloan's doorway.

Smiling up from his desk's computer, he said. "Terrific."

"Start him off by sending him over to the museum to see if it has descriptions of Matilda's jewelry. If so, distribute them to local hockshops and jewelry stores. And fax the state police and the NYPD and request they distribute them to their most likely places for the unloading of hot goods."

"Will do. As for me, I thought I'd canvas Ollie Allen's old stomping grounds on Riverfront Road tonight, in case anyone has seen him around recently. Who knows? Maybe I'll turn up a lead on his partner."

"Those are chancy characters over there, Sloan. They can spot a cop a mile away. Why don't you wait till Richards is on board? I'd feel better if you went to Riverfront with a partner."

"I'll be fine."

"Tuck a cellular phone in your pocket. And don't hesitate to call in the Newtown Police if you smell even a hint of a need for backup. Should you want to talk to me, I'm goin' to be here for quite awhile. Benson's put me on the night shift."

Cocking rearward in his chair, with the back of his head in the cradle of interlaced fingers, he made a clucking sound and teased, "That's your penance for being so delinquent with your paperwork."

She stepped into the office and closed the door as if she possessed a wonderful secret to share. "He's taken the handcuffs off the Duncan investigation."

155

Sloan lurched to his feet. "How'd you manage that miracle?"

"I hit him in the three spots where he is most vulnerable. One, male ego. I made a not-so-subtle suggestion that by pussyfooting with Elizabeth Hollander, he's let himself be intimidated by a woman. Two, his duty to his oath of office, by questioning whether he's being derelict in it. And lastly, the old standby with him, a deep compassion for the victim that's rooted in his Jewishness, which, whether Aaron Benson realizes it or not, is why he's a DA."

Sloan laughed. "You are a pistol."

"Yeah. Also a bitch."

"So why's Benson got you working tonight?"

"What else could it be?" she replied as she left the office. "Lots and lots of paperwork."

Presently, as she worked on the memorandum justifying a formal reopening of the Duncan case, Sloan poked his head through her doorway and announced, "I'm off to Riverfront."

"Carefully, Peter Sloan," she said without looking up.

Ten minutes later, he parked his county car in the lot behind the Depot restaurant. Noticing the presence of a court van used to transport jurors to meals during deliberations or to hotels in cases in which a jury had been ordered sequestered, he began the short walk toward the Hudson River on an evening with hints of autumn. Two more minutes brought him to the corner of Hempstead Street and a road older than the town.

Long before Dutch settlers invaded the territory that became Stone County to establish the village of Newtown a trail had been tramped beside the big river. It passed beneath a steep hill that even then was called the Heights and ran northward in a nearly straight line to a beautiful sheltered cove where a clan of Iroquois had created a settlement that thrived on fishing. When the British held sway, the village became a town. The nineteenth century saw it bloom into a small city, while the trail provided a bed for the tracks of a railway and the parallel road named for its geography.

Lined with mercantile establishments, Riverfront Road had once boasted three hotels and shoulder-to-shoulder saloons. But on the evening Peter Sloan turned into it, the hotels were gone, most of the stores had FOR RENT signs in the windows, and the saloons had dwindled to three. Eagle's Nest had been renovated into a sports bar named after the symbol of the Newtown Consolidated Schools athletic teams. Virtually unchanged in a hundred years, the Black Horse proudly claimed to be the workingmen's bar. In Major André's, a man might find companionship with another man that promised a more intimate outcome than a few hours of drinks and idle talk about sports or one's job. And he could do so, as so many of his predecessors throughout most of the bar's history could not have, without fearing a raid by the Newtown Police Department's ever-vigilant and usually brutal vice squad. Now, the only times the police arrived were in response to urgent phone calls from the bartender, reporting a breach of the peace. Or when a detective like himself was working an investigation, which hardly ever had anything to do with the sexual orientation of the bar's patrons, as in the case of the detectives who responded several years earlier to a charge of an armed robbery, alleged to have been perpetrated by Oliver Allen.

With a Newtown PD mug shot of him in the pocket of a blue blazer, Sloan pushed through a windowless wooden door into a long, dim room thickly fogged by cigarette smoke and pungent with the smell of beer. Speaking softly in a baritone range, young men and older ones clustered in pairs and trios along a bar with a picture on the wall behind it of the British spy whose ignominious name had been commandeered. In back of a bewildering display of liquor bottles ran a mirror that created the surreal effect of a slightly clouded mural of men drinking at a bar. A few patrons struck intimate poses at tables for two along the opposite wall and beneath framed black-and-white photos of celebrities who had become elevated to gay iconography. James Dean looked surly with a cigarette dangling from pouty lips and a rumpled and half-open denim shirt exposing a hairless chest. Next to him hung his moody costar in *Rebel Without a Cause,* Sal Mineo, offering come-on eyes of an adult in a pubescent face. Judy Garland wore black leotards and a haunted expression. Others held the chiseled faces and torsos of a latter-day fame and desirability: a shirtless Tom Cruise; a fully clothed but seductively eyed Matthew Broderick; Another Matt, Dillon—the actor, not the town marshal of *Gunsmoke*— with opened shirt and half-shut eyes; and John Travolta in a black cowboy hat, tight shirt, and even tighter blue jeans. On a small rectangular dance floor at the back of the dim room, couples were lighted by the yellow glow from a jukebox blaring rock and roll, surrounded on the wall by pictures of boys in bands. Stepping to the bar, he had a feeling of being looked at and studied by them, the customers, Major André, and the bartender.

Tall, broad-shouldered, and muscular enough to look capable of handling trouble without calling the police, the bartender asked, "Will it be a drink first? Or whatever it is you want to ask me about?"

Sloan leaned a side against the bar and scanned the faces nearest to him. "You do a good middle-of-the-week business."

"People get thirsty on Wednesdays, too."

Facing the bartender, Sloan said, "Who says I have something to ask you?"

"Like everybody in here, I know a cop when I see one."

As the two men nearest him picked up their drinks and moved to a table, Sloan smiled. "What you said is a real coincidence. Somebody told me just a little while ago that there are people who can do that. I'll have a beer first."

"Bottle or tap? Tap is only Budweiser."

"Bud's fine, as long it's not all head."

"I run an honest bar," he said, drawing the beer.

"You're the owner?"

"I didn't say I own. I said I run."

"What's your name?"

"Mr. Bartender."

Served the beer, Sloan laid the photo of Oliver Allen before him. "Do you know him, Mr. Bartender?"

He gave it a glance. "Sure. Really bad picture, though."

"When's the last time you saw him in person?"

"I'm not interested in being a witness, Mr. Policeman. It's not that I don't believe in doing my civic duty. It's just that I ain't got time. And it might be bad for business."

"Why should you be a witness?"

"You're not looking for Ollie to ask him for a dance. But if you'd care to invite me for a whirl, I just might take you up on it. You are kind of cute. For a cop."

The next-nearest drinker snickered. Reflected in the mirror, he was a willowy youth with bleach-streaked brown hair and eyes that met Sloan's in the glass and quickly turned aside.

"So, Mr. Bartender," Sloan said, "are you going to tell me when's the last time Ollie was in? Or are you going to make me go down the bar and all around the tables disturbing your patrons by showing them my badge and asking them when was the last time they saw him?"

"It was maybe a week and a half ago. Midweek."

Sloan took a sip of beer. "Was he around a lot before that?"

"I'd see him two or three nights a week since he got out on parole. He was always in Saturdays. Making himself available. You'd think after time in Attica, he would have lost some of his looks. Hell, he looked better than ever. He was always on the skinny side before he went away. I guess he worked out a lot with weights while he was upstate. He had no trouble making new pals, young and older. Of course, the older ones have money, so Ollie usually glommed onto them."

"Did you notice if he made one new friend in particular?"

"I don't suppose you'd let me in on what this is about?"

"You don't suppose right."

"The reason I asked is that I read in the paper that Ollie's mother was the old lady they found dead up at the lake and that I haven't seen Ollie coming around Riverfront since then. Come to think of it, I ain't seen his new friend, neither."

"Did the new friend have a name?"

"Everybody has a name. Quite a few have lots of names. You don't pay much attention to names when you're behind this bar. The one that I knew Ollie's new friend by was Bobby."

"How about a last name?"

The bartender shrugged.

"Was Bobby what you'd call a regular customer?"

"He breezed in sometime back in June, I think. I guess you could call him a vacation regular. I figured he was a summer camp counselor or a busboy in one of the Catskill hotels."

"Give me a ballpark age. Description."

"Twenty something. Not bad-looking. Medium height, weight. Peroxided short hair. A bit swishy for my taste. He probably has a wardrobe stuffed with neat little cocktail numbers and stunning gowns for Saturday nights. But since we don't serve drag queens in here, I couldn't say for sure."

"Can I count on you doing your civic duty enough so that if I left you my card and Ollie and/or Bobby put in an appearance, I could expect a phone call?"

"If I don't lose the card, why not?"

Sloan produced one. "Office, home, and beeper."

"What? No toll-free eight hundred number?"

Sloan slapped a quarter on the bar. "A token of my confidence in your good citizenship. How much for the beer?"

"Four and a quarter, plus tip. Dance with me once and you can forget both."

A five dollar bill went onto the bar. "Sorry, but regulations say no dancing on duty. Nice talking to you, though."

With a final glance in the mirror as he turned away from the bar, he noticed the bleach-haired youth's eyes dart aside again. Five minutes later, leaning against a parking meter half a block north of the bar, he saw the youth emerge, look his way, hesitate, and then saunter south toward First Street. Stopping near the corner, he turned, looked back, shuffled feet and hands nervously, and ducked into the shadows of a doorway.

Strolling past a defunct shoe store with a FOR SALE sign barely readable through a grafitti-decorated show window, Sloan heard a youthful voice. "Walk up First. I'll catch up."

Pausing, Sloan whispered, "You do know I'm a cop?"

"I'm not trying to pick you up, for crissakes."

Presently, as he fell into step with him, Sloan said, "What have you got for me?"

"Ollie's friend is Bobby Mitchell. That's his real name."

"What's yours?"

"Jimmy will do."

"Okay, Jimmy it is. Do you know where Bobby lives?"

"He used to be with his family up at Stone Light. Then his old man tried to beat him up once too often. Instead, Bobby beat the crap out of him. That's when Bobby came to Newtown and lived with me. Then he met Ollie Allen and moved in with him."

"Were they lovers?"

"Not in the way Bobby and I were. Bobby liked it rough. I guess his old man beat liking getting slapped around into him. That's why Bobby left me. I'm not into sadomasochism. Bobby liked being an *M*. I guess in Ollie, he found the perfect *S.*"

"Do you know where they lived together?"

"At first, it was a rooming house on Old Quarry Road. But a couple of weeks ago, Bobby bragged that he'd moved and was living high on the hog out of town."

"Did he say where?"

"Yes. But I didn't connect it until I heard that the cops finally identified the old lady who was killed up at the lake."

"Do you think Bobby had something to do with it?"

"Look, mister, whoever you are, I don't want you thinking I'm ratting on Bobby because he dumped me. This isn't some game of revenge. I'm only telling you this because maybe it will help Bobby, because I will never believe that Bobby Mitchell had anything to do with killing an old woman."

"Then what's the connection you made, Jimmy?"

"When he told me he was living high on the hog, he said they moved into Ollie's mother's mansion up on Traitor's Lair Road."

"If you think Bobby wasn't involved why talk to me?"

"I don't think he was involved . . . willingly." His voice wavered and light from a streetlamp sparkled in a teardrop trickling down a cheek. He gulped breath. "I think he was in a master-slave thing with Ollie, so if he was involved, Ollie forced him."

"I know this is difficult for you, Jimmy," Sloan said as he gripped the trembling youth's arm. "But I've got lots of things I need to know. Did one of them have a car?"

"Ollie had a . . ." He choked again and wiped away tears. "He had a beat-up old station wagon."

Loosening his hold, Sloan spoke quietly. "When's the last time you saw either of them?"

"Saturday night. They were in André's a couple of minutes."

"The bartender said he hadn't seen them for over a week."

"Saturday nights, André's is real crowded. I guess he didn't notice them. They were there just a few minutes, as I said. They were on their way to New York. Ollie was driving a maroon BMW."

"Jimmy, you've been a big help to me. And maybe to Bobby."

"He's all I'm interested in."

"Jimmy, the best thing you can do if you see Bobby is to get him to turn himself in."

Turning back toward Riverfront Road and breaking into a run, Jimmy sobbed, "I only hope he's still alive."

As the slender, fleeting figure disappeared around the corner and

Sloan continued along First Street toward Holmes Street, the beeper on his belt chirped. Removing it beneath a streetlamp, he read a digital display. Recognizing Flynn's office number, he realized he had disobeyed her order and left his portable cellular telephone in the car.

Seeing a public phone booth two blocks away, he dashed to it and dialed her number. Picked up on the first ring, he identified himself gaspingly and asked, "What's up?"

"You can quit the pub crawl," she answered grimly. "Oliver Allen has been located and positively identified."

With a viselike tightening in his chest, he blurted, "What do you mean *identified?* That sounds like he's dead."

"A homeless woman collecting discarded bottles and cans to turn in for refunds found the maroon BMW in high weeds at the Old Brewery, with him in the driver's seat. It looks like he blew his brains out. Meetcha there."

31

Carnival

PARKED ASKEW, THREE cars belonging to Sheriff Todd Himes and his deputies flung flashing red and yellow lights on a knot of men in uniforms and in streaks across the weathered brown brick facade of the long-abandoned brewery. A mainstay of employment in Newtown for more than a hundred years, it had been closed in the 1980s, its Old Brewery and Hudson's Half Moon brand names and two-hundred jobs absorbed by a Baltimore beer manufacturer whose managers had found a cheaper labor force in the South. Adding to the carnival atmosphere as Sloan parked his car and bounded out, yellow POLICE CRIME SCENE NO NOT ENTER streamers fluttered on a stiff breeze off the river.

In the houndstooth jacket with turned-up collar, Arlene Flynn momentarily diverted her attention from District Attorney Aaron Benson to greet Sloan with a little jerk of her head in the direction of an expanse of weeds and a splash of light. "As soon as Dr. Plodder finishes doing his thing, we can go over and have a glimpse," she said. "Meantime, I was just briefing our leader."

"Why don't you start over, for Pete's sake?" Benson said, blithely oblivious to his unintentional pun.

Flynn swung an arm in an arc between the dark hulk of the old brewery and the glow in the weeds. "The woman who spotted the car is apparently one of several squatters," she said. "They go in and out of the first floor of the brewery through a loading dock around to our left. For some reason, tonight she'd exited on the opposite side and noticed something red in the high weeds off to the side of the access road."

She pointed to a stretch of badly deteriorated blacktop.

"She decided to have herself a look," she continued, "found the car, peeped in the front, and saw a man's body at the steering wheel. She called the sheriff's office and reported having seen a bullet hole in the right temple and a pistol in the hand. Lucky for us, the first of the deputies on the scene had had a couple of run-ins with Oliver Allen and recognized him right away. Then he recalled the alert for the BMW. Sheriff Himes phoned me personally."

"So Oliver has saved us all a lot of work," Benson said with satisfaction. "It's pretty obvious, isn't it, that he found out he could not live with himself after killing his mother? So he drove in here and drilled a hole in his head."

"That's certainly possible, boss," Sloan answered, his eyes again toward the light in the weeds. "But I think someone ought to have a look around for evidence of someone else being with Ollie. We might even find another body."

Flynn and Benson exchanged startled looks.

"Ollie definitely had himself a partner," Sloan continued. "Name of Bobby Mitchell. I've got a confidential informant who says they were shacking up at Matilda's house. The CI told me Ollie and Bobby enjoyed an S-M relationship. So it occurred to me they might have sought the ultimate experience. Since Ollie was the *S* and Bobby was the *M,* I thought Ollie might have plugged Bobby out in the weeds and then turned the gun on himself."

"My God," gasped Benson. "I thought Arlene was the one with the wildly macabre mind."

"Murder and suicide. It's certainly an intriguing theory," Flynn said, tugging her lip.

Sloan sighed and jammed balled hands on hips. "All right. Except for *what?*"

"Except for . . . *why.* A sexual thrill? I find that hard to accept. But I can see Ollie wanting to rid himself of a potential state's witness against him. But why should he shoot himself?"

"Guilty conscience," Benson exclaimed with disgust. "The guy didn't murder just any little old lady. He murdered his mother."

"No need for a jury summation now, boss," Flynn gibed.

"Surely, Arlene, you don't doubt he did? If so, why in hell have we been looking for him? Besides, I believe we can toss the presumption of innocence out the window, given all that you two have turned up. Plus the suspect being dead by his own hand. How much evidence do we need?"

A chubby figure lumbered out of the weeds.

"The single gunshot wound in the right temple appears to be self-inflicted," Zeligman said, breathing heavily and mopping his forehead with a sleeve of his topcoat as he reached them. "There's the requisite scorching around the wound and gunpowder residue. Naturally, I'll need to verify all this at autopsy. He's been there three or four days, maybe more." He stuffed the handkerchief into his breast pocket. "This cool night and I still sweat. Maybe I should retire."

"Come on, Ted," she replied. "A crime scene wouldn't seem at all proper without . . ."

Zeligman's lips formed a Kewpie doll smile. "Without Plodder plodding around? Now you tell me something, my dear Flynn. Why is it all your crime scenes are impossible to get to without ruining my shoes? See for yourself. But watch your step. This veritable mud puddle is riddled with chuckholes. Will my full report in a day or two suffice?"

"I do need to know something right away, Ted."

"Naturally!" He made a courtly bow. "Your wish. My command."

"Fingernail scratches on face, neck, arms."

He thought a moment. "Say! Are you thinking this is the guy who killed the old lady at the lake?"

"I won't know for sure till I hear about scratches."

"Well, at least that's not going to keep me up all night."

"Call me as soon as you know. If I'm not at the office, I'll be at home. Never mind the hour."

As Zeligman plodded away, she signaled to Benson, Sloan, and Sheriff Himes to follow her into the weeds.

Falling into step beside her, Himes loomed more than a foot taller than she and had to adjust his naturally long gait as they proceeded with all the caution Zeligman recommended. Nearing the car, he said, "Shouldn't we all wait till Sam Mason's crime-scene team gets here, Arlene?"

Proceeding ahead, she said, "I'm only going to take a quick peek inside the car. I'll walk in Ted's shoe prints."

Standing half a foot from the left-front window, she found herself

165

looking directly into the face. The head tilted rakishly to the left, slightly backward, eyes open as if surprised, mouth slightly agape, and tongue lolling from its left corner. Because the head was turned, she was able to see a circular spattering of congealed blood at the right temple and the rivulets that had coursed down his cheek and neck, staining the shirt collar. The head had hit the closed window so hard, the glass had cracked. That it had not shattered indicated the bullet had remained in the skull.

Edging closer and slightly to her left, she barley managed to see through the windshield to view the body's slack right arm and what appeared to be a Smith & Wesson .38 snub-nosed revolver in the up-turned and loosely opened hand.

Carefully retracing Zeligman's path, she said, "Gentlemen, when you see for yourself, note the gun's in the right hand."

"Of course it is," Benson said. "Zeligman said he'd blasted himself in the right temple."

"That's very odd," Sloan said.

Benson's expression wrinkled with worry. "I don't follow."

With a slowly upraising left hand, Sloan said, "Ollie was a southpaw."

"No use hanging around here," Flynn declared. "Let's get back to the office, where Peter Sloan will report on his pub-crawling expedition and share with us everything he found out concerning Bobby Mitchell."

Walking to their cars, she found a familiar silent hubbub as the arriving state police CSU methodically unloaded from their van all the paraphernalia of their arts and crafts. Soon, they would be swarming over the car in which a deserving Oliver Allen had met a fate he had inflicted on his undeserving mother. But with this thought came another, drawing her mind for a moment to the murder of a younger woman and positing a tantalizing but unanswerable question. Upon dying, had Oliver Allen's immortal soul floated out of his body to hurtle through the black tunnel and into the blazing light that had welcomed Sebastian Duncan? If he had, might Matilda Allen have been awaiting his arrival?

If she had been, what might she have said to him?

As Benson, Sloan, and she reached her car, a hurried movement beyond the state police van caught her attention.

Chugging toward them on stubby legs and in a white suit that created for him an aura as spectral as Washington Irving's headless horseman, Marty Katz bellowed, "Wait up a minute."

Benson moaned. "Oh hell, not him."

Sweating to a halt, Katz puffed, "Do you have a statement for the *Clarion?*"

Brushing past the newspaperman, Benson replied, "I have nothing tonight, Marty. I'll have something ready in the morning. Come see me at the office."

The red of Katz's face deepened to purple. "Come on! You know the *Clarion* goes to press at midnight."

Benson glanced searchingly at Flynn. "The statement will be available tomorrow?"

She gave a quick nod and stifled her amusement.

"But I need something now," Katz demanded. "Whose body have you got in there?"

Realizing he had missed the point, Benson said, "Ah, you're asking about the body."

"What in hell did you think I was asking?"

With a slight elevation of eyebrows and a tiny embarrassed smile toward Flynn, who smiled back knowingly, he said, "The body is that of Oliver Allen. He appears to have shot himself in the head. Despondent over the loss of his mother, probably."

With Flynn nodding approvingly, they proceeded to their cars. Forming a small parade, they rolled through abandoned downtown streets to an empty parking lot behind the darkened courthouse. Admitting them through a side entrance, an elderly watchman said, "Good even', folks, workin' awfully late tonight," and offered a salute.

"Well, I almost put a foot in my mouth out there, didn't I?" Benson chuckled as he settled behind his desk. "When Marty Katz asked about getting a statement, the only one I could think of was the release we're planning on the Duncan matter. Arlene, I hope I didn't lie when I told him we'd have it in the morning."

"I was dotting *i*'s and crossing *t*'s when Himes called."

"Good. I'll go over your draft first thing and have Connie put it in the computer and have it ready for Katz and anyone else in the press who's interested."

"Oh, they'll all be interested," Flynn said. "What interests me is the reaction its release might provoke from James Duncan. He'll probably

167

come thundering down from Traitor's Lair Road in feathers and war paint."

"Don't forget Elizabeth Hollander," Benson said, feigning a shudder. "Once this hits the paper, Sebastian is bound to know. Then I suppose I can cross Elizabeth off my contributors list."

"If it wasn't against the law," Sloan replied, "Arlene and I would chip in."

"The more intriguing result to contemplate in announcing an investigation into Jennifer's death is the effect, if any, it has on the people on our short list of suspects," Flynn said. "In any event, we'll soon find out the truth of the maxim that the press has its uses if you know how to go about it."

"Is that another precept of Flynn's Law?" Sloan asked, yawning.

"Sherlock Holmes. Don't you remember 'The Adventure of the Six Napoleons?' "

"I never read any Sherlock Holmes. But I did see a few of the old movies and most of the television series. Who was better in your opinion? Basil Rathbone or . . . whatever this new guy's name is?"

"Jeremy Brett. Apples and oranges, Sloan. That's like comparing radio and television. Or, much more relevant to your experience, my typewriter with your computer. Should you decide to correct the gap in your literary education, I'll pick you up a copy of the complete Holmes the next time I pay a call at the It's a Crime bookstore."

"Better yet, you could ask the people at Computer Center at the mall if Holmes is available on CD-ROM."

Benson drummed fingertips on the desk. "Can we get back to business? We were talking about the statement."

"Putting out releases like this would be easier all around," Sloan interjected, "if they were word-processed in the drafting stage. Connie would get a diskette and wouldn't have to rekey."

"It's a very short statement," Flynn retorted. "Shall I get it and read it to you, boss?"

"Leave it on my desk on your way home." He glanced at his wristwatch. "Look at the hour! You and Peter have had a very long day. If you want to sleep late, be my guest. In fact, I insist on it. As for me, that damned Davis jury still hasn't reached a verdict, so I'll have to be in when court convenes at nine. However, I don't see anything on your agenda that can't wait a couple of hours. Do you? What's the next step in the Duncan case, Arlene?"

"I think I should talk to the woman who was butler, maid, and cook that weekend. Cornelia Stewart. I'll do that first thing."

"I presume tonight's event out at the Old Brewery takes the urgency out of the Matilda Allen case," Benson said, turning to Sloan.

"Except for Bobby Mitchell. We don't know what role he had in the murder. His last known address prior to hooking up with Ollie was his parents' home up in Stone Light, I figured I'd go up there bright and early."

Flynn nodded assent. "Take Richards along as backup."

"I thought he was to go to the museum about the jewelry."

"With Ollie dead, the gems are probably a moot point."

"Okay. The team of Sloan and Richards will be checking out Mitchell," Benson said. "What if he's at home? Do we bring him in or what? Is there any evidence putting him in Matilda's house?"

"We're going to need a set of his fingerprints to send to the feds for comparison to the unidentified set lifted from the bureau drawer in Matilda's bedroom," Sloan said.

"If he's at home, arrest him. If the prints clear him, I'll apologize to him in the middle of the town square. Does that wrap up this meeting?"

"I'm serious about you taking Eddie Richards along to Stone Light, Sloan. I don't want you tackling Mitchell without backup," Flynn said as she rose from her chair and shouldered her bag.

"Scout's honor," he said, holding up three fingers. "Your order will be carried out to . . . the . . . letter."

"Like you carried out my order to put a cell phone in your pocket when you went over to Riverfront Road?"

As Sloan opened his mouth to respond, the last in a line of lights on Benson's telephone winked and another phone could be heard ringing in the distance. "Your line, Arlene," Benson said. Picking up the receiver and punching the blinking button, he held it out to her.

She answered, "DA squad. Investigator Flynn."

"Good, you're there," boomed Dr. Theodore Zeligman's gruff voice, loud enough to be heard by the two men. "Now, about those scratches on the body in the car. There were none."

Part Six

Flynn's Law

"With me it's more than a feeling, it's a law."

—Stephen Greenleaf, *Death Bed*

32

The Press Passer

I 'M HERE TO pick up a statement," growled Martin Katz.
For the benefit of a startled young man seated behind the reception
desk, he waved a robin's egg blue plastic-laminated Stone County
Court press credential bearing his photograph with a bulldog expression he purposely affected for ID pictures.

The lilting voice of Constance Hardwick wafted from her office.
"I've got it for you in here, Marty."

Filling her doorway, he cast a glance into Benson's office and found
an unoccupied desk. "He's not in yet?"

Hardwick's thumb pointed downward. "Court. The jury in the
Davis case asked for a read-back of testimony."

"The Davis jury? I figured them for a verdict last night, or this
morning at the latest."

"So did the district attorney," Hardwick replied, handing Katz a single sheet of paper. "I believe this is what you want."

Taking it, he read:

OFFICE OF STONE COUNTY DISTRICT ATTORNEY AARON BENSON
1 Hempstead Road, Newtown, New York
STATEMENT FOR THE PRESS   *For Immediate Release*
Stone County District Attorney Aaron Benson
announced today that as a result of a routine review of office
files, an investigation is to be conducted into the circumstances
surrounding the death last year of Jennifer Hollander Duncan.

Katz blurted, "Hole-lee cow-a-bunga," and read on:

Benson said, "I am persuaded by this review that it will be in the best interest of the people of Stone County that a further probe is warranted into Duncan's death, which had been attributed to an accidental overdose of a powerful sedative. This in no way criticizes the findings at that time of Stone County's medical examiner, Dr. Theodore Zeligman, or the New York State Police and Stone County Sheriff's Department investigators, who had not had access to the information that my staff's routine review of files produced."

Asserting that there are no plans at the moment to present the case to a grand jury, Benson indicated that the inquiry will be conducted informally under his direction by Special Investigator Arlene Flynn.

Shifting his eyes from the release to Hardwick, Katz demanded, "Is she in her office, Connie?"

Without looking away from a computer screen, Hardwick asked, "Is who in her office?"

"Don't be cute, Con. How many women work here?"

Flashing eyes shifted from the screen to him. "There are four. And we all work very hard, for your information."

"You know whom I mean. Flynn."

"She's not expected in before noon."

"Is she at home?"

"I don't believe so."

"Well, do you know where she is?"

"No, I do not."

He angrily stuffed the statement into a side pocket of his white coat. "Would you tell me if you did?"

"If I had authorization to do so, I'd be delighted to tell you," she said, returning to her work. "But I don't."

"Can I take that to mean you do know where she is?"

"Take the meaning anyway you like. You usually do."

"What about Detective Sloan? Is Pete on the premises?"

"Any questions you have about the statement should be directed to Mr. Benson himself."

"Forget the statement. Now I'm following up on the body that was found at the Old Brewery last night. It was Oliver Allen's body, in case nobody told you. I know Sloan was out there because I saw him. So is he in or not?"

She picked up a phone. "A moment and I'll find out." Unanswered, she put the phone down. "Apparently not."

"If you happen to see him, or Flynn, or Benson, or anyone else who even remotely qualifies to answer the questions I have to ask on behalf of the readers of my newspaper about either the Duncan or the Allen case, tell 'em they won't be able to duck the press and the public by hiding behind your skirt forever."

Her nimble fingering of the keyboard stopped and her eyes drilled into him. "I find that remark deeply offensive, Marty. Nobody's ducking you. They're busy people who were up half the night carrying out their duties, not only for the benefit of your readers but on behalf of *all* the people of Stone County. Now, if I may, I also have the public's work to do. Have a good day."

Shaking his head and chuckling as he passed the receptionist, he said to the wide-eyed young man, "When it comes down to telling someone off, kid, Connie Hardwick is the cream of the crop. And I should know, pal. I've been told off by the best."

Except for three years in the uniform of his country, he had carried a press pass for three and a half decades. In seeking to describe the who, what, where, when, why, and hows of human folly, he had been pushed around, threatened, glad-handed, backslapped, conned, cajoled, flattered, insulted, and often scared to death. A variety of credentials had admitted him to corridors of power of government and smoke-filled rooms of party politics, into lavish festivities in hotel ballrooms, to city tenements where murders had been committed, and to a muddy, weed-filled lot at an old brewery, all in the name of the public's right to know.

In that cause, he took the stairs down to the second floor of the Stone County Courthouse. Pausing at the double doors of one of the chambers, he peeked through a small square window and saw Benson seated at the prosecution table, listening intently as a clerk droned through a transcript of the Davis case testimony. Stepping into the room, he approached a uniformed court officer and whispered, "How long is this going to take, Tommy?"

A familiar burly court presence for as long as Katz had been cov-

175

ering county trials, he whispered back, "Till the lunch recess at least, Marty."

At a lobby pay phone, he fished a thick black notebook from the pocket containing the Duncan statement and flipped through its dog-eared alphabetical pages to *F.* The third ring of Flynn's phone triggered her answering machine. Hanging up, he muttered, "Oh where or where can you be, my little colleen?"

Leafing forward to *Z,* he found a single entry and dialed the number for the office of the medical examiner.

An unmistakable voice answered, "Coroner."

"It's Katz at the *Clarion,* Ted."

"If this concerns my report," Zeligman said, sounding harassed, "the autopsy on Oliver Allen's not even started yet."

"Is there any doubt he was killed by a bullet to his head?"

"I once autopsied a body with two bullets in the head, but it was a coronary that was the cause of death. The guy was literally frightened to death by a gun at his head. So don't go jumping to conclusions, Katz. If you want the Allen report, call tomorrow."

"I'll do that, Ted. But for now, I'm wondering if you have a comment in reaction to DA Benson's statement?"

A moment passed before Zeligman replied, "What statement?"

"On his investigation of the death of Jennifer Duncan."

"Oh, that. Other than standing by my report in that case, I'll have no comment."

"As I recall, your report concluded that—"

"She died of a massive overdose of a prescription sedative."

"Am I correct in remembering that you'd found the overdose had been accidental?"

"What other reasonable conclusion could I have drawn?"

"I can think of two. Suicide. Homicide."

"I said *reasonable* conclusion."

"Apparently, Benson differs with you."

"Did he say that?"

"Not exactly. He's just issued a press release saying . . ." He pulled the crumpled statement from the pocket. "It states, and I quote exactly, 'I am persuaded by this review that it will be in the best interest of the people of Stone County that a further probe is warranted into Duncan's death, which had been attributed to an accidental overdose of a powerful sedative.' "

"That is accurate."

"Benson goes on, 'This in no way criticizes the findings at that time of Stone County's medical examiner, Dr. Theodore Zeligman, or the New York State Police and Stone County Sheriff's Department investigators, who had not had access to the information that my staff's routine review of files produced.' End quote. Do you have any comment on that?"

"I'm grateful he's not criticizing me."

"Care to speculate on what his *information* might be?"

"Nope."

"Or what the source could be?"

"Well, that's probably . . ."

Katz felt a tightening in his chest. "That's probably who?"

"It's not my place to speculate. That's your job, Marty. You know as much as I do about that case. Hell, you probably know a lot more. All I did was the autopsy. The only person speaking to me was Jennifer Duncan, through her remains. From what I remember of your newspaper's coverage of that tragedy, you must have talked to everyone who was at her house that weekend. And a bunch more who were not there, I believe. Including Jennifer Duncan's mother, who was all the way up in Rochester that night. If Elizabeth Hollander knew nothing then, what could she possibly know now? If you need comments about Benson's statement, I suggest you talk to people who were actually there."

"Thanks, Ted. I will be getting back to you about the Oliver Allen autopsy results tomorrow."

As he hung up the phone, Zeligman's provocative question was burned into his mind: "If Elizabeth Hollander knew nothing then, what could she possibly know now?"

Dearest Dr. Plodder, you darling old gentleman, he asked himself as he thumbed rapidly through his notebook to entries at the *H,* whatever did you mean by that? Did you misspeak? Or did you inadvertently reveal that you have an idea as to the source of Benson's information?

Finding Hollander listed at a Rochester number and himself out of quarters, he slipped the book into his pocket and hurried out the Jail Street door of the courthouse and raced as well as his legs permitted, passing the Scales of Justice and turning right on Fourth Street for another block to the corner of Main and its dominant landmark, the century-old redbrick Clarion Building.

Occupying the entire second floor, the city room bristled with computer stations that had relegated the clatter of press association wires and the rat-a-tat-tat of typewriter keys and end-of-a-line bells to history. Crossing the cavernous heart of the newspaper to his office overlooking Main and Fourth, he heard a quiet as daunting as that of the library that Andrew Carnegie's largesse had provided a full two decades after the first *Clarion* had rolled off noisy basement presses, long since replaced by the irresistible march of a technology speaking in whispers.

A Touch-Tone telephone that felt as weightless as a feather put him through to Rochester without the intervention of a long-distance operator. To his surprise a live human male answered by saying, "Hollander residence."

He pictured a butler in cutaway coat and white gloves. "May I speak with Mrs. Hollander, please?"

"I'm sorry, sir, Mrs. Hollander is away at the moment."

"When do you expect her back?"

"I can't say, sir. She's out of town."

"This is Martin Katz of the Stone County *Clarion* in Newtown. Can you tell me where she might be reached?"

"Why, she's down there, sir, staying at the George Washington Inn."

33

Getting to the Light

FINDING ROOM FOR legs and feet under a dashboard crowded with radios set to frequencies of the state police, sheriff, and various Stone County town and village police and emergency units, Investigator Edward Richards had settled his bulky frame into the passenger seat of Sloan's plain olive green county-owned car at eight o'clock, extended a seat belt to its full length, snapped it closed, and asked, "How come you're driving this wreck?"

"Because mine was practically totaled over the weekend by an anonymous kamikaze in the lot at the mall," Sloan said bitterly as he pulled away from Richards's Stanley Street boardinghouse. "And now what's left is being held hostage by my insurance company. It claims my policy covers only eighty percent of the repair job. If I had all I've laid out in premiums all this time, I could junk the wreck and buy a brand-new car. Where's the justice for the honest, hardworking people like you and me, Eddie?"

"There are two lessons to be learned from this sad experience, partner. Don't own. Lease. Don't go to malls. Do all your shopping from catalogs."

"Easy for you to preach. You're not married."

Where Stanley ended in an intersection with Town Line Road, they looked ahead to the charred skeleton of a two-family house that had been destroyed by a fire, for which a case of arson had been brought by District Attorney Benson. It had been proven, in Richards's opinion. Yet, mystifyingly, a jury still had not come in with a finding of Harlan Davis's guilt. But on an unseasonably cool August morning, he had a new case, involving one Bobby Mitchell, who might or might not be found at their destination.

Some twelve miles due north of Newtown, the village of Stone Light had sprung into existence on a rocky finger poking into the Hudson from the west bank and providing an ideal location for a wooden tower with a bonfire on the top to advise navigators in the nineteenth century of the proximity of their boats to the hazardous shoreline. Rebuilt of steel and given an electric lamp at the turn of the new century, the beacon identified on charts as Stone Light had been rendered obsolete by radar during World War II. Yet, as Sloan and Richards neared the village from the west via a two-lane blacktop road, the tower remained, a quaint anachronism but a sure guide to a hamlet that technology and transportation systems had bypassed.

History had also reduced Stone Light's police department to a front-room office in the home of its only officer. Greeting his unexpected visitors at the door, the village constable, George Athens, was a deeply tanned middle-aged beanpole of a man. He wore the the symbol of his authority in the form of a six-pointed brass star on a red-and-blue plaid shirt. Standing in the open doorway with police radios chattering in the room behind him, he studied the identity cards presented to him by the pair of plainclothes detectives. "The DA squad," he gasped in astonishment. "What brings you around?"

"We're hoping you can give us the address of a family named Mitchell," Sloan answered.

Athens shook his head. "What's Bobby done now?"

Sloan smiled. "I figured he wouldn't be unknown to you."

"That kid's been a one-man crime wave. The last I heard, he took off a couple of weeks ago after a big dustup with his old man. I didn't know he was back in town."

"He may not be. We're here to find out."

"Who did he kill?"

"Why did you think he killed someone?"

"I've been expecting it. He's just like his old man. Both have a violent streak a mile wide. If they're not beating up on other people, they're clobbering each other. I figured it would be just a matter of time till one of them grabbed one of their guns and went the whole nine yards."

"Tell us about the guns."

"Their house is an arsenal of rifles, shotguns, and pistols. But there's nothing I can do about them. The long guns are all legal for hunting. And the pistols all have licenses. Don't ask me how or why they got them. They just did."

"May we have directions to the Mitchell house?"

"I could show you the way."

"Thanks, Constable, but we'd rather check out the place on our own."

"So as not to attract attention," Richards explained, "which your showing up in the vicinity might do."

Shrugging broad, bony shoulders, Athens looked crestfallen. "Far be it from me to tell the DA's men how to do their job. The Mitchell house is the gray clapboard at the corner of Light and Riverside, two blocks in the direction your car is parked and three more to the left. There's a Mobil station on the opposite corner. You can't miss it."

"Who lives in the house, besides Bobby and his father?"

"That's it. The mother skipped out years ago."

"Is Mr. Mitchell likely to be at home?"

"He works as a janitor at one of the big stores at the mall and leaves about six-thirty every morning."

"What kind of car does he have?" asked Richards.

"He's got a Ford pickup truck."

"Does Bobby have a car?"

"The kid has a Harley. He's a motorcycle freak who gets a kick out of tooling around town and riling up everyone with the noise. Or gunning it past the state police barracks to make them take off after him. By the time they catch up with him, he's well within the speed limit. A real jerk, you know? But vicious. So be careful if you do find him at home. Which is why I think I ought to go over there with you to back you up."

"If we find we need a backup, Constable," Sloan said, "you can count on hearing us call for it on the countywide emergency frequency."

Returning to their car, Richards said, "How would you like to be a one-man band, Pete?"

Sloan started the car. "It's probably got rewards. I imagine big-city cops wonder why anyone would want to do the kind of policing you and I do. Yet Flynn gave up the big town downriver in favor of Stone County."

"But only after a lot of years in the NYPD. Have you ever asked her why she did it?"

The car turned into Light Street. "None of my business."

"I think it was a woman thing."

Sloan shot him a sidelong look of amazement. "A *what?*"

"My guess is, she found out there was only so far a woman could go in that cop shop. Up here, she runs the show."

"And very well, too," Sloan snapped.

"Hey, who's saying she doesn't?"

The car slowed at an intersection.

"Light and Riverside. And there's the house," Richards said, nodding at a small gray structure that had seen better days. "No pickup truck that I can see. No Harley, either. Shades are down in the windows, up and down. It looks to me as if nobody's home. We could stake it out. But we'll stick out like a sore thumb."

"We'll go ahead and see if we can get a look into the side yard, then around the block to have a look at the back," Sloan said. Easing through the intersection, he proceeded slowly to the far corner of the house. Looking right, his eyes went wide.

"Eddie, my pal, you're the expert," he said exultantly, "Is that thing parked in the yard what I think it is?"

Richards tapped Sloan's shoulder with a fist. "You can take the word of one who used to own one. That baby is what is known in the biking fraternity as a Harley hog."

34

Detour

FLYNN'S SLEEP HAD been hard to come by. When it did, but in a halfhearted way, at the crack of dawn, she'd dreamed a phantasm of right-handed guns and left-handed men. Of no scratched faces when there ought to have been. Of old women who had died quite differently on the same Sunday. And of sons, one forever beyond the pale and another who traveled back from the other side. The click of the timer in her bedside clock radio had awakened her a second before the start of the six o'clock news.

The news began with a story about a body found in an automobile on the grounds of the Old Brewery. The man had a gunshot wound in the right temple.

"Stone County Sheriff Todd Himes identified him as Oliver Allen, a thirty-nine-year-old parolee," the newsman said. "Himes noted Allen had been released from Attica prison in January after serving three years for armed robbery. He was the son of murder victim Matilda Allen, whose nude body was found in a wooded area on the shore of Ichabod Crane Lake several days ago. She had been strangled with her stockings. The sheriff declined to say if her son had been considered a suspect in her death."

"Hooray for small favors," Flynn said aloud as she rolled out of bed.

"But," the newscaster continued, stopping her in the middle of putting on slippers, "crime reporter Martin Katz writes in today's edition of the *Clarion* that the car in which Allen's body was discovered may be Mrs. Allen's BMW. It had been reported by state police headquarters as missing from her home on Traitor's Lair Road."

"You have a good memory, Marty," she said, moving toward the bathroom.

"However," the news story went on, stopping her again, "the *Clarion's* account interpreted the presence last night at the Old Brewery of District Attorney Aaron Benson and his chief criminal investigator, Arlene Flynn, as an indication that Allen may have been sought for questioning in his mother's death."

Switching on the lights of the bathroom mirror, she mumbled, "Good guesswork, Marty," and faced her daily confrontation with mortality. Studying her face, she wondered why, if Matilda Allen had struggled and clawed her attacker's flesh while fighting for life, Zeligman had found no scratches on Ollie's face, neck, and arms.

From the bedroom, the newscaster said, "In the trial of Harlan Davis on arson charges, the jury is to resume deliberations at nine o'-clock this morning with a read-back of testimony. Court observers had expected that District Attorney Benson's summation yesterday would result in a quick guilty verdict."

"Nothing's easy," she said, splashing cold water into her face. "Flynn's Law."

"Now the weather outlook," the radio continued. "The forecast is for temperatures to rebound after their sudden dip last night. They will rise to near ninety today and continue in that range the rest of the week."

"Swell," she said, switching off the radio.

Breakfast had been Beethoven and Schumann on FM, a toasted bagel, orange juice, black coffee, and questions about the iced coffee Jennifer Duncan had been drinking on the final night of her life. Had it been black? With cream and sugar? Or cream only? Did she use sugar? Or had she preferred an artificial sweetner? Who had made the coffee? Iced it? Put in the other ingredients, if any? Did she do all that herself? Or had someone served it to her? Had iced coffee been part of Cornelia Stewart's duties that fateful night?

With breakfast done and the kitchen cleaned up, she stepped out into a morning that exhibited every intention of turning into the sweltering day promised by the radio. Starting her car, she heard the awakening squeal of the police and emergency services radio beneath the dashboard. As it came on, a red light flashed and danced, restlessly scanning all the frequencies. Were one to transmit, the light stopped, signifying by its position which of the services was on the air. Next, she felt the rush of warm, then cool, and finally cold from the air conditioner. The hands on a clock on the control panel, which Peter Sloan constantly derided as incredibly old-fashioned, registered seventeen before eight. On Sloan's preferred digital clock it would have read 7:43 A.M. Punching the play button on a built-in tape machine, she could not remember what she had left in it and was pleased to hear that she would be enjoying the companionship of Wolfgang Amadeus Mozart in the form of Symphony No. 29 during the drive up Traitor's Lair Road to the home of Cornelia Stewart.

The direct route to the southwest side of Crane Lake would have been Old West Point Road. But she had decided to have one more look at the crime scenes that marked the beginning and the apparent ending of the Allen case by visiting them in reverse order: the Old Brewery first, then Matilda's house.

The route through town took her east on Fourth Street, past Marty Katz's newspaper, behind the courthouse, and in front of the building with Tim Flynn's law office. Turning north, she followed Heights Boulevard, passed the Depot restaurant, and crossed Cove Road and the dividing line between the town and the former industrial section that had been superceded by Mountain View Industrial Park, where Jennifer Duncan had envisioned her daring new venture.

On her right she came to the Old Brewery, its haunting quiet restored with the retreat of the previous night's swarming police presence. Stopping at the roadside and remaining in the car, she saw that the tall weeds in which the maroon BMW had been parked had been flattened in the process of removing and towing it to the storage compound at the state police headquarters at Stone Light for further investigation by criminalists. Had a homeless woman not been so inquisitive, the car might not have been found for months, perhaps years. And the murder of Matilda Allen might have slipped into a bourn that was more tantalizing for cops than that which William Shakespeare's Danish prince had pondered. Hamlet had contemplated a question for which he would inevitably have to discover the answer: What followed life? But a homicide cop with an open case might die without being able to respond to the age-old query of real life and detective fiction.

"Who done it?" she asked of the flattened clump of weeds. "Was it you, Ollie?"

And having done it, did you, as Aaron Benson surmised, feel the sting of a sin so unfathomable that your only penance was to take your own life?

If so, why do it with the gun in your right hand?

"To tease me, Ollie?" she asked. "Was that why you shunned your left hand for the right?"

A revenge against those who had been his life's nemesis, the police? By shooting himself with a pistol in his right hand did he hope to have the last laugh on the cops?

Driving on, she came to the ruin of a cookie bakery that had burned down one night in her youth, casting over the whole town a peanut butter–colored cloud that scented that wintry night with the tantalizing aromas of her mother's kitchen in the week before Christmas. Baking had been her favorite Christian observance until an old priest at Sacred Heart had mounted the pulpit at a Christmas Eve Mass when she was a girl to declare, "You must never forget while you gaze with joy upon the Christ Child that the manger of Bethlehem was the start of a journey which led him inevitably to the Cross of Calvary and the even greater promise of Easter Sunday. For God loved you so much that he sent his son to die for *your* sins so that *you* might have eternal life."

Until then, she had not considered herself a sinner.

As she followed the winding path of Traitor's Lair Road and wondered what sermon the new young priest at Sacred Heart would deliver on next Christmas Eve, a crisp, urgent voice beneath the dashboard rudely interrupted Mozart.

"Clear all frequencies. Clear all frequencies."

Another male voice came on. "Ten-thirteen. Ten-thirteen."

She gasped. "Oh my God, that's Eddie Richards."

"Officer in need of assistance. Officer down. This is DA Four. Officer down. Ten-thirteen. Officer is down. Location, Stone Light. Corner of Riverside and Light. Officer under fire."

She heard it in the background.

Pop-pop-pop-pop.

Pop. Pop.

Pop-pop-pop-pop-pop.

Automatic-rifle fire answered by a pistol.

Pop-pop-pop-pop-pop-pop-pop-pop-pop.

Pop. Pop.

"DA Four requests assistance all units," Richards said. "Request ambulance immediately."

"Oh God, it's Sloan who's down," she moaned.

The first voice returned to the air. "All units vicinity Stone Light. All units respond. Officer down. Officer under fire. All units respond corner Light and Riverside, Stone Light."

Silence.

Looking down, she saw the red radio light scanning.

"Trooper Six responding. Two miles south."

"Trooper Four. Responding from Indian Creek Road."

Central asked, "Estimated time arrival, Trooper Four?"

"ETA, five minutes."

"Constable Athens, Stone Light, ETA, one minute."

Central said, "All sheriff units respond."

"Sheriffs Three and Five on route from Newtown Mall."

Looking left as she crossed Valley Road, she saw the lights of the two white cars darting from the mall parking lot. As they turned in her direction, she heard the scream of their sirens. A moment later, they swerved past her.

Flooring the accelerator pedal, she reached under the dashboard, groped for and found a red globe light, slapped it onto the dashboard, flipped its switch, and raced after them, wishing her Plymouth had a siren, as well.

"Athens on scene."

Pop-pop-pop-pop-pop-pop-pop.

"Good for you, Athens," she exclaimed.

"Trooper Six. ETA, one minute."

"Go, go, go, Six."

"Stone County Medical Paramedic One. ETA, fifteen."

"To officer requesting assistance. Units on route. Ambulance on route," advised Central's voice.

No response.

"Officer requesting assistance? DA Four? Officer requesting assistance? Come in, DA Four," Central begged.

She pounded the steering wheel. "He's busy, for crissakes."

"Trooper Six out."

Pop-pop-pop-pop-pop-pop.

"Go around the side," Richards blared.

"Thank God." She sighed.

Ahead at the crossroads of Traitor's Lair and Indian Creek, she saw flashing lights swing left and then heard a voice say, "Trooper Four. My ETA Stone Light, three minutes. Request directions to scene."

Someone answered, "Straight six blocks, hang left two."

"Roger."

"Trooper Six at scene and out."

"Good, good, good," she shouted as the leading sheriff's cars darted across a small bridge over Indian Creek.

"Sheriffs Three and Five, eight minutes away."

"DA Four. This is DA Four."

"Eddie! Great," she cried.

"DA Four. Perp in custody."

"DA Four, repeat."

"DA Four. Man in custody. Where the hell's the ambulance?"

"Paramedics on route."

"DA Four. I'm bringing him myself. Request escorts."

"This is Paramedic One. We'll meet you."

"Paramedic One, stand by. DA Four? Medic One will rendezvous with you."

"DA Four. Roger rendezvous. Tell those guys to floor it."

"Sheriffs Three and Five?"

"Sheriffs Three and Five."

"Sheriffs Three and Five, roadblock Traitor's Lair and Indian Creek."

"Sheriff's Three, Five. Roadblocking Traitor's and Indian."

"DA Four and Paramedic One, you read?"

"DA Four, Central. Read you."

"Paramedics read you, Central."

Just past Indian Creek Road, the sheriff's cars executed U-turns as she pulled to the shoulder and waited anxiously.

35

Touch and Go

WEARING A GREEN skullcap, baggy green pants, and a white short-sleeved shirt that revealed almost hairless muscular arms as he stepped out of the emergency room on the ground floor of Stone County Medical Center, the doctor appeared to Flynn to be even younger than Father Brennan. "Mr. Sloan is in a coma," he said. "He has a serious head wound. Fortunately, the bullet that struck him had ricocheted. A good deal of its force had spent. It also was tumbling. The result was that it did not penetrate the skull. But it caused a fracture, and that has resulted in swelling of the brain. It's going to be touch and go. Should the swelling worsen, we'll have to go in to relieve it. He also got a wound in the upper-left chest. It passed cleanly through and exited via the armpit. Which hand does he use?"

"He's right-handed. Why?" Flynn said, dreading the answer.

"Had he been a lefty, he wouldn't be tossing around a football for a while. Why wasn't he wearing a bulletproof vest?"

"I pray I'll be able to ask him," Flynn said. "And then chew him out royally about it."

The doctor pressed a fingertip to his left cheek. "There was also a grazing wound here."

"Will it leave a scar?"

"Plastic surgery should take care of it nicely."

"If I know Pete Sloan," she said with an affectionate laugh, "he'll probably think it makes him interesting and keep it."

"It will be awhile before we know about the swelling. Meanwhile,

189

there is no sense in you two waiting around here. Should the situation change, we'll notify you immediately."

"Thanks, Doctor," Benson said. "If you do have to reach me, I'll be at the Sloan residence for the next hour or so, then in my office."

"I was told that when Mrs. Sloan was informed of what had happened, she collapsed," the doctor said. "Is she okay?"

"She's been sedated and is being attended to by the family physician," Flynn said. "Pete's kids don't know anything about this yet."

"Pray that when they do, the crisis is past," said Benson.

"That must have been one hell of a shoot-out he was in. What happened to the bad guy?"

"Not a mark on him," Flynn said bitterly. "So far."

Benson forced a little laugh. "She's joking, Doctor. We did away with rubber hoses a long time ago. We've got him locked up safely in the county jail."

"In case you need to contact me, Doctor," Flynn said. "I'll be over at the jail questioning the murderous son of a bitch."

Arriving on the third floor of 100 Jail Street, she was met outside a small interrogation room by the man whose voice she had heard on the radio in a dramatically different tone from the one with which he greeted her now. Then, he had been urgent yet controlled. Now, he was hushed and gentle, more priest than policeman. "How's Pete?"

She tugged her lower lip. "The doctor says it's touch and go, Eddie."

A shrug lifted his large arms, revealing a shoulder holster that jail security regulations required be emptied of its weapon. "Hell, it's just a head wound," he said bravely. "You know just as well as I do, Arlene, that Pete Sloan's head happens to be his least vulnerable spot."

She tilted her head toward the windowless door of the interrogation room. "Has he been read his Miranda rights?"

"He has indeed. I read them myself."

"On tape?"

"Video and audio."

"Has he asked for a lawyer?"

"He hasn't uttered a peep since he yelled, 'I give up. I'm coming out,' up at the house."

"Who's in there keeping an eye on him?"

"Two of the guards. Tinney and Raphael. He's still cuffed."

"Has an assistant DA been called?"

"Jean Detwiler. She was held up in court while the jury in the Davis case was reporting its verdict. She's on her way over here now."

"Good. Now, Eddie, while we're waiting, tell me, please, what the hell happened up at Stone Light?"

"An ambush, pure and simple. Pete and I knocked on the door of the house, completely by the rule book, and Mitchell opened it as sweet as pie. We ascertained his identity and asked to talk to him. He invited us in. In a split second, he had a pistol in hand and was blasting away. Pete got hit and fell back right onto me and we both tumbled out the door. I dragged him off to the side and took cover and radioed for assistance. By then, the kid was peppering the door with shots from the pistol. There was a second or two of quiet that let me get Pete off the porch and into some bushes, and then all hell broke loose from a semiautomatic rifle from a window off to my left."

As he finished, Assistant District Attorney Detwiler came off the elevator. Short and trim, she had on what she called her court duds—a white blouse with a lank black bow tie, gray double-breasted jacket, matching mid-thigh skirt, and low-heeled black pumps. "Davis was found guilty on all counts, in case you were wondering," she said. "Now, what about Bobby Mitchell? Has he been Mirandized?"

"He has," Richards said.

"Did he ask for an attorney?"

"Nope."

"Who's going in with me?"

"I am," Flynn said.

"What's the charge going to be?"

"He's under arrest for assault with a deadly weapon, assault on a police officer, and attempted murder," Richards replied.

"However, I intend to start with his possible role in the death of Matilda Allen," Flynn said. "We have reason to believe he was an accomplice before, during, and after her murder. That's why Eddie and Pete wanted to talk to him."

"Okay," Detwiler said, opening the door to the interrogation room. "Let's get on with it."

36

Precept Thirteen

H E SLOUCHED IN a white T-shirt and blue jeans at a table at the
far end of a long room brightly illuminated to accommodate
a small television camera situated to record him from the front and
show a calendar with the day's date in large black numerals and a clock
on the wall behind him. Handcuffs linked his right wrist to the arm of
a metal chair.

"I am an assistant district attorney," Detwiler said as she and Flynn
entered the room. "I believe you have been advised of your constitu-
tional rights. Is that true, Mr. Mitchell?"

As he answered with a nod, Flynn studied his expressionless face
and noted scabby scratches forming a little ski trail down his right
cheek.

Detwiler continued. "Do you wish to speak to an attorney at this
time, Mr. Mitchell?"

"What for? There must a been a hunert cops to say I shot at them,
so no lawyer's gonna get me out of this, is he?"

"You are still entitled to legal counsel."

"Forget about it."

"If you should change your mind, all you have to do is tell us and
this interview will cease immediately."

"Let's get it over with. These cuffs hurt."

Detwiler turned to Tinney and Raphael. "I'm sure it will be fine
if you remove them, gentlemen."

"If we do," said Tinney with a frown, "one of us has to stay in here
with you."

"Well, at least loosen them," Flynn said impatiently. "Then you both can leave."

With the guards gone, Detwiler said, "Concerning your right to an attorney, Mr. Mitchell, I must advise you that the events of today will not be the only matter you'll be questioned about. You will also be asked about your relationship with one Oliver Allen and the circumstances of the death of his mother, Matilda Allen. Do you still wish to proceed without an attorney?"

His face remained a blank. "I don't see that it makes much of a difference."

"For the record, then, are you waiving at this moment your right to consult with a lawyer?"

He nodded slowly.

"This is being recorded and will be transcribed in written form, which you will have to sign. Please answer yes or no."

He sighed. "Yes."

"You will be interviewed by Special Investigator Flynn of the Stone County district attorney's office. Again, should you change your mind about a lawyer—"

"Yeah, yeah," he grunted. "I got it, lady."

Flynn sat opposite him, her hands linked at a right angle and flattened on the green felt table pad. "For the record, you are Robert William Mitchell of Stone Light, New York?"

Flexing the fingers of the cuffed hand, he grunted, "Yep."

"May I call you Bobby?"

He shrugged. "Everybody does."

"Including Oliver Allen?"

He cracked a smile. "He doesn't call me Bobby anymore, does he? Since he's deader'n a doorknob."

Flynn thought of the fingerprint on Matilda Allen's bathroom doorknob. "How do you know Ollie's dead?"

The smile became a smirk. "I heard it over the radio this morning. It said he shot himself in the head."

"Yes, he was shot in the head. But I don't believe he did it himself. Do you believe it, Bobby?"

"Why shouldn't I?"

"What if I told you he was shot point-blank in his right temple and the gun was in his right hand?"

"Then I'd say he shot himself."

"The problem I have is that a left-handed person would be expected to shoot himself in the left side of the head."

"Since he's dead, what's it matter?"

"It matters a whole lot. It means someone else shot him."

He smiled again. "Meaning what? That it was me?"

"Why would you shoot him?"

"You tell me."

"I've got a few ideas."

"Such as what?"

"How about a lovers' quarrel?"

"Oh, lady," he said, chuckling and shaking his head, "you've got some imagination. Are you saying Ollie and me were queer for each other? Listen, lady detective, I'm straight."

"All right, forget that idea. Let's try this for size. You and Ollie had a falling out over splitting up the proceeds of the money and jewelry the two of you took from his mother's house."

"This gets weirder and weirder. I was never in his mother's house. I don't know where you came up with that. Next, you'll have us screwing in the old lady's bed."

"If you weren't in that house, you have nothing to worry about. Except, of course, all that shooting you did this morning. That's serious enough. The detective you shot is in very grave condition and may not pull through. If he dies, you're looking at a count of first-degree murder." She turned to look at Detwiler. "Is that right, Jean?"

Detwiler nodded. "That's the law. Kill a law officer of any kind and it's murder one."

"Therefore, what really puzzles me," Flynn continued, "is why, if you had nothing to worry about from the police at your door this morning, you decided to start shooting?"

"They pulled their guns on *me.*"

"As you said, Bobby, this gets weirder and weirder," she said, shaking her head. "They did not pull guns on you, Bobby. The man you shot and who could die still had his weapon holstered when paramedics put him in the ambulance. I was there. I saw it. So stuff like 'They pulled their guns on me' is malarkey. Okay?"

"You still can't put me in that BMW and shooting Ollie in the head. And there's no way you can put me in that house up on Traitor's Lair Road."

"How'd you know where Matilda Allen lived, Bobby?"

"I read it in the paper."

"How'd you hurt your cheek, Bobby?"

"Shaving."

"Those aren't razor cuts. They're scratches. Like the sort fingernails might leave. Here's something you didn't read in the newspaper, because it wasn't in the paper. When Matilda Allen was being strangled from behind with her own stockings, she managed to reach up and back with her right hand and scratch whoever it was who was attacking her. There were bits of shredded skin under two of the fingernails of her right hand. That happens to fit the two scratches on your right cheek."

"I got these scratches screwing."

"I see. Then whoever scratched you can testify to that."

"I don't remember who did it."

"Could it have been Ollie Allen?"

"Who gave you this crazy idea that has you insisting that I'm gay?"

"My information that you met Ollie Allen in the gay bar over on Riverfront Road called Major André's was erroneous?"

"Absolutely. If anybody ever saw me in a gay bar, it was because I went in there to take a leak or use the phone. Besides, I hardly knew Ollie."

"Where did you meet him?"

"I don't remember. What's it matter?"

"It doesn't. But I'm one of those people who likes to tie up all the loose ends. For instance, what you just told me is one more loose end that's going to bother me till it's tied. If you hardly knew him, how is it the two of you roomed together?"

"Who says we roomed together?"

"I say, on the basis of what people like me and Assistant DA Detwiler call 'information and belief.' That's cops' and lawyers' talk for 'We have a witness.' "

"He's lying."

"Someone's lying. And who said the witness is a he?"

"I say. It has to have been Jimmy Paxton. He only said it to get even with me."

"For what?"

"Who knows?"

"Did he want to get even with you for dumping him in favor of taking up with Ollie Allen?"

"Don't be ridiculous. Why would I want to take up with him?"

"To put a little thrill in your life?"

"You take the cake, lady. What thrill?"

"The thrill of somebody a few years older and with a whole lot more experience. Someone much stronger and more domineering than Jimmy Paxton?"

"Domineering? What's that supposed to mean?"

"I heard you liked rough sex."

"Lady, you are a sicko."

"I think you were looking for someone with an edge of danger to him. Suddenly, here's a guy fresh out of Attica. Even better, this ex-con had big ideas about squeezing money from his mother, an old lady living alone in a very secluded area."

"You know, you should write mystery programs on TV."

"It's funny you should say that. When I was in college, on my way to becoming a police officer, I wrote a thesis about mystery programs on TV and on the radio, long before your time."

"Fascinatin'. Only we're not on TV, are we?"

"Sort of," she said, raising a hand and pointing backward to the television camera. "But I think I'm safe in saying that the tape of this interview is not going to be the basis of a made-for-television movie. There wouldn't be enough suspense to keep the audience from grabbing their remote-control units to change the channel. In fact, there's no mystery at all. I believe I've got enough evidence to permit Assistant DA Detwiler to prosecute you not only for the shooting you did this morning but for strangling Matilda Allen. I don't think I can prove that you put the bullet into Ollie's head. But that won't matter. There's more than ample evidence to persuade a jury to find you guilty of the murder of his mother."

"If you're so sure, what are you sittin' here wastin' your time talking' to me for?"

"On account of the loose ends."

"Screw your loose ends."

"There was also the possibility you might show me that I'm wrong in the way I see this case turning out. You mentioned that I ought to write mystery programs. If you've watched them, and I assume you have, you know that they often have a surprise twist at the end. But that's made-up stuff. This is real, isn't it? A true-life murder. True life doesn't have twists. Flynn's Law."

"What?"

"That's precept eight of what I call Flynn's Law."

"What the hell's that?"

"It's my collection of the rules that govern our lives and deaths. For instance, take Flynn's Law, precept thirteen."

"You take it."

"I believe it may apply to you, Bobby. I numbered it thirteen because I learned it when I was thirteen years old. Being a teenager, I did a stupid thing. I stole a lipstick from a store."

"Big deal."

"Well, it looked awful on me. And there was no way I could wear it without my parents wanting to know where I'd gotten it. But the worse thing about stealing it was that I felt damned guilty about it. I had a feeling that everyone who looked at me knew what I'd done. I laid awake at night worrying. So I went to my dad and confessed. My penance was to take the lipstick back and admit what I'd done to the store owner. And since I'd used a little of it, I had to pay for it, deducted from my allowance. So, precept thirteen of Flynn's Law goes this way. 'If you've got a guilty secret, let it out or it will eat you up.' "

"That's a lovely story, lady. Only I ain't got no guilty secret to let out."

"I believe you do. But it is not your murders of Matilda Allen and her ne'er-do-well son. It's the fact that you are a homosexual and can't accept it. That's why, even now when you may face at least two counts of murder, what truly upset you was when I touched on the subject of your being gay. You are more afraid of that fact getting out than you are of being charged with the murder of Matilda Allen. And maybe the murders of Ollie and a detective of the DA squad. My squad, by the way."

"Why should I be afraid of something that's not true?"

"It is true, Bobby. And I think you're afraid your father will find it out. You're more afraid of him than you are of the penalty for murder."

"You think you're so smart, don't you? Well, you ain't. You have it all wrong about who killed the old lady. Ollie did it."

The two women exchanged astonished glances.

Prevented from raising his right hand to his face, he lifted the left and touched the ski-trail scratches. "I got these from her all right," he said with a crack in his voice. "But I got them trying to *stop* Ollie from killing her. I kept pulling at him and telling him there was no need to kill her. We had all of the stuff we wanted. Why kill her? But Ollie was too strong. He was built like a bull. He held me off with one hand and choked her with the other. And after he did it, he looked at the scratches on me and laughed. He said if the cops ever caught us, all he had to do was point them out and tell them I was the one who did it."

"Did he tell you why he did it?"

"He was too damned pleased with himself not to. He told me everything went just the way he'd planned it and that if we carried out the rest of the plan, we'd both wind up being rich."

"What was his plan?"

"He said he thought of it a few years ago. How to get rid of his sister and mother and have all the old lady's money for himself. He said he'd already gotten her to change her will once and he could do it again. Only when he brought up the subject when we were having breakfast that morning, she refused. Mommy sat there and said, 'No.' It was his mommy saying no that set him off. He decided to wait till she was getting ready to go to church and then go upstairs and kill her. The plan was to make it look as if some stranger did it. I was supposed to give him an alibi by saying he couldn't have killed her because we were shacked up together at the time of the murder."

"Wait a minute, Bobby," Flynn interjected. "Back up and tell us again what you said about the sister."

"Ollie said he killed her. He made it look as if she drowned when her boat capsized on the lake. He said he drowned her first and rowed her out, dumped her, overturned the boat, and swam back. But even then something went wrong."

"What went wrong?"

"The old lady accused him of killing the sister. They had a big fight about it and the old lady fell down the steps. At first, he thought she was dead. But when he saw she wasn't, he got her to the hospital. All she had was a crushed hip. Shortly after that, he got arrested and sent to prison, so his big plan had to wait."

"He picked you only so you could be his alibi."

"That's right."

"Tell us the plan he had for killing his mother."

"The idea was to kill her and dump her somewhere to make it look like some sicko did it. But he needed help. The helper was to get all the money in the house and a lot of jewelry to tide the helper over until Ollie collected from her will. Then they'd split the proceeds. Unfortunately, that old junker of a car that he'd stolen in the city broke down when we got back to the house after dumping the body. It wouldn't start. So we ended up taking her car. Only we learned that the state police were looking for it. That's when we drove it to the Old Brewery to hide it. And that's when the bastard tried to get rid of me. I think he was hoping to make it look as if I did the old lady."

"How did he try to get rid of you?"

"He pulled a gun and was going to shoot me. Only I grabbed his hand and arm-wrestled for it. When it dropped to the floor, I got to it first, jammed it to his head, and that was that. Then I stuck it in his hand and took off. I hitched my way back to Stone Light. When I heard on the radio that he was found and that the police said it looked as if he'd killed himself, I figured I was home free."

"Until two detectives knocked on your door this morning."

He sighed long and deeply. "Right."

"What happened to the jewelry Ollie gave you?"

"It's in a toolbox buried at the foot of the old light."

37

※

Guessing Game

WHEN THE VIDEOTAPE of Bobby Mitchell's confession ended, District Attorney Aaron Benson stared across his office at the blank television screen. With a pained sigh, he said, "In the Torah, Job says, 'Let the day perish wherein I was born, and the night in which it was said, "There is a man-child conceived." ' "

His smooth boyish face wrinkled into a scowl.

"How the devil can a man kill his mother?"

Flynn removed the tape from the player. "In spite of this," she said, shaking it, "I'm nowhere near persuaded that Ollie did kill his mother."

Benson's scowl gave way to openmouthed amazement.

"I believe Bobby killed Matilda," she said, dropping into a chair with the tape in her lap. "Bobby Mitchell is the sociopath in that odd couple. He's a much better fit to the profile of the sociopath. Now, I have no doubt that Ollie talked about killing his mother. I'm sure he would have been happy to see her dead. But Bobby did it, as sure as I'm looking at you."

"I'm the jury," Benson said, tilting back and steepling fingers beneath his chin. "Show me beyond a reasonable doubt."

"First, the scratches. His story that Matilda clawed him while he was trying to help her is ludicrous. I stood inside that bathroom. It's very small. I can't see three people squeezed into it as Bobby said they were. Matilda scratched him while he was strangling her, not helping her."

"Duly noted. But not conclusive."

"Secondly, if Oliver had really wanted to kill his mother to cash in on her will, he could have done it long before that Sunday. He had a

200

perfect opportunity that day three years ago when she fell down the stairs and lay there helpless with a shattered hip. He could have snapped her neck like a twig. What did he do?"

"He took her to the hospital."

"Bobby would also have us believe that somehow Ollie forced his mother to change her will."

"But she did change it. She put him back in it,"

"Yes. But what did Ollie get? An annual allowance and the rest of his inheritance in a trust fund, to be his when he turned forty. *If* he'd already killed his sister to clear the way for his getting everything, why didn't he force the old woman to revise the will to make him exclusive beneficiary?"

"You said, 'If he'd already killed his sister,' as though you don't believe he did."

"The only evidence on that score is Bobby's word. I'm sure Bobby knew about the sister's death. Ollie probably told him of it. Ollie may even have made up the story that it was not a boat accident on the lake."

"Why would Ollie say he killed her if he didn't?"

"I'd have to guess. And guessing is destructive of the logical faculty."

"Humor me."

"Ollie was being the macho man. Playing *S* to Bobby's *M*. I am guessing, keep in mind."

"You guess very well."

"Can't you picture a scenario in which Ollie hoped to use Bobby to carry out an act that Ollie knew he could never achieve himself? In young Mr. Mitchell, we have a casebook sociopath if ever there was one. I doubt that Ollie had it in him to kill anyone. But in Bobby, he found his hopes fulfilled in spades."

"Yet Ollie tried to kill Bobby in that car."

"Nonsense. There was no struggle for a gun in the front seat of that BMW. Bobby had the gun. Bobby planned to use it. And that's what he did. What did he need Ollie for? He had Matilda's jewelry and probably whatever money she might have had in the house. And there was the very real possibility that if Ollie got himself into a scrape with the law, he would carry out his threat to give up Bobby for the murder. The man-child in this tragedy who deserves Job's curse is not Ollie Allen, though he has sins aplenty to account for on Judgment

Day. The bad seed was Bobby Mitchell. Only Ollie's dead and Bobby's the one who'll be doing the talking to the jury. And they won't want to hear guesswork. They'll want facts. The only ones I can provide you when you go to court are those that prove Bobby Mitchell shot Pete Sloan. I don't see how we can prove he killed the Allens."

"I can certainly make a case for him being an accessory to Matilda's murder," Benson said, dismantling the steeple. "And the taking of Matilda's jewelry makes that into felony murder, which means a minimum sentence of twenty-five years to life. This morning's shooting spree will be added to that, to run consecutively, I'm sure. If, God forbid, Pete should die—"

Rising abruptly, Flynn cut him off by tossing the videotape onto his desk. "If you're going to have what you need to put Bobby Mitchell away for good, I'd better get started on putting it all down on paper while it's still fresh in my mind."

"Speaking of paper," Benson said, picking up a sheaf of pink telephone message slips. "While we were at the hospital, Connie took a call from James Duncan. He requests an urgent meeting."

Flynn managed a smile. "That sure didn't take long."

"It gets better. He's bringing a lawyer. It's none other than Simon Cane, Esquire."

"He's not a criminal lawyer."

"I infer that James Duncan has a civil suit in mind." Fanning the pink slips in his hand like playing cards, he said, "It gets worse. These others are from our friends in the press. The entire pack has been baying into Connie's ear all morning long. They want me to let them up here for a press conference on all that's happened today."

She looked at the slips with disgust. "Sharks. The smell of blood and they come circling."

"There were four calls from the great white."

"Marty Katz?"

"But the first of his calls had nothing to do with the big shoot-out up at Stone Light. He requests an immediate meeting with you and me on the subject of what Connie noted on the slip as 'information he has obtained from a *highly reliable source*'—Connie underlined it— 'connected to the Jennifer Duncan murder.' "

Flynn tugged her lip. "Did he actually use the word *murder?*"

"Connie's got it in quotes. She wrote, 'information he has obtained from a *highly reliable source* connected to the Jennifer Duncan murder.'"

She sat. "He's got to be guessing. Everyone I've talked to pledged me complete confidentiality. He's bluffing."

Benson let the call slips float to the desk like autumn leaves. "If I call a press conference on what happened at Stone Light, Katz will be there in the front row. And you know damn well he's not going to let me get away without asking about the Duncan matter, whether he's bluffing or not."

She rose. "Can you hold off plunging into the shark pool for a day or so?"

"I haven't held on to this job these many years without having learned to dance. I am an expert at the politician's finest footwork. The duck and shuffle sidestep. What have you got in mind?"

"I'll see what I can do about sticking a harpoon in Jaws."

"What about Simon Cane and his client?"

"I'll be there to lend you moral support, but you'll have to do the heavy lifting."

Looking down at the pink slips, Benson murmured, "Oh, Lord, thy sea is so great and my boat is small."

Part Seven

Awakenings

"A person who is tired of crime is tired of life."

—John Mortimer, *Rumpole of the Bailey*

38

❦

It's a Crime

THE RAUCOUS BACKGROUND sounds through the phone signified it was the lunch hour at the Scales of Justice. Over them as Marty Katz filled the phone booth at the rear, she said, "Let's you and I have a chin-wag, Marty."

He shouted above the din. "Come on over. I'll be at my usual spot near the front door."

"Not there, my ink-stained buddy. Meet me in half an hour at It's a Crime."

"My, my," he said, chuckling. "The mystery bookshop. Now is that appropriate, or what?"

"It's only you I want to see, Marty. This isn't going to be a press gang bang."

"I didn't get the nickname 'Scoop' for nothing. And my mom didn't raise a fool for a son."

Sons and mothers, daughters and fathers, she thought as she hung up. What were the mystical bonds that so often seemed to be stronger between a boy and his mother than with his father? And a girl's to her dad rather than to her mom? The Book of Proverbs said, "A foolish son is the heaviness of his mother." And Ezekial stated, "As is the mother, so is her daughter." Sophocles in *Phaedra* pronounced, "Sons are the anchors of a mother's life." Poet Dinah Maria Mulock Craik had penned, "Oh, my son's my son till he gets him a wife / But my daughter's my daughter all her life."

Getting into her car, a nursery rhyme came into her head:

Mother, may I go out to swim?
Yes, my darling daughter:
Hang your clothes on a hickory limb
And don't go near the water.

Being a good daughter, it had not been Jessica Duncan, but her brother, who dared the dive from the far side of Horseman's Head Rock and claimed to have come face-to-face with Jennifer Duncan.

Five minutes early, she parked her Plymouth in a small lot beside the bookstore and tried to recall mysteries she had read in which a son or daughter turned out to be the guilty one, and who might be the more likely suspect in a matricide. Although no title sprang to mind, she felt certain she would find at least one were she to look to Agatha Christie. Entering the store, she thought of the evil bastard son of the Duke of Holderness, whom Sherlock Holmes had unmasked in "The Priory School." But he had not murdered a parent. The sin of Cain had been his intent.

For an estimate, if not the exact number, of homicidal sons and daughters inhabiting the pages of mystery novels, she might have asked the proprietor of the store. Fittingly funereal in a black frock coat he never failed to don purveying books, Charles Carew was the opposite of the grim pose. Tall, red-haired and red-faced, and Irish by birth, he greeted her in a genuine brogue.

"And where have you been so's I haven't seen you in ages, Arlene, moy loov? I was afraid you'd gotten tired of crime and quit your job, or died and gone to heaven, it's been so blessed long."

"Get tired of crime, Charlie?" she said as he draped long arms about her in a bear hug. " 'A person who is tired of crime is tired of life.' And heaven wouldn't have me."

"There's a suspicious character in a white suit lurkin' in the stacks, and he's been askin' about you, my dear. I was about to toss him out, he's that criminal-lookin'."

"That's because he's a newspaperman, Charlie."

"That explains it, sure." He laughed.

She found Katz browsing. Looking as blanched as a ghost in his hallmark suit and matching hat, he skimmed his nimble fingers across titles of horror novels. He spoke without looking at her. "How's Pete Sloan doing?"

She sighed. "It's touch and go."

"I'll say a prayer for him."

"I didn't realize you were a praying person."

"You can find me at temple as often as you go over to Scared Heart. You're there Christmas Eve and Easter. I go for Rosh Hashanah and Yom Kippur."

"Do you think it will do either of us any good?"

"I figure it couldn't hurt."

He took down an inexpensive fat compendium of Stephen King stories. Leafing through it, he whispered, "I heard a fascinating story yesterday that this guy could turn into a real hair-raiser."

"King could turn the Yellow Pages into a hair-raiser."

He replaced the volume. "I have a question for you along the line of some things that you asked me the other day in the Scales of Justice. Do you believe that people can communicate from beyond the grave, Arlene?"

"This detective stands solidly upon the ground and does not believe in ghosts."

"Then explain to me why you've been dashing all around the county like you were Bill Murray in *Ghostbusters.*"

"Being Catholic, I'd call it performing an exorcism."

"Okay, you're not Bill Murray. You're . . . whoever it was in that movie."

"Jason Miller. Who's the main character in your story?"

"Are you asking my source?"

"Indeed I am."

"That would be telling."

"I never feel comfortable on one-way streets, Marty." She spun away. "Have a nice day."

He caught the sleeve of her houndstooth jacket. "Before I go with what I've got for the next edition of the *Clarion,* I decided that I should talk to you first, in keeping with my journalistic principles."

"Journalistic principles. There's an oxymoron," she said as she moved down a narrow aisle to the Sherlock Holmes section to look for a complete collection of the fifty-six short stories and four novels by Sir Arthur Conan Doyle to present to Peter Sloan for hospital reading.

Katz sidled next to her. "I also figured that for all the times you've been fair to me, I have to be fair to you."

She decided upon the grandfather of Holmes collections, the brown-jacketed hardcover Doubleday edition of *The Complete Sherlock Holmes*. Opening it to the introduction by the late Christopher Morley, the Sherlockian who had joined in founding the New York Holmes society, the Baker Street Irregulars, she read, "We must begin in Baker Street, and best of all, if possible, let it be a stormy winter morning when Holmes routs Watson out of bed in haste. The doctor wakes to see that tall ascetic figure by the bedside with a candle."

She closed the weighty book, tucked it under her left arm, and completed the passage herself. "Come, Watson. The game is afoot."

Somewhere in that foggy London, Professor Moriarty plotted crimes worthy of the Napoléon of crime, perhaps a subterranean raid on a cache of gold in a supposedly unassailable bank vault or the theft of the crown jewels from the Tower of London. Within 221B Baker Street, Dr. Watson scribbled notes of his most recent adventure alongside the best and wisest man he had ever known. Slouched into a cane chair by a coal fire and packing his third bowl of tobacco as he pondered a three-pipe problem, Holmes kept an ear tuned for the rattle of a hansom cab drawing up to Mrs. Hudson's rooming house. Footfalls racing up seventeen steps might belong to young Wiggins, scampish leader of the original unofficial police force known as the Irregulars; a mysterious young woman with a delicate problem of blackmail; a minister of Her Majesty Queen Victoria's government worried about a missing set of blueprints; a foreign potentate in a disguise that could never fool Holmes; or Inspector Lestrade, the best of Scotland Yarders, who were known for thoroughness and method but were forever found to be wanting in imaginative intuition.

Katz's insistent voice summoned her back from the memories of her own magical journeys up the steps to that romantic sitting room in a nostalgic country of the mind when the year was always 1895. "Let's cut out the verbal fencing, Arlene," he said, "You know precisely what's on my mind."

Moriarty once had said much the same thing to Holmes and got this reply: "Then everything I have to say to you has also crossed yours." She chose not to answer.

Face reddening, Katz demanded, "Do you deny that there is more to the sudden interest of the DA's squad in the death of Jennifer Duncan than something you stumbled across in a routine tidying up of the files?"

"I appreciate that you're a hopeful author yourself, Marty," she said, moving to a display of a new thriller by Clive Cussler. "But I think you may be letting your imagination run away with you." She leafed through the novel about the latest adventures of underwater salvage featuring Cussler's hero, Dirk Pitt. "How's the work on your long-awaited novel of life in a small upstate New York town progressing, by the way?"

"Fine. I just started on a chapter about a wealthy woman whose grandson comes to her with a fantastic story involving a near-death experience. It's quite a coincidence, since that was the subject of your questions to me the other day."

"It's a small world," she replied, keeping the Cussler book as a second gift for Sloan. "Now I'm even more eager to read your novel. When do you expect to finish the writing?"

"I keep finding my fiction sidetracked by true life. And by life's inescapable partner, the Grim Reaper. And what might lie at the end of our worldly journeys."

"It is that 'bourn' from which 'no traveller returns.' "

"If we're to believe these near-death experiencers, some of them apparently do come back."

"But from where, Marty? Have those people really come back from death? Or did they simply make an excursion into the equally fascinating but fantastic and complex land of the imagination and troubled memory?"

"Which do you think it is?"

"Look around us, Marty. All these books. All these imaginative individuals who possess the wonderful gift of being able to entice their readers into a suspension of belief. Imagination is a mighty thing, isn't it? And never more so than in our childhood. When I was a kid, I had a vivid sense of fantasy. I had an imaginary friend, name of Noreen. Yet she was as real as could be. Do boys have imaginary friends, Marty?"

"I was born with a reporter's notebook in hand. My friends were and are called Who, What, Where, When, Why, and How."

"They are a detective's friends, too. But they happen to be extremely shy when they are in a detective's company. They don't like to go out in public or be quoted in newspapers unless they are also with the detective's other friend, Mr. Evidence. I bet your friends, the five Messrs. W. and Mr. H., feel the same way about their companion. I believe his name is Mr. Be Careful About Your Sources. I mean, think of their embarrassment if it should turn out their names got into print prematurely and they had to deal with a not-so-pleasant guy by the name of Mr. Retraction, Also known as Mr. Egg on Your Face."

"Look, Miss Chief Investigator of the DA squad," Katz said in a burst of impatience, "is you is or is you ain't looking into whether the death of Jennifer Duncan was a murder?"

The rise of his voice lifted eyebrows among half a dozen lunchtime book browsers and the store's proprietor.

With a stern look at Katz, she whispered, "Let's continue this conversation outside, shall we?"

As she paid for Holmes and Cussler, he paced the sidewalk. When she emerged, he grumbled, "When I covered that woman's death a year ago, I thought something smelled fishy. Newspapering tends to give you a feeling that when a rich dame dies mysteriously, it might be a good idea for somebody to look into whether the hubby did it. Nobody did. Then all of a sudden, you're snooping around. I think you've got reason to believe as I did one year ago—that James Duncan killed his wife. Am I right?"

"Marty, are you still beating your wife?"

"The hell with you, smart-ass. I gave you a fair chance. Now I'm going with my story."

"What story? That Sebastian Duncan told Elizabeth Hollander that he died and talked to his mother and she told him that she'd been murdered?"

"I don't recall mentioning Elizabeth Hollander."

"You didn't have to. She never liked her son-in-law. She's always believed he killed Jennifer. She's in town this week. And you start acting like Sherlock Holmes. It's obvious she's been bending your ear. Marty, my dear friend, if you print what she told you about Sebastian's supposed near-death experience, you'll never live it down. You won't be able to show your face in the Scales of Justice again, especially after I parade out Mr. Evidence and knock your story into a cocked hat. Therefore, if you choose to commit journalistic suicide and end up writing stories about flying saucers and dogs with six heads for super-market tabloids, go ahead."

He glared across Hempstead Street at a knot of men coming out from lunch at the Depot. When his eyes settled on her after a long, thoughtful moment, he cracked a sly smile. "Has anyone ever told you that there are times when you can be a real bitch?"

She thought of Sloan. "The epithet is not unknown to me."

His eyes studied his black-and-white wing tips a moment and returned to hers. "Here's what I'm going to do. I'll sit on my story for a couple of days and give you a fair chance to bring me compelling evidence that I should spike it forever."

"You've got a fifth friend with the initial *W.* serving you, as well, Marty," she said, playfully pinching his chin. "His name is Mr. Wisdom."

39

❊

Angry Words

THE ANGRY WORDS of a man spilling from Benson's office and through the double glass doors assaulted Flynn as she stepped from the elevator.

"This is an outrage. A slur on my wife, my family, and me."

Entering the reception room, she found the law intern looking at her aghast. Beyond the next door, Constance Hardwick had an expression of bottled-up fury as she nodded toward Benson's open door and silently mouthed, "James Duncan."

Braced on props of rigid arms and balled fists, he leaned across the desk and almost into Benson's astonishingly composed face. "Where do you get the temerity, the gall, to dare to drag up something that was settled to the satisfaction of everyone, including you, over a year ago?"

Rearing back with uncurled fingers next to his hips like a gunfighter in a Western at a Roxy matinee, he was shorter than she had imagined, but much handsomer than in the photograph that had accompanied Marty Katz's story on the death of his wife.

"Are you doing this because it's an election year?"

"Politics has nothing to do with it," Benson said calmly. A rightward glance revealed Flynn at the door. With a little smile twitching the corners of his lips and the relieved expression of someone in that same cowboy movie who had glimpsed the arrival of a rescuing hero, he blurted, "Arlene, please come in."

Duncan turned abruptly toward her. "You're the person who's helping in the perpetration of this atrocious slander."

Entering the office, she nodded in greeting to a third man.

Reserved in tailoring and bearing but with a face as darkly hand-some as a soap-opera actor, Simon Cane had left the top-floor suite of the law offices building, crossed Fourth Street, and come to the up-permost floor of the Stone County Courthouse. In his capacity as se-nior partner of Cane, Liberman, Hawkins and Berger, Attorneys at Law, he had attested with a flamboyant signature on the final page of Jennifer Duncan's last will and testament as to its veracity and validity. Although she had never encountered him in a criminal case, she had seen him frequently in corridors outside civil-court chambers. Smil-ing, he came halfway out of his chair with a cherry "Hello, Arlene."

"As your able lawyer will tell you, Mr. Duncan," she said, coming into the office, "no one has slandered either you or anyone in your family."

"The implication of the statement issued by this office in which your name figures prominently," Duncan said, seething, "is that I had something to do with my wife's death."

"I fail to see how you can possibly draw such a meaning," Benson retorted.

Duncan took a folded paper from his pocket. "Then explain this to me," he said, opening it. "You say it will be in the best interest of the people of Stone County that a probe be conducted into a death that had been attributed to an accidental overdose of a powerful sedative. If that is not a way of saying Jennifer was murdered and that I had something to do with it . . ."

Benson stood. With manicured hands on his hips, he looked like a kid pretending to be a western gunslinger. "Sir, your name is not even mentioned in that statement."

Duncan crumpled the paper and flung it to the desk. "It's certainly between the lines. I demand an immediate end to this travesty, a re-traction of that statement, and the issuance by you of a public apology."

Cane shifted slightly. "The portion of that statement that caught my eye is the line at the end of the second paragraph," he said calmly. "It speaks of information in your files that was not available either to the coroner or the Stone County Sheriff's Department. This raises fasci-nating questions. First, why was it not available? One might deduce that it was not because it is new information. That raises my second query. What is this fresh information?"

"We never discuss with outsiders details of an investigation while it is in progress," Benson replied. "To do so would be an injustice. An investigation involves data from a wide variety of sources that must be checked out and verified."

"In other words, rumors and hearsay," Cane interjected.

"That's it exactly."

"For example, the category of hearsay might include totally unsubstantiated allegations of criminal activity against a particular individual of otherwise impeccable reputation in the community. For instance, a man like Mr. James Duncan."

"An excellent example," Benson said. "Hypothetically."

Duncan exploded with anger. "Hypothetically, hell. Why don't you come right out and admit you're investigating me? And you can also admit why. This so-called information came straight from the poisonous mouth of my mother-in-law. That woman has been all over Newtown, spreading a venomous lie that I had something to do with Jenny's death. I think she even came to this office with it. And that's what's prompted this farcical waste of taxpayers' money."

"Murder is not a farce, Mr. Duncan," Flynn declared.

"Nobody murdered Jenny. She took those damned pills to kill herself."

Flynn tugged her lip. "I find that very hard to believe."

"Your coroner believed so. The only reason he didn't rule it a suicide was the absence of a note."

"Many people kill themselves without stopping to write and explain why. But the absence of a note permitted Dr. Zeligman's sentimentality to influence his verdict. He ruled 'accidental overdose' in order to spare the children the traumatic experience of believing their mother had abandoned them."

"Suicide or accident," Duncan said. "What does it matter?"

"It matters because each of those explanations flies in the face of logic. From all that I've ascertained so far, your wife had everything to live for. And asking me to accept that she took all her pills at once, inadvertently, stretches credulity to the breaking point I do believe your wife *was* murdered, Mr. Duncan. I'll stake my reputation on that. Proving it is my first problem. Second is finding who did it."

"Therefore, I am your easiest nominee."

"You certainly had means, motive, and opportunity."

He snorted a bitter laugh. "What motive?"

"Let's make it plural. You had millions of motives in the form of your wife's money. Not to mention the added inducement of her real estate, stock holdings, and the like. And dare I say the other woman?"

"Now you are telling us that you are acting on the basis of slanderous gossip?"

"Gossip qualifies as slander only if it's false. If gossip concerning an affair with Madeline Trainor is wrong, you have the right to sue whoever spreads it. And you've got an excellent attorney."

"That's a fool's errand, Arlene," Cane interjected. "And you know it. And so is, I might add, your idea that my client murdered his wife because of another woman. If that was true, why has he not collected his winnings in this great gamble on murder and married her? Madeline Trainor as a motive falls apart."

"That still leaves me the first."

"I'm a civil litigator, Arlene. The last time I tried a criminal case was moot court in law school. Nonetheless, I believe I detect a huge hole in your first motive. And it is this. If James had been determined to profit by his wife's death, roughly in the amount of ten to fifteen million dollars, why would he not have bided his time by waiting a couple of years? By then, the cosmetics venture would have been in full operation and bringing in ten to fifteen million a *year*. That's according to the most conservative of estimates."

"Your proposition might hold water, save for one interesting bit of information that's come to me from a disinterested and, therefore, highly reliable source. The night Jennifer died, she warned your client that if he did not break off his affair with Trainor, she would cut him out of her will and see to it that he'd never get to see their children again."

Duncan blared, "Whoever told you that is a liar."

"Do you deny you had quite a row at the boat landing? The blush in your face is our answer, I think."

"What husband and wife don't fight?"

"I'm sure most do. But how many would pick so public a place to do it? And on such an auspicious occasion?"

"Your logic in attributing motive to my client is a slender reed, Arlene," Cane said impatiently. "Furthermore, it collapses under the weight of the third and most important element if you are to prove a case of murder: opportunity. Please explain for my client's benefit,

mine, and District Attorney Benson's when, where, and, most importantly, how James enticed or tricked Jennifer into ingesting that entire
bottle of pills."

"An excellent question, Simon."

"What's your answer?"

"I have none—yet."

"And you never will have one," Duncan exclaimed. "Because
there's no way I could have. I was nowhere near the kitchen when
Jenny took her pill. Ask Cornelia Stewart."

"I shall. Meanwhile, why don't you tell me where you were in the
house at the time Jenny said she was going to bed."

Blush seeped into his face again. "I wasn't in the house."

"Were you still at the boat landing?"

Duncan fidgeted. "I was not."

"Were you on the deck with the guests?"

His face had become crimson. "Not there, either."

"Then where were you?"

He sighed deeply. "I'd gone out for a drive to cool down a little
after the fight with Jenny. I got in the Jaguar and just took off."

"Produce an eyewitness for me and I'll believe you."

Duncan looked anxiously at his lawyer. "Do I have to?"

"Of course not," Cane said. "You have waived none of your con-
stitutional rights by being here. However, if you have such a witness,
I believe you should reveal who it is. But privately to me, first." He
looked at Benson. "Aaron, is there a room where my client and I can
talk for a moment?"

Benson nodded at a door opposite his desk. "The grand jury room
is at your disposal." As the door closed behind them, his eyes turned to
Flynn. "Any guesses about what Duncan is telling him? Oh, sorry. I
forgot. You don't like to guess."

As the door of the grand jury room opened a crack, Flynn whispered, "That was quick."

Observing Duncan as he crossed the office and sat for the first
time, she noted his expression had changed from surly to sheepish.

"Before my client proceeds, Aaron," declared Cane, "I insist that I
receive your assurance that should Arlene's investigation develop a
compelling need for her to talk to the individual to be named that I

be permitted to produce that individual and that all questioning be done in my presence."

Benson nodded. "Agreed."

Cane turned to Duncan. "Go ahead, Jim."

Duncan gulped breath. "I went for that drive with Maddie."

"Madeline Trainor?" Flynn asked.

"That's correct."

"Forgive me, gentlemen, but I'm a cop. I wear a cop's thinking cap. And what occurs to me is, to put it bluntly, You lie and she swears to it."

"That's very offensive, Arlene," Cane objected. "May I propose that before you utter something equally as insulting you let my client finish his statement?"

She held up her hands as if surrendering. "Sorry."

"There is someone to back up what I've said," Duncan continued, his voice wavering nervously. "Ask the night desk clerk at the motel on Old West Point Road."

"This was over a year ago, Mr. Duncan," Flynn said incredulously. "Why are you so sure he'll remember you?"

"Maddie and I registered under the names Mr. and Mrs. James Farley. But I was afraid the clerk recognized me, so I tipped him fifty dollars in the hope he would be discreet. You can check the motel's records. We had room fifteen. We checked in about ten and stayed only till midnight. That's another reason I over-tipped."

"I believe that a review of the coroner's report will show that Jennifer Duncan excused herself from her guests, took her pill, and went to her bedroom within that time frame," Cane said. "In fact, I believe the report notes that Cornelia Stewart puts the hour between eleven-fifteen and eleven-thirty."

"Excuse me," interjected Benson, "but the pills could have been dropped into Jennifer's coffee earlier than that."

Flynn shook her head. "No, boss. That's not possible. If the pills had been added to the coffee, Jennifer would have found the bottle empty when she took the one pill we know from all the evidence that she removed from the bottle herself. The others had to have gone into her glass of iced coffee virtually simultaneously."

"Therefore, she took them all herself," Cane said. "And that means suicide. I trust that spells an end to this ill-advised investigation and that Mr. Duncan may go on with his life without further embarrassment."

"I will be talking to your housekeeper."

"Cornelia Stewart is now a suspect? God, you are amazing!"

"I'll be calling on her at her home, if that makes you feel better." The two men rose to leave.

"One more question, please, gentlemen?"

Duncan glared angrily. "What is it?"

"Why were you so quick to cancel Jennifer's project?"

"For the simple reason that I knew nothing about and had no desire to get involved in the cosmetics business."

40

Music by Mozart

Looking down from his window, the district attorney of Stone County observed Simon Cane conferring on the steps of the courthouse with his client and asked, "Do you buy Duncan's alibi?"

"It's too rich in the details not to," Flynn said from her chair. "But I'll send Eddie Richards up to the motel to have a look through the registration files and have a chat with the night clerk, if he still works there."

Benson returned to his desk. "How went your meeting with Marty Katz?"

"We had our usual chess match."

Benson smiled. "You checkmated him, I trust?"

"I'm afraid it was a draw. But I won some time. He's going to sit on the story your friend Elizabeth Hollander fed to him about Sebastian's NDE"

Benson groaned. "She didn't."

"She did. But I told Marty that if he went with Sebastian's tale, he would become the laughingstock of his buddies at the Scales of Justice. I also hinted I was close to making an arrest. I thought I was until Duncan came up with an alibi."

"If it holds water."

"I expect it will."

"Elizabeth is going to be a sorely disappointed."

"Not to beat a dead knight, to carry on the chess analogy, but you and I were rooked by a brilliant opening gambit by the queen of the game. I refer, of course, to Elizabeth Hollander and her story of Sebastian's supposed near-death experience."

"I'm sorry. I don't follow you. Supposed? There's no doubt that kid was pulled back from the brink of death."

"Yes. But did he have the near-death experience his grandmother told us about?"

"Are you saying the kid lied to her?"

"I'm saying Elizabeth lied to us. I believe she made up the story for her own purpose."

"I'm sorry, Arlene, but that's quite a reach."

"Is it? You will recall that she told us she'd heard people talking about near-death experiences on television talk shows. I think that when she learned of Sebastian's drowning experience, she saw in it an opportunity to bolster her contention that her detested son-in-law was a murderer. And then to get you to take another look into Jennifer's death. It was a brilliant tactic. She knew you well enough to know she would get the investigation. Then she made sure word of it got to the right people. She talked to Ted Zeligman about it even before she came to see you. And to be doubly sure of results, she gave the story to Marty Katz."

"I'm embarrassed to say it, but I think you're right."

"Her only risk lay in somebody discovering Sebastian did not go down that dark tunnel and into the light, to find Mommy waiting for him with a tale of murder."

Benson thumped a fist on his desk. "That's why she was so adamantly opposed to you interviewing the kid."

"I believe Elizabeth did some quick research into the phenomenon and learned that people who claimed to have had an NDE almost invariably told someone about it immediately. Sebastian did not. She said he'd waited until he spoke to her a couple of days later, ostensibly because he had been instructed to do so by his mother. I think that was Elizabeth's invention. She is an extremely clever woman. By keeping us away from Sebastian, she effectively fitted us with blinders. Speaking of tunnel vision!"

"She counted on your investigation to come up with evidence of murder."

"With that, Sebastian's story of an NDE would be rendered irrelevant. This is pure speculation, of course. I have no way of proving it."

"The irony," Benson said, "is that Elizabeth was right about Jennifer having been murdered, but wrong in choice of suspect."

Flynn left her chair and crossed the office to stand at the window. "The horror to contemplate is that James Duncan was also my prime suspect."

"Mine, too. All the circumstantial evidence pointed to him."

"I was this near," she said, turning and showing Benson an almost-closed vise of finger and thumb, "to arresting him."

"Does that put us back to square one?"

She moved to the door. "Not at all. The roster of suspects has been greatly reduced, but we still have people with motive. If Sloan were here, I'd talk the case through with him. Nothing helps in a case as much as thinking it out loud with someone."

Benson looked wounded. "I'm available."

"No offense intended, boss. But I'm talking about cop think. You do DA think."

He rolled his eyes. "Dare I ask what the hell that means?"

"I know the difference, but I'm not sure if I could explain it to you."

He smiled impishly. "I'm fascinated. Give it a try."

She thought for a long moment. "Will an analogy do?"

"I'll try to keep up."

"If you were to look at the criminal justice system as if it were a concert by a philharmonic orchestra, the detective would be Mozart, coming up with the notes—clues and evidence. The DA is the maestro who arranges all the instruments—witnesses and so forth—and conducts them. The difference is that our audience is not a packed concert hall, but twelve people in the jury box. And our problem is that at the moment you and I have got ourselves an unfinished symphony."

"I'm sure you'll complete it," he said confidently as she went out the door. "And I'm positive it will be another Arlene Flynn masterpiece."

With the two books she had bought for Sloan lying beside her on the seat of her car and a Mozart cassette playing as she drove toward the hospital, she thought of Dr. Watson's best and wisest friend. Not only a very capable performer on violin but a composer of no ordinary merit, Sherlock Holmes had been pictured by the doctor while Sarasate's violin filled St. James's Hall. Seated in the stalls, he was wrapped in the most perfect happiness, gently waving long, thin fingers in time to the music, while his gently smiling face and his languid, dreamy eyes were as unlike those of Sherlock Holmes, the sleuth hound, as relentless, keen-witted and ready-handed a criminal agent as it was possible to conceive.

Before she entered Sloan's private room, his doctor made an inadvertent joke. "The swelling of the brain appears to have been arrested."

Placing Holmes and the Cussler novel on the bedside table, she said, "Well, Sloan, at least someone's made an arrest in this damn case of ours."

She looked for a flicker of amusement in the lips and eyes of a head swathed in mummylike white wrappings that ballooned to proportions of the grotesque jack-o'-lantern on the shoulders of Washington Irving's fearsome horseman in pursuit of the fictional figure for whom a deep and perilous lake had been named. Plastic tubes streamed out of the nostrils and from adhesive patches on his bared chest and arms, slack at his sides. A bandage covering his chest wound encompassed his entire left shoulder. He seemed to be barely breathing. But a monitor next to the bed displayed reassuringly moving zigzag lines and emitted little beepings at comfortingly regular intervals.

"I brought you books," she said. "There'll be a quiz on the canon. In case you don't know it, that's what we Sherlock Holmes nuts call the complete collection of Dr. Watson's accounts of the adventures. I haven't had time to find out if they're available on—what was it?" She thought a moment, remembered, and answered for him. "CD-ROM."

Whatever the hell that is, she thought.

Could he hear her? If yes, neither his pulse nor the monitor indicated so.

"I'll be stopping at the Newtown Mall tomorrow on my way up to see Cornelia Stewart," she continued. "I'm going to drop in on the pharmacist who filled Jennifer Duncan's prescription. It's a detail, one of those loose ends that need tying up in any case."

In two and a half years, how many cases had they worked?

"You were occupied with something else during the investigation into the body that was found in the boathouse on the old Troy estate. The clue that clinched that one was mud on the back of an Oriental carpet that was where it shouldn't have been. But I told you about that already, didn't I?"

Giving her a cockeyed look, he had said, "Only a woman could have noticed something like that."

"Like spotting breakfast dishes that had been washed but not put away," she said, searching hopefully into Sloan's sleeping eyes for a sign of wakefulness. "I was correct about them, by the way. Bobby Mitchell said the three of them had had breakfast together—he, Ollie, and Matilda. But I was wrong in thinking Ollie killed her. It was Bobby. I can't prove it, though. However, it doesn't matter, because Bobby admitted shooting Ollie in the car. He also confessed shooting you. Not that an admission was needed. We'll have witnesses galore at the trial, including you, if it goes to trial. Benson will probably get a plea and save the county a bundle in court costs."

She studied the chest bandaging.

"Why the hell didn't you wear your vest, dummy?"

Her eyes drifted up to the wrapped head.

"Of course, a vest is no protection against a head wound, is it, Flynn? That's what you'd be saying if only you could, isn't it? You and your wiseass lip. Well, Peter Sloan, keep in mind that favorite saying of Benson's from World War Two. 'Loose lips sink ships.' Speaking of loose lips, one pair almost sank the Jennifer Duncan case."

The thought prompted a glance at the Holmes book.

"In 'A Scandal in Bohemia,' Holmes matched wits with an adventuress by the name of Irene Adler. Watson described her as a woman of dubious and questionable memory. But to Sherlock, Irene would always be *the* woman. Well, to me, Elizabeth Hollander will always be *that* woman. She was blabbing all over town. She went so far as to tell Marty Katz about Sebastian's purported near-death experience."

Her thoughts returned to the mystery bookstore.

"Marty asked about you. Your name was the first word out of his mouth, so he has to be as concerned about you, as we all are. I managed to talk him out of going with his story, at least for a while. By then I hope to have the case wrapped up. Incidentally, cross James Duncan off our list of suspects. He appears to have an alibi. It turns out he could not have laced Jennifer's iced coffee with her entire prescription. He was otherwise engaged in room fifteen of the motel on Old West Point Road. Three guesses who kept him company. Hint. Her initials are M.T. So she has an alibi, too. Not that she ever ranked high on my list of likely murderers."

It would require a supreme confidence in one's feminine allure, she thought, for any woman to murder her lover's wife in the expectation that he would be so grateful that a proposal of marriage would just tumble from his adoring lips.

"There was always a problem with James Duncan, you see. Why would he decide to kill Jennifer on an evening when their home was crowded with guests? Then I learned of the big argument on the boat landing and figured that James went into a panic and did it. Instead, he and Madeline hopped in his Jaguar and then into bed in a motel."

Consequently, the question remained: Who killed Jennifer?

"With our suspect list shrunken by two, Sloan, who's left?"

The Rudermans? Desirous of aborting their deal with Jennifer and going forward on their own?

Viable candidates.

The import-export man, Borrero? And the other international businessman, Schack?

Very long shots.

The woman who licked barbecue sauce from her fingers?

Tom Pierce was probably right. In a mystery novel, Darlene Devonshire would be an adornment.

The banker? The only motive for murder more frequent than money was love.

The victims of Jennifer Duncan's takeover of their company, Lester Troy and his chemist, Alexander Umlauf?

The figure whom Tom Pierce had shunned? Mr. Dominic Perillo, the beard? Might he have done the deed on behalf of the young woman he had brought to the party?

What of Pierce? How much of a leap might it have been to go from poison pen to poisoned coffee?

The affable artist, ignored by everyone and passing the time sketching the kids?

"If he did it," she said, "it's definitely time for me to retire and keep bees."

The all-purpose other woman on the scene, Cornelia Stewart?

Insufficient data, though she surely had the opportunity.

"Whoever did it, Sloan," she said, "the trick was getting the rest of those pills into a glass that Jennifer apparently had in her hand."

The door opened and a nurse entered the room bearing a tray with three small bottles and three syringes.

"It's time for Mr. Sloan's shots," she said. "I'm afraid I have to ask you to step out for a moment."

"It's quite all right. We've finished our talk."

Startled, the nurse blurted, "He's been talking?"

"I am so sorry. I did the talking. Thinking out loud."

The nurse laid the tray on a high table. "I see."

Flynn looked at Sloan. "Do you know if people who are in his condition can hear?"

"I've been nursing long enough to have learned not to answer questions like that. It has also been my experience that speaking to someone who is comatose is always an expression of faith. And I will never sell that medicine short."

"Then you won't think I'm foolish if I tell him good night?"

"Certainly not."

"I'm going home now, Sloan," she said, patting his arm. "I'm going to take a long, hot shower. Dinner will be microwavable and eaten accompanied by Mozart on the stereo. In the morning, I shall pay a call on Mrs. Cornelia Stewart in hopes of finding out, to paraphrase the old song, 'who was in the kitchen with Jenny.' "

As she rose, she watched the nurse fill a syringe from one of the three bottles.

"Excuse me," she asked. "How do you know which one of those he gets first?"

"The patient's chart contains his neurosurgeon's detailed instructions. Mr. Sloan is receiving wonderful drugs. But if they were mishandled, they could prove fatal. The chart lists the times for administering the medications, the proper order of injections, and the dosage. When the doctor draws up the instructions, he also goes over the procedures with everyone treating the patient."

"Did you hear that, Sloan?" Flynn said as the first needle went into him. "I'm leaving you in excellent hands."

41

Right Way Up

FLYNN PAUSED IN the middle of her living room, crowded with
mementos and souvenirs of her private and public lives, records,
and books. Many dated to her girlhood, for she had never been one to
discard anything that had either brought her pleasure or added to her
knowledge. In that, she had been her father's student.

"Throw something out," he had taught, "and the very next day
you'll want it."

Her mother had been the opposite. Consequently, her grown-up
daughter had spent a small fortune in antique shops on Ina Street and
at flea markets looking for replacements for items tossed out with the
death-knell pronouncement, "No sense in hanging on to this dust collector."

Timothy had grown up to be just like her, inquiring of his sister on
a regular basis, "Why do you keep all this stuff?"

She invariably answered, "In order to drive the executor of my estate crazy getting rid of it. Namely, you."

His equally fastidious wife, Celeste, had ventured an opinion on the
clutter only once. "You have so many beautiful things, Arlene, but I'd
sure hate to be your housekeeper."

"Oh good Lord, I'd never have anyone in to clean," she had replied
with a shudder. "I've heard too many horror stories from my boss
about things being dropped or upset and broken. The only event more
destructive of one's possessions than a maid or housekeeper is a moving man."

In the relocation from Gribetz Street to her new house, she had counted six items of furniture scratched, the glass of three picture frames smashed, and an umbrella stand lost forever.

But her greatest aversion to having someone in to clean was the probability of her things not being returned to their proper place. In sharing compulsive Hercule Poirot's "finicky tidiness" she expected to find that everything she owned was exactly where it belonged. Poirot had achieved fame by solving a famous case while straightening ornaments on a mantelpiece. She had unraveled the murder of a renowed author by noticing that an Oriental carpet had been put down before the movers had come.

Now, like Poirot, Miss Marple, Sherlock Holmes, and countless other detectives in fiction and real life, she thought as she placed her shoulder bag in its proper spot next to the front door, she had on her hands a murder case in which a housekeeper was about to move into the limelight.

With Mozart on the stereo and domestics on her mind, she ate a microwaved turkey dinner while rereading Poirot's mystery of the missing Clapham cook.

"Let me tell you a servant's every bit as important as a tiara to a woman in my position," said the offended Mrs. Todd as Poirot brushed aside her demand that he take steps to locate her decamped employee. "A good cook's a good cook—and when you lose her, it's as much to you as pearls are to some fine lady."

Presently, Poirot told Mrs. Todd's maid, Annie. "You alone can shed any light on the case. Without your assistance I can do nothing."

Finally, Poirot said to Captain Hastings, his version of Dr. Watson, "A disappearing domestic at one end—a cold-blooded murder at the other." To Poirot, the vanished domestic had been one of the most interesting of his cases.

In addition to neatness, she shared with Poirot a religion. Brought up as a *bon catholique,* he had been observed in crossing himself on momentous occasions. He had once chastised a witness with the warning, "You tell your lies and you think nobody knows. But there are two people who know. Yes—two people."

One was *"le bon Dieu"* and the other was Hercule Poirot.

Yet it had been in an Anglican church while singing words of a hymn, "The proud have laid a snare for me," that he saw that a trap had been set for him in the case under investigation. Now, suddenly, he found himself looking at it the right way up.

That other deductive reasoner, Sherlock Holmes, who had been Agatha Christie's inspiration in creating Poirot, had warned all his emulators, imaginary and not, that circumstantial evidence was a very tricky thing. It might seem to point very straight to one thing, but if you shifted your own point of view a little, you could find it pointing in an equally uncompromising manner to something entirely different.

She had fallen into exactly that trap. Her suspect in the murder of Jennifer Duncan had been the husband. She had been embarrassingly wrong.

Setting aside the Poirot book, she thought of Peter Sloan in the intensive-care unit of the hospital. A coma and bandaging had turned him into a mummy, while plastic tubes made him into a tied-down Gulliver. Recalling the nurse sticking a needle in his arm, she winced and wished she had not asked the nurse such a stupid question.

"How do you know which one of those he gets first?"

Yet in the face of the insult, the nurse had been patient in explaining the chart containing the neurosurgeon's instructions for administering wonderful drugs that, if they were mishandled, could prove fatal. "The chart lists the times for administering the medications, the proper order of injections, and the dosage," she had said. "When the doctor draws up the instructions, he also goes over the procedures with everyone treating the patient."

Had Sloan been awake, she thought as she went to the kitchen for the after-dinner cleanup, he would have had a good laugh. But as she placed the dinner plate, knife, fork, spoon, and coffee cup into the sink and turned on the hot water, her thoughts skipped to the kitchen of the Duncan house on the night Jennifer had been murdered.

Who had been in the kitchen with her?

That was the crucial question to be put to Cornelia Stewart in the morning.

Who had had the opportunity to drop a fatal dose of pills into her coffee?

Whoever did it had done so as readily as she in adding a few drops of dish-washing liquid to the water in the sink.

Closing her eyes, she tried to picture the act of picking up the bottle of pills. Were they first shaken into a hand. Or had they been dumped from the bottle into the glass of iced coffee, swiftly and deftly, in the moment following Jennifer's taking the first one herself?

Who had had that split-second opportunity?

Who among Jennifer's guests could have known how to sieze that singular moment?

"Oh my God, Peter Sloan," she gasped. "I have been such an incredibly stupid bungler. I've been looking at this murder from the wrong angle. I've been thinking about who had the opportunity to kill Jennifer Duncan. What I ought to have been looking for was who had the *knowledge* to do it."

42

Prescription for Murder

NCHORED AT OPPOSITE corners by Sears and Macy's, New
town Mall testified to the richness of choices available to the
Stone County consumer, with the convenience of abundant parking
spaces and a shelter from the elements that had not been available to
shoppers along Main Street on Arlene Flynn's childhood Saturdays. Yet
lacking in all the conveniences was a feature of that time—as quintes-
sential as matinee movies at the Roxy. Bright and shiny, the Newtown
Mall Pharmacy was nothing like the store that had stood upon the
southwest corner of Main and Fifth, for Feicht's Drugstore had a soda
fountain that even then had been old-fashioned.

Entering Feicht's, she had breathed in the smells of medicines in
huge brown jars behind a counter at the rear and heady perfumes and
soaps in glass showcases to her right. But it had been to the left that she
turned, looking for an unoccupied stool at the fountain if she was
alone or with a friend. Accompanied by her family, she looked for a
booth. But alone or with companionship, she had always had a sundae
of vanilla ice cream topped with a thick and oozing mixture of peanut
butter and marshmallow syrup that, despite years of trying, she had
never been able to reproduce in her kitchen.

Certificates and licenses on a wall identified the young man at the
rear of the mall pharmacy as Kim Myung Rho. She recognized a Ko-
rean name, although he spoke in flawless English. "Certainly I remember filling that prescription," he said. "How could anyone in my
position ever forget that the tablets that passed through his hands took
someone's life? It is even worse to know it was a suicide."

"The coroner's verdict was accidental overdose."

"Impossible. The directions on both the prescription and the label were unequivocal. I have the distinct memory of explaining the dosage to Mrs. Duncan. I can see her now, standing where you are, with her husband at her side, their delightful children, the housekeeper, Mrs. Stewart, another couple, and Les Troy and Mr. Watson from the bank. There was no way she could have made that mistake. Unless she had been drunk at the time."

"She was not an imbiber. She preferred coffee."

"There you are! It had to be suicide."

"You mentioned another couple had been with her when she was here picking up her prescription. Did you know them?"

"I never saw them before. I assumed they were Mrs. Duncan's business associates."

"Why did you assume that?"

"I knew about her plan to go into the cosmetics business by taking over Troy Chemicals. Since Les Troy and a banker were with her that day, I figured they'd been at the plant for a meeting on the matter and that they all came to the mall for lunch and she took the opportunity to pick up her prescription. I was guessing, as I told you."

"I understand the pills came directly from Troy Chemicals in the proper dosage."

"That's correct."

"Did you transfer the proper number of pills from the bottle they came in from Troy Chemicals and put them in one of your own containers?"

"It wasn't necessary. This was not a common prescription. It was not a medication that I acquired in bulk, such as a commonly prescribed blood pressure regulator. Should a refill be required, Dr. Granick had to write a fresh one. I just applied to the Troy bottle one of my labels containing Dr. Granick's dosage instructions."

"Did it carry a warning label like the kind you find on an across-the-counter product?"

"In a situation in which the medication is considered in an experimental stage, information such as a warning against abuse or misuse is provided directly by the manufacturer in an insert. And the prescribing physician goes over the dosage with the patient. There is just no way that Mrs. Duncan could not have known the dangers in taking more than the recommended dosage."

"Can you show me the kind of container they came in?"

"No problem," he said. Turning to a shelf of bottles of all sizes, he took down a small white one. "This is a standard Troy Chemicals bottle—plastic, two inches tall and one inch in diameter. This one contains glynase, small blue tablets used for treatment of diabetes. In providing these to a customer, I would transfer the prescribed number of tabs to one of my own containers."

"How large were Jennifer Duncan's pills?"

"The tablets were roughly the size of a vitamin pill or an antacid, white in color."

"Easily dissolved?"

"I really couldn't say. Shall I call Les Troy and ask him?"

"No need to disturb him. Like you, he remains painfully aware that one of his products caused a tragic death. And he has the additional distress of having been present at the time."

"Yes, it was an awful experience for him. But in a way . . ."

"Please complete your thought, Mr. Rho."

"I was going to say that in a way, the death of Mrs. Duncan was a good thing for Les. God, that sounds awfully heartless. But it is ironic that her dying kept Les from losing his business."

"Death is full of ironies that we all have to live with, Mr. Rho. Thank you for your time and your help."

Leaving the mall, she drove to Old West Point Road, turned north, and presently passed the motel where Duncan had established his alibi in the form of Madeline Trainor. When the road swung by Ichabod Crane Lake, she again glanced at the huge rock from which Sebastian had leapt, giving an excuse, she felt certain, for his wily grandmother to concoct a tale of a near-death experience in order to provoke a damning investigation of her son-in-law.

Parked in front of the Duncan house as she drove past was the Jaguar in which James had fled his wife's threat to divorce him and strip him of any chance of seeing his children. Barely half a mile beyond, she turned into the short driveway of the older and considerably more modest home of the Duncan housekeeper and frequent caretaker of Sebastian Duncan and his sister.

A boy whom she estimated to be about fifteen years of age answered the doorbell. Wide-eyed at the sight of her identification card, he turned and yelled, "Hey, Ma, there's a lady cop at the door."

Cornelia Stewart promptly appeared at the end of a hallway, drying hands on an uplifted apron and striding toward the front door with an exasperated "who's bothering me when I'm busy getting dinner on the table" expression Flynn had observed many times on her mother's face. "If it's about what happened to Mrs. Duncan," she declared defiantly, "I have nothing to say to you, lady."

"I'm sorry, Mrs. Stewart, but you have no choice. This is a murder investigation."

"Murder? Baloney. That poor thing killed herself. So go away and leave her, the Duncans, and me in peace."

"Mrs. Stewart, you can either talk to me now," she said with a glance at the agitated boy at her side, "or do so in my office in answer to a subpoena from the district attorney."

Stewart stepped back and aside. "I heard you were a hard-as-nails woman."

"Who told you that? James Duncan?"

"Never mind who it was."

"Whoever said it was right."

"You'll have to talk to me in the kitchen. I've got things baking in the oven that are almost done."

Flynn sniffed the air. "Apple pie?"

"Apple tarts. I make them for Sebastian Duncan."

"They're Sebastian's favorite," the boy said. "Mine, too."

"This is none of your business, Richard," Stewart said as they entered the kitchen. "So get outside and find something to do."

Pouting, he sidled away.

"I'll try not to keep you long, Mrs. Stewart," Flynn said. "But I believe you happened to have been a vital witness to what went on in the Duncan house on that awful night last year. Specifically, about who came into the kitchen."

"Everybody was in the kitchen at one time or another."

"I'm only interested in who was there when Jennifer took her headache pill."

"She didn't take the pill in the kitchen. She took the pill and her glass of coffee up to her bedroom. At the time, I thought she only took the one. But she obviously took all of them up with her, because when we looked inside the bottle in the morning, it was empty. She must have emptied the bottle while everybody was too busy to notice."

"Who was everybody?"

"Well, let's see. In the kitchen at the time were Sebastian, Jessica, me, and that jerky Italian man."

"Would that be Dominic Perillo?"

"It was him that dropped a tray of leftover appetizers all over my floor. He was getting them out of the refrigerator by himself instead of letting me do it when Mrs. Duncan came in to get a pill. She had a fit. Screaming at him. At me. That's why everybody got busy. Me and Sebastian and that damn man were all hurrying to pick up the stuff. Mrs. Duncan even tried helping. But then she just got more upset and yelled some more and picked up her glass and stormed out."

"I'm trying my best to picture the scene, Mrs. Stewart. Who was in the kitchen before Mrs. Duncan came in?"

"That man. Myself. Sebastian."

"Dominic Perillo was at the refrigerator?"

"That's right. The damn greedy pig."

"Where were you?"

"I was at the sink, rinsing out the drink glasses."

"By the way, what were the guests drinking that night?"

"Mostly white wine. The Italian was downing martinis like they were going out of style. He kept saying to me that nobody made a better martini than me, all the time trying to put his hands on me. I believe the painter had ginger ale. I didn't see much of him because he was down by the boat landing most of the time making sketches of the kids. Of course, Mrs. Duncan was not a drinker. She had her iced coffee. I had a big pitcher of it in the refrigerator."

"When she came in for her pill, was her glass full? Or did she have to get more from the refrigerator?"

"I think it was about half-full. Anyway, I know she didn't get any from the pitcher on account of that man was practically inside it looking for more food. I never saw any man eat like that. And the worst table manners you ever saw. For the life of me, I don't know why they ever let him in the house. But he was with Miss Trainor, a really classy lady, so I suppose they could not just kick him out."

"Back to what people were drinking. Did anyone else have the iced coffee?"

"Definitely not."

"Okay. Now, check me on this. When Jennifer came into the kitchen, Perillo was rooting around in the refrigerator. You were at the sink."

"That's right."

"Where was Sebastian?"

"He was at the refrigerator and very much amused by what was going on. Then everything went on the floor, just after Jennifer and Jessica came in."

"Excuse me. Jessica came in with Mrs. Duncan?"

"That's right."

"Then what happened?"

"Jennifer went to the cabinet for the pills."

"Where was the cabinet?"

"To the right of the sink. It's a wall cabinet. She always kept the pill bottle on the top shelf and away from the kids. Even though they both had been told they were not to mess around with them because they were so strong, you never can tell about kids, can you?"

"Very prudent indeed. Did you see her take the pill bottle down from the cabinet?"

"Oh yes."

"What did she do with it?"

"She opened it and took one out. Then all hell broke loose at the refrigerator and Sebastian howled with laughter. Then we all rushed to pick up."

"Including Jennifer?"

"I told you. Yes."

"And yourself."

"Naturally!"

"Plus Sebastian."

"Sure. He was right there, laughing his head off."

"What about Jessica?"

"Oh, she's a good girl. She must have helped, too."

"I'm sure she's the perfect little lady. But do you have a clear memory of Jessica helping with the mess?"

"Well, I was awfully busy myself."

"Think hard, Mrs. Stewart. It's essential that you be clear on this point."

"It was over a year ago."

"Let me approach this from a different angle. Do you recall what Jennifer did with the pill bottle and her glass of coffee when she started to help in the cleanup?"

"I know she put the glass on the counter."

"Where was the pill bottle?"

"Right there on the counter, too."

"When Jennifer stopped helping you all clean up, did she pick up the glass and the pill bottle? Think hard, Mrs. Stewart. Try to picture it."

She closed her eyes tightly. "Yes."

"Yes what?"

"Yes, she just picked up the glass."

"Not the pill bottle?"

The eyes opened. "No. It was on the counter."

"Where were you?"

"Standing by the refrigerator."

"And Perillo?"

"Down on his knees, still picking stuff up."

"Sebastian?"

"He was with that man, doing a little duckwalk and picking up the appetizers."

As Flynn sucked in a deep breath of air rich with the aroma of baking apples, she closed her eyes, picturing the only image possible. Opening them, she noticed her hands trembling. Tugging at her lower lip, she asked, "Mrs. Stewart, where was Jessica?"

Stewart's ruddy face went pale. "Oh, now look here, lady, if you're thinking that sweet little girl could have . . ." She shook her head violently. "Jessica murder her mother? No, no, no!"

While the little girl Flynn would always be in part of her mind railed that she had to be wrong—horribly wrong—the portion of her mind that thought like a woman and would always be a cop insisted, "When you have eliminated the impossible, what remains, however improbable, has to be the truth."

As Stewart sobbed, the chief investigator, Stone County DA squad, quietly inquired, "May I please use your telephone?

43

Daddy's Little Girl

D ISTRICT ATTORNEY AARON Benson stood in front of a massive fieldstone fireplace flanked by picture windows affording views of Ichabod Crane Lake and the shadowy hulk of rock outcropping called Horseman's Head. Before him in an arrangement of three white glove-leather chairs and a matching sofa sat Arlene Flynn, Simon Cane, and James Duncan.

"After receiving a call from Investigator Flynn this morning, Mr. Duncan," Benson said, "I took the extraordinary liberty of phoning Simon and insisting that he accompany me to this meeting with you. The half hour it took us to get here was, believe me, the longest, most difficult, and by far the saddest automobile trip of my life."

Fury welled in Duncan's eyes as they glared past Benson and Flynn to his attorney. "Simon, what the hell is going on here?"

"It's a serious situation, Jim. Aaron will spell it out for you. Then I'm sure we can reach an accommodation."

"An accommodation? Accommodate what, for crissakes?"

Benson answered. "There's a strong likelihood your daughter, Jessica, was responsible for your wife's death."

Duncan sat mute.

"We all want to work this out in the best possible manner for you and Jessica," Cane said. "I'm confident from what Aaron said to me during the drive up here that he hopes a trial can be avoided. What Jessica needs is help."

Duncan gulped air. Wide, teary eyes slowly took in the three grimly immobile faces around him. Square shoulders suddenly went limp. He gave a quick, slight nod and spoke in a barely audible reedy tone. "All this time, I've feared that's what happened. But I thought it would have been Sebastian." He sobbed and buried his face in the chalice of his upturned palms. "He was the one Jenny gave a hard time to. Yelling at him for spending so much time at his computer. Hanging out with Rick Stewart and the Fulmer boys." He looked up at Benson pleadingly. "It just never occurred to me that it was Jessica. How can you be sure?"

Benson turned to Flynn. "Arlene?"

"For whatever comfort it may be for you, Mr. Duncan," she began quietly as she stood by the fireplace. "I believe Jessica did it for love. To assure herself of your love."

"My love?" he cried. "I have never not loved that girl. She is the light of my life."

"She didn't do it as a plea *for* your love, Mr. Duncan. She did it because she was terrified of losing it."

He moaned and pounded the arm of his chair "That makes no sense at all."

"Jessica was afraid Jennifer would divorce you and arrange things so that you could never see Jessica and Sebastian again."

Duncan barked a laugh. "That's insane. Where would Jess get such a preposterous idea?"

"She heard it from Jennifer's own lips. When you and your wife had your big row by the boat landing, Jessica overheard you. So did Sebastian. But he was an eight-year-old boy, and that is not the same thing as being an eleven-year-old girl. Having been in that predicament, I can assure you that there's no one in the world as precious to a girl of that age as her dad. I was thinking about that phenomenon the other day. A bit of a poetic wisdom came to mind. It goes, 'Oh, my son's my son till he gets him a wife / But my daughter's my daughter all her life.' I'm afraid it was written before divorces became commonplace, rather than the exception. As to how I can be sure it was Jessica, I can't be certain without talking to her. Where is she?"

"About half an hour ago, Rick Stewart came tearing up on his bike and Jessica, Sebastian, and he took off to go swimming over at the rock."

Turning slightly and peering through a window, she saw them atop

Horseman's Head Rock. Too far away to hear them, she thought they looked like figures in a silent home video.

"As to how," she said, facing the three men again, "I've got a pretty good theory. But I must stress that it is just that. I do not have direct evidence. I do not know if there was an eyewitness. But I think it is very possible that Sebastian saw what happened. He may have dismissed it as child's play. He could well have understood what was going on but he was afraid to tell what he'd seen. I can also see him realizing it and refusing to believe it. He buried it so deep in his subconscious that nothing could bring it back. Well, almost nothing."

She glanced at Benson and remembered him at his desk, looking worried as he listened to Elizabeth Hollander in royal blue raiment relating a fantastic tale of a young boy's near-death experience. She saw Kevin Albert, the expert on the phenomenon, and his fearless son playing in the yard. Dr. Eric Lyle surfaced from her recent past, expounding on repressed and recovered memory.

"If Sebastian saw what happened," she continued, "there is a chance that he can recall it through hypnosis."

Duncan shook his head violently. "I'll never submit my son to mumbo jumbo like that."

"As to what Sebastian may have seen, I believe this is what occurred. It began with Jessica overhearing the argument and your wife's threat that if you didn't break off your relationship with Madeline Trainor, she would divorce and disown you and cut off all all contact with the children. It could be that Jessica observed you and Miss Trainor leave together, thus indicating to her that Jennifer's threat might, indeed, become a reality. This must have left Jessica terrified and angry. But her anger was not directed at you. She could never really be angry with Daddy, you see. But Mommy? It was easy to be angry with her, especially when Jennifer vented her own anger on the children. After you and Miss Trainor departed, she was quite sharp with Sebastian, Jessica, and Jessica's boyfriend, Rick Stewart."

"How do you know all this?"

"There were witnesses, Mr. Duncan. I talked to them."

"Trying to pin Jenny's murder on me," he replied bitterly. With a deep sigh, he added, "Dear God, now I wish you had."

"Regarding how Jessica did it," Flynn continued, "I have no doubt she did not suddenly say to herself, I think I had better kill Mommy. She simply saw in Jennifer's taking one of her pills an opportunity to get back at her. In a moment of utter confusion in the kitchen, when Jennifer set down the one pill she had taken from the bottle, the bottle containing the rest of the pills, and her glass of coffee, Jessica seized the chance and dumped all the pills in the coffee. A moment later, Jennifer picked up the pill and glass and went to bed, with no idea she would never wake up."

She looked again at the children on Horseman's Head Rock.

"Jessica knew the pills were powerful, of course," she said as she watched the girl teasing Rick Stewart. "But I prefer to believe she simply expected Mommy to get sick awhile. Not die."

As Flynn sat, Benson rose and said, "Mr. Duncan, I think we should have a talk with Jessica now."

Duncan stood. "Of course," he said with an astonishing calmness. "Come with me to the landing and I'll call her over."

As Flynn followed the men down wooden stairs to the landing, a Longfellow poem recited by her own mother long ago came to back mind.

> There was a little girl
> Who had a little curl
> Right in the middle of her forehead;
> And when she was good
> She was very, very good,
> But when she was bad she was horrid.

Reaching the end of the dock, she saw Jessica seated with the boys, a slight figure in a blue bathing suit.

The suit she had wanted to bring home from Macy's had been canary yellow, Rick Stewart's favorite color. It was a wonderfully skimpy two-piece. But her mother had said, "Not on your life, my dear. You're much too young." So she had been forced to settle for a one-piece as blue as a robin's egg that would show off her suntan. As long as she did not spend too much time in the water, wads of paper toweling gave shape to her chest. But next summer, she had felt certain, her daddy would buy her the one she wanted. Meanwhile, she intended to pray

242

that at the age of thirteen she would not need to pad it. Rick would have to take more notice of her then, for sure.

"Me, I'm a tit man," she had overheard him say often enough to the Fulmer twins. "I am crazy for girls with huge balloons. I just love to bury my head down between 'em when I'm getting' laid. Of course, there's a lot to be said for legs. Those long, slender, and silky ones that can wrap right around you."

Judging hers woefully short, she also prayed for improvement and imagined them wrapping satisfyingly about him while wondering what glories she might discover as she looked up into his dreamy brown eyes and felt the moving of his body upon and within her.

Once long ago, she had glimpsed her daddy and mommy that way. But their bedroom door had been open only a little and Sebastian had almost caught her looking. Yet in that momentary vision, she had marveled so much over what she had seen of her daddy that she had found it difficult to sleep that night. And when she did, she dreamed that she had been the one in bed with him.

The next year, they had moved to the new house by the lake, and on the first good day for swimming she had seen Rick Stewart rising out of the water and onto Horseman's Head Rock. Lithe and lovely, his muscular torso had been beaded with droplets of water that glistened like diamonds. Now, the shy thirteen-year-old boy she had fallen instantly in love with was a swaggering young man full of bragging stories nobody believed about being with girls with big tits and long legs.

On this sultry August afternoon, he had come barreling up to the house on his bicycle. Wearing faded cutoff blue jeans, bare-chested and sweating, he had been so excited that he leapt from the bike and stormed onto the sundeck, where she and Sebastian had been eating sandwiches for lunch. "Let's go out to the rock," he said breathlessly. "I heard somethin' you gotta hear. Specially you, Jess."

She had quickly changed from shorts and a tank top into the blue swimsuit, stuffing it with paper, and returned to the deck, to discover Rick and Sebastian already at the rock. Swimming out and climbing up to them, she found them sitting with backs to her and their legs swinging over the lip of the far side. As she sat beside Rick, she asked, "What did you hear that's so important and who said it?"

He looked at her sidewise. "It was a lady cop at my house. Talking to my old lady in the kitchen. But I was right outside, so they didn't know I was listening."

"Eavesdropping is not very nice, Rick," she said haughtily.

"Maybe you won't think so when you hear what she said."

He paused for effect.

"Well?" she demanded with an elbow poke to his ribs. "What was it you heard?"

He turned full face to her. "She was talkin' about you. And what you did to your mom."

Jessica's shrug jutted forth her padded breasts. "I don't know *what* you are talking about."

"The lady cop thinks it was you that put somethin' in your mom's coffee that killed her. And she thinks Sebastian saw you do it. *That's* what I heard her say."

She shook her head and tossed long blond hair "Oh, Rick, that is so crazy."

He peered down at the water. "Oh, is it? Well, that lady cop didn't think so. I wouldn't be surprised if she showed up around here and arrested you for murder."

Leaning forward slightly, she looked at her brother. "It's him that should be arrested. I loved Mommy. He hated her."

Sebastian gasped. "I did not hate Mommy."

"Oh yes you did. Because she was always picking on you."

He scrambled to his feet. "You're the one she was always yelling at, on account of you always hanging on Rick."

"Hey, don't drag me into this," Rick protested as he shot to his feet. "I didn't have nothin' to do with killin' your mom. Besides, I was nowhere near the kitchen that night. Remember? Your old lady had a big argument with your old man and threw one of her fits and ran me off." He grinned down at Jessica. "Is that why you killed her, Jess? Were you mad at her because she kicked me out of your house?"

She stood defiantly. "That is not why I was mad."

"Oh no? Then what were you mad at, enough to kill her?"

"I didn't."

"I gotta hand it to you. That was a slick trick, putting something in her drink."

From the shore, she heard her father calling her name, and as she and the boys turned to look, she saw that he was not alone.

244

"The woman with your old man," said Rick, raising an arm and pointing toward the dock. "She's the lady cop."

Jessica felt a surge of terror.

"Don't worry, Jess," Rick said with a laugh. "When they put you on trial, your lawyer can say you were insane."

"Jessica, I have to talk to you." Daddy's voice was urgent. "Jessica? Come here, Jessica. This minute."

With Rick's laughter booming over the water and echoing back while her father waved his arms and repeatedly called her name, she drew back. "Watch out," Sebastian cried in alarm. "You're too close to the edge."

With a cry of "Daddy," she went over the edge. But her going off the far side was nothing like Sebastian's beautiful, arching, graceful bird in flight. She alternately hit the sheer black face of the other side and cartwheeled all the way down, plunging into the purple water with a huge splash.

Staring down in disbelief, Rick mumbled, "Holy Christ."

A few moments later, her body reappeared, bobbing up out of the darkness and into the light.

Epilogue

The Convalescent

WELL, LOOK AT you, Peter Sloan," Flynn exclaimed as she barged into the room. Most of the bandages were gone. "Richards was right. Your head is your least vulnerable spot."

He rolled toward her in a wheelchair. "You're not getting rid of me that easily. Thanks for the books. I'm already up to chapter four of *A Study in Scarlet.*"

"What do you think of good old Sherlock? The truth and only the truth. Flynn's first precept."

"Frankly, I think Watson was a fool. The man he picked for a roommate was an insufferably arrogant snob."

She laughed deep in her throat. "Of course he was! That's the basis of his enduring charm. And it's why he was such a great detective. If he'd been a woman, he'd have been a bitch."

"I've heard a rumor. In other words, I've had a visit from Marty Katz. He said that while I was deep in slumberland, you wrapped up both our cases."

"Not as tidily as I'd have liked," she said, frowning as she sat on the edge of his bed. "But both are officially closed."

"Then why the long face? Aren't you satisfied?"

"There are still a few loose ends. Alas, I'm afraid they'll never be tied up. Bobby Mitchell owned up to killing Ollie, but he still insists he didn't strangle Matilda. And it would have been nice to have talked with Jessica Duncan."

"Her accidental fall off that rock was a bad piece of luck."

"That, my dear Sloan, is one of those damn loose ends. Was it really an accident?" She shrugged. "We'll never know."

"Have you been allowed to talk to Sebastian?"

She laughed. "At length."

"And?"

"And . . . that's the irony. He would have been a lousy witness. He said he didn't see a thing. He was too busy helping Dominic Perillo and Cornelia Stewart clean up the mess on that kitchen floor to pay any attention to what his sister was doing. Without an eyewitness, there would have been no way to prove that Jessica put the pills in Jennifer's coffee. And you tell me, Peter Sloan. What jury would ever convict a twelve-year-old girl of murdering her mommy without an eyewitness?"

"Did you ask Sebastian if he had a near-death experience?"

"I did indeed. He looked at me for a moment as if I were out of my mind. But then this funny look came into his eyes and he said, 'Oh, you're talking about when I drowned and saw Mommy.'"

After a long moment of silence, Sloan grinned. "Come on, boss. The kid was pulling your chain."

"Was he, Sloan?" She tugged her lip. "Was he?"